"It's alive... *Alive!!!*"

A soldier shouted in fear as the radio crackled with startled cries and the rat-a-tat of gun fire. A long hiss followed as the signal went dark. The old man lowered the walkie-talkie and surveyed the work of his team. Below the high cliff where he stood, sirens began to wail as gun fire and explosions wracked a lonely military base nestled between the painted hills of the Nevada desert. Above, heat lightning sizzled as a far off bunker crumpled in a roiling cloud of dust.

Emerging from the fog of destruction obscured by the darkening twilight, a massive creature stomped. Its eyes burned an evil green. Spot lights glared down trying to track the rapidly moving monster. Men in military uniforms scurried in pursuit. Tanks fired and machine gun studded Humvees crisscrossed the tarmac trying to halt its progress. Explosions threw up gouts of concrete, fire and steel but the creature was impervious to attack. The machines of war and heavily armed soldiers were like playthings. The giant swatted each aside easily.

The monster bound forward making a steady path toward the outer fence line leaving a path of destruction and chaos in its wake. The creature plowed thru the electrified fence tearing a massive hole that arced with blue lances of electricity. The heavy clomps of its footfalls echoed off the cliffs as it stomped into the darkening wastelands leaving only deep rectangular footprints in the desert sands to mark its passage.

"Master..." the radio hissed.

The old man raised the receiver eyeing the burning guard towers, smoking tanks and flashing emergency lights below.

"Report," he whispered, his voice dry and ancient.

"The creature has been freed."

"I can see that," the old man allowed himself a rare smile. "Did you retrieve the object?"

WHOOMP!

"There were… complications…" his minion said nervously as a large concrete tower evaporated in a column of flame. "The woman was here… she proved… difficult."

The old man growled, "*Mina Harker…*" He gripped his radio tightly, his gnarled fingers whitening, his momentary smile melting into a frustrated scowl.

"We barely escaped her." A long pause. "What are your orders, Master?"

A small mushroom cloud blossomed on the horizon as the Monster encountered a final group of American resistance. The destruction soothed the old man's nerves helping him to refocus. His grip on the walkie-talkie loosened.

"We will deal with the object and *that* woman later. Meet me at the rendezvous point in five minutes."

"Yes, Master…" the radio squawked a final time.

The old man sighed as he watched the fires burn below reflected in the dark sunglasses he always wore, the deep lines on his face relaxing.

So, the mysterious Mina Harker was here. That would mean she too would be tracking the monster, *his* Monster. So much the better. The creature once released would track down those he sought, the heirs, like a dog to his bone. And once he had them and the powers they

2

possessed… he would be invincible. But he would need to act quickly. He would need to make plans.

The old man watched as another section of building dissolved in a sheet of flame. His men had done well. While not a complete triumph, the release of his creature would prove decisive. Years of toil, sacrifice and planning would soon be paid back one hundred-fold. His mind raced with the needed preparations for the final stage of his master plan.

"Come if you will Mina Harker, my old friend," he whispered. "Doctor Victor von Frankenstein and his Monster will be waiting for you."

He chuckled as another explosion wracked the night… a night that reminded him so much of one long ago. The night that had set him on his path to destiny. The night Frankenstein met his Monster.

Chapter 1: Mina

Roswell, New Mexico... Spring 1938.

"Keep your britches on, Brady! The old RCA is warming up!" The young girl shouted, waving away her little brother.

The two sat in the sitting room of their small farmhouse far on the outskirts of Roswell, a forgettable hard-scrabble farming town in the middle of the New Mexico high desert. Momma was in the kitchen nearby, finishing up with the dinner dishes, humming a new Count Basey tune while their lazy, flabby-skinned blood hound snoozed in a corner, far away from the soft glow of their large RCA radio.

"There!" Selma announced, satisfied she had got the dials just right. She settled back on the threadbare love seat snuggling into their mamma's latest knitting project. Her four year old brother came to join her, one strap bravely holding up his over-sized coveralls. His face was still plastered in spaghetti sauce from dinner.

"Brady, your face is a mess!" Selma protested.

He used a section of Mamma's crochet to wipe off both cheeks. Selma gave him the stink eye as he managed to hide the evidence deep in a crevice of one cushion.

The radio crackled to life with a dramatic announcer's voice. "The Adventures of Flash Asteroid brought to you by Oval-Aid with new saccharine flavor crystals! It's like sugar... but from the future!"

A giant slurping sound.

"*BY THE GALACTIC LEGIONS, I LOVE IT!*" Flash Asteroid announced in a loud baritone.

"I hope Momma gets us some Oval-Aid from the Piggly-Wiggly..." Brady confessed in hushed tones as they listened raptly.

An orchestra introduced the show, punctuated by sound effects of alien mind rays, rumbling rockets, and shouting space marauders.

"Then you better hope she doesn't check her knitting before she heads to the store..." Selma smiled, hugging her little brother close. "Now hush, the show's starting!"

"When last we left Flash Asteroid and his faithful companion, talking Martian super dog, Buck Barkstar, they had been captured by nefarious alien scientists with a secret plot to conquer the Galactic Legion," the narrator intoned. "Flash and Buck now find themselves strapped to a lab table in the Alien mothership hovering high over Earth as the Aliens prepare to do their worst."

"At last I have captured you, Flash Asteroid!" the Alien Commander shouted in a sniveling voice.

"You don't scare me, you eight-armed coward!" Flash replied bravely. "Let me out of these space chains and see how a real American fights!"

"You are now a prisoner of the marauding Pirates of Uranus!" the Commander replied. "We are going to poke you and probe you for all of your precious Galactic Legion's secret defense codes!" The Commander cackled loudly as only evil radio madmen know how.

"Ron't rell him anything, Rash!" Buck Barkstar yelped.

"I won't, faithful companion," Flash reassured his canine sidekick. "It will take more than words to break Flash Asteroid!"

"We'll see about that…" the Alien Commander chuckled. "Bring out the Probe-o-tron!"

Nefarious music played followed by an evil buzzing and chirping of a robot entering the scene.

"Start with the dog…" the Commander muttered grimly.

"Selma!" Momma called from the kitchen.

"Momma, Flash Asteroid is on! Can't it wait for Little Orphan Annie?"

"You come in here this instant, young lady, ya' hear!"

"Alright…" Selma sulked as she got up slowly.

She returned a few minutes later, finding her brother leaning in close to the radio. The Probe-o-tron was beeping and whirring as Buck Barkstar yelped. Suddenly, a fight broke out as Flash broke free of one of his many-armed captors. He crashed the Probe-o-tron into a control console and the ship's emergency horn began to blare.

"Curse you, Flash Asteroid!" the Alien Commander wailed. "Now we are all doomed! This ship will crash into your Earth's atmosphere, demolishing everything it hits and us with it!"

"Come on loyal companion!" Flash announced to Buck. "Quickly, let's get to the escape pods and warn the Galactic Legion before it's too late!"

"Selma!"

"Momma! *What?*"

"Go outside and get your Papa, please."

"But this is the *best* part, Momma!" Selma wailed, exasperated.

"Now!"

"You better tell me what happens!" she hissed at her little brother who looked at her wide-eyed.

She stormed out of the front door toward the barn, stomping thru their dry yard. She paused, looking up in the sky as a shooting star flashed brightly overhead, followed by another close by.

"I'll be!" she wondered.

The first star shot rapidly thru the clear night sky. It was bright green. The second followed close on its heels, a deep scarlet. The two were as rare as they were pretty. Selma sighed loudly as she admired their beauty. But then something odd happened. The stars changed course. Selma did a double take.

In the sky overhead, the shooting stars zigzagged erratically like two biplanes in a space age dogfight. Lights flashed brightly as the two objects zoomed past each other, making pass after pass. Suddenly, the red one ignited in a far off explosion. It descended in a sparkling trail falling far, far to the east. Its green opponent limped along on the edge of the sky. It slowed as if damaged and began to fall growing larger, coming closer and closer...

Suddenly, the dark yard lit up as bright as day. Overhead, a huge emerald light roared by, shaking the tree with Selma's favorite tire swing and the plants just starting to peak out of Mamma's garden. Their scarecrow bucked wildly, buffeted by the raging wind.

"Papa!" Selma screamed, as the light became overwhelming. It whooshed by as quickly as it came followed by a large hollow boom in the valley distance. The yard grew quiet and dark once again.

CREAK...

Selma screamed as she saw the rusty door to the outhouse rattle and her father emerge, his overalls down by his knees, shuffling toward his daughter to find out what had just happened.

"Selma, baby!" he shouted. "Are you alright!"

She turned to her father, her face stricken with fear.

"Papa, put your britches back on!" she wailed. "Or the Pirates from Uranus will get you with their Probe-o-tron!"

*****

"Can we change the channel?" Mina asked, as they rattled down the old dusty highway.

"Why? I wanted to find out how Flash Asteroid escapes the Pirates from His Anus?" Edgewick Stoker replied, in his pleasant Irish lilt.

"Ach, be serious for once, Edge. It's Uranus," Lonn Cheney scoffed, his thick German accent struggling as it wrestled with the eighth planet's name.

The slender Irishman smiled. "I can't help myself, lad. Uranus… truly the butt of all humor in the solar system!"

Mina reached forward and flicked the radio off. It was the only new thing in Lonn's beat up Ford flatbed.

"Can we please stop talking about that mindless radio show?" she asked, brushing back a strand of her thick black hair.

"Ever since you and Lieutenant Murphy started dating, you have been absolutely no fun, lass," Edge teased.

Mina shook her head. "How much longer, Lonn?"

"The mine should be a few miles down," the rangy German replied, scanning the horizon. "Peter said to meet us there. He and Ian should be close behind."

"Good. They should have lights and equipment from the observatory so we can look around." She looked out the window of the Ford as the dark Roswell valley streamed by. "This could be the find of a lifetime."

The three had set out from Roswell a half hour earlier after seeing a strange object falling from the sky. After a brief set of goodbyes with friends and family, they set off to chase the UFO, or Unidentified Flying Object, which they estimated had impacted in the far western portion of the valley they called home. They were each researchers working at a US Army Air Corps observatory. Lonn was their boss, a professor of astrophysics at a nearby university. Edge was a visiting professor from Ireland. Mina was a PhD student working at the observatory for her research.

Joining them would be two others. Peter Murphy, the base executive officer and Mina's recent boyfriend and a strange, weaselly fellow, Ian van Helsing, another PhD student.

"Don't get your hopes up, Mina," Edge replied, yawning. "I admit that what we saw in the sky was remarkable... but finding the remains of a meteorite would be extraordinary... still, it beats sitting at home on a lazy Sunday evening!"

"Here is the mine," Lonn commented, as he turned off the main road onto a bumpy gravel driveway. A sign read *Roswell Salt Flats Mining Company, Founded 1896*.

The place had seen better days. The gravel path they travelled down led to a scramble of abandoned wooden mining buildings far off the main road. The buildings were built in a semi-circle near a collection of sheer walls ringing this part of the valley. Closed since the early days of the Depression, the mine was abandoned with few visitors, mostly kids who used the odd intact window for target practice. Lonn pulled in front of what once was the Head Office and applied the emergency brake to his weathered truck. He turned off his headlamps.

"We should wait for Peter," Lonn said.

Edge leaned forward and clicked the radio on. "Well I, for one, would like to be regaled by more mindless American radio drama."

Mina sighed loudly and laid her head back on the seat in mock desperation.

"This is a strange place we find ourselves, Buck Barkstar," Flash Asteroid fretted. Eerie alien music played in the background.

"The Pirate Commander said we were crash landing on Earth, but this is like no Earth I've ever seen..." Footsteps crunched loudly as the duo traversed the alien landscape.

"Rare roo you think we are, Rash?" Buck whispered, nervously.

"I fear when we hit the Galactic Legion's defense shield, Buck, we and those dastardly pirates were transported to..."

DUH... DUH... DUUUUUUUHHHHH!

"THE OMEGA ZONE!" Flash's voice echoed.

Headlights beamed brightly behind them. Mina reached forward and twisted the dial on the radio, flicking it off.

"Thank goodness!" she exhaled, pushing Edge to exit. "We've been saved by the *real* Flash Asteroid!"

They piled out of Lonn's pick-up as an olive-brown Army sedan pulled alongside. The emergency brake crunched as two men exited. The first was pale and scrawny with bony arms and a receding hairline. He had close set, bookish eyes and a glass jawline set in a semi-permanent scowl.

"Ian!" Lonn greeted, patting the smaller man on the back heartily.

Ian looked up with a distrusting expression as he rubbed the shoulder the big German had clapped.

"Professor Cheney," he replied. "If you wouldn't mind, I prefer not to have my joints reset each time we meet." Lonn looked at him confused.

"It means he'd rather you not rattle him to death with those ham-sized fists of yours, you Teutonic brute," Edge quipped, nudging his bigger friend jokingly.

Lonn looked down at his oversized hands and shrugged.

Joining Ian was a fit and handsome young man in a tan military uniform. His skin was sun-kissed and his face hale with a thick mop of curly blonde hair. He reached out and grabbed Mina by the hand, pulling her in close.

"Did you miss me?" Lieutenant Peter Murphy whispered.

Mina gave him a peck on the cheek and unwrapped herself. As handsome as Peter was, she was his equal with stunning, long black hair, deep crystal blue eyes, beautiful alabaster skin, and fine chiseled features. Peter always told her if she ever got tired of being a rocket scientist, Hollywood would snap her up in a heartbeat.

"Take it easy, tiger," she said, smiling. "We could use that youthful vigor to find a UFO!"

Peter smiled at her slyly before opening the trunk of the base staff car and passing out lanterns to each of them.

"So, what are we looking for?" the Lieutenant asked. "Little green men? Flying saucers? Probe-o-trons from Uranus?"

"You were listening to Flash Asteroid, too!" Edge enthused.

"Unfortunately, he doesn't miss a single episode," Mina sighed. "But no... nothing as flashy as what the radio can dream up. It's probably a large rock... hopefully still glowing from the heat of atmospheric entry."

"Heat of what?" Peter asked.

"The friction created when an interstellar object collides with the particles of our atmosphere, Lieutenant," Ian interjected, clearly irritated. "How, exactly, did you become executive officer of a planetary observatory if you don't know basic facts about astronomy?"

"Got caught kissing the wrong General's daughter, I guess," Peter shrugged.

"Oh really?" Mina asked, one eyebrow arched.

"Darling," he said, without missing a beat, "you know I have eyes only for you."

Peter turned to Ian. "I'm here because the Army asked me to be, Professor van Helsing, I'll leave the pointed head work to the professionals. Just point me in the right direction and I'll try to lend a hand." Ian grunted and turned away.

Peter leaned over to Edge and Lonn, whispering, "Good thing the General never found out about his daughter."

Edge and Lonn snickered while Peter grinned wolfishly. Mina looked on darkly.

"Alright, *boys*," she emphasized the later word. "Let's spread out and find this thing. We have a lot of ground to cover. I'll go with Edge and Lonn. We'll cover the western section. Peter, you and Ian take the cliffs. We'll meet back in an hour."

"*For the Galactic Legion!*" Peter crowed, as he left with Ian who stumbled over an odd scrub brush.

"I like him!" Edge enthused as he, Mina, and Lonn made their way thru the mining buildings to the open terrain beyond.

"Yeah," Lonn agreed, nodding. "He is a good catch, Mina. Well done!"

"You act like I'm looking to settle down?" Mina said, searching the ground for clues of fallen debris, her lamp shining weakly.

"If you don't snap him up, dear, I will!" Edge replied, turning his lantern beam from side to side. "Now, that may prove a challenge with Mrs. Stoker, but I think she can be reasoned with."

"Ha!" Lonn boomed as the three separated, each scanning their own piece of scrub-laden terrain.

They searched for several minutes, moving further and further apart. Soon the mining complex was completely wrapped in the darkness of night and the only sign of one another was the feeble rays of light emitting from their portable lanterns.

"Edge, come here!" Mina called. She had just rounded a large boulder several hundred meters from her friends.

Edge followed the weak beam of her portable lamp and picked his way thru the desert underbrush. As he neared, he could make out a faint glow behind a hill in the distance.

"Do you see it? It's coming from just beyond that rise!"

Edge stopped and whistled.

"Yes, I do." He turned and hollered, "Lonn, I think we've found something. We could use a spare light."

Edge lowered his lantern and stared.

"Follow our lanterns! The way is pretty clear."

"What do you think it could be?" Mina whispered.

"I don't know, lass, but I think we are about to find out." They heard Lonn jogging over.

"Ready?" Mina said, as Lonn's light joined their own, illuminating a path forward.

"Yes," Lonn replied.

The three picked their way through the scrub brush and rocks cresting the rise of the hill, anticipation building with each step. What they saw was like something out of an H.G. Wells novel.

"Jesus, Mary, and Joseph!" Edge whispered, crossing himself.

"That's no meteorite," Mina breathed. "That's a ship!"

"We should get Peter and Ian," Lonn murmured in awe.

Below them in a crater extending well into the night was a giant metal disc, its nose burrowed deep into the ruined hillside. The disc was the size of a small house and badly damaged with scorch marks and jagged holes, marring its once shiny and smooth body. The exterior was silver metallic with a beetle-like opalescent sheen. There were no windows or seams in the body beyond the holes of twisted metal that dotted the craft. It gave off a faint, pulsating light that tinted everything around it a wicked metallic green glow.

"We should get closer," Mina declared. "There could be survivors who need our help!"

"Mina, no," Lonn shook his head. "We don't know what that is or where it has come from. We should send for help."

"I'm taking a look. There could be people hurt." She started to pick her way down the slope. "You can wait here or go back to the car for Peter. Up to you."

"I'm with the lass on this one," Edge said, clasping his colleague on the shoulder. "Flash Asteroid would do it!"

Lonn grumbled in German, "The dog has more sense than Flash..." but followed anyway.

The ship's eerie green glow lit the way, putting stark relief details on the ship's surface, twisted alien metal, mysterious symbols, and pulsing lights. As they approached, Mina could make out a strange green gas rising from the ship's belly, mixing with the dust from the settling hillside.

She stopped a few feet in front of the nose of the ship, which was buried in the hill. She peered into the desert and saw the long swath of destruction from the disc's crash. A trail of faint wisps of green light, scattered rubble, and smoldering plant life went on for miles lighting the valley floor.

This was no unmanned object. Someone had piloted this landing in an attempt to avoid total destruction.

"Where is the pilot?" Lonn asked, as if reading Mina's mind. "The impact should have destroyed the craft and the better part of the valley."

He paused, thinking. "There was intelligence behind this landing."

"Aye…" Edge muttered, scanning the vessel for clues, "this only gets stranger and stranger."

He scanned the vessel's exterior from a safe distance, its eerie green light giving everything a spooky hue.

"There doesn't appear to be a door or hatch of any kind. All I can see are glowing green electronics like the inside of a radio."

Mina stepped past Edge and Lonn and placed her hand on the craft's fuselage.

"Mina, no… you could be burned!" Lonn warned, trying to stop her.

"It's OK."

She passed her hand down a length of the alien vessel's midsection.

"It's cool to the touch… at the speed it fell, it should be blazing hot."

"Mina, this is not a radio show!" Lonn gushed. "Be careful."

"Relax, Flash Asteroid," Mina huffed, continuing to study the outer shell of the vessel. "It's not like this is from outer space. This must be from the government… Maybe Peter will be able to explain it."

She paused as her hand felt a faint tickle. "Hold on… what's this?" As her hand passed over a section of the fuselage, a square of soft light lit up a hidden panel under her palm. The light shone thru her fingers growing in intensity. Mina pulled back her hand instinctively.

The light grew hotter and more intense, bathing the three of them in emerald. A narrow pure white beam emanated from the center of the portal and scanned them left to right, up and down. Mina swallowed and stared hard as Edge and Lonn began to back away.

"Mina, I'm all for being a chancer, but maybe a tactical retreat would be in order," Edge whispered.

The craft began to whir as the lights on its sides strobed brightly.

"And maybe this isn't from the government," Lonn gulped.

Mina nodded and followed her two companions as they backed away. The ship seemed to respond. The scanning stopped and the emerald light grew stronger, harsher. The portals dotting the vessel blinked rapidly. Mina, Edge, and Lonn turned to dash up the hill as the whole craft flared brilliantly. The three friends stumbled and fell, blinded by the intense electric green glow, crying out in alarm.

And then… darkness.

*****

"What was that?" Peter exclaimed, as he saw a flash in the distance.

"What was what?" Ian replied, poking his head up from behind a tumble of rocks hugging the cliff side.

Another flash, this time followed by a piercing scream that echoed throughout the mining complex.

"Mina!" Peter shouted.

Another pulse of light and then darkness again.

Peter scrambled forward. "Come on, Ian! It came from that far hill. Mina and the others need our help!"

Ian picked himself up from the rocks he was inspecting. He followed the dimming light of the Lieutenant as he deftly picked his way thru the rocks and underbrush that seemed to snarl the hapless scientist with every step.

They scrambled across the field and climbed the hill as quickly as possible. Peter crested the rise expecting the worst. What he saw took his breath away.

Below him Mina, Lonn, and Edge lay on the ground in a crater next to a strange alien disc emanating soft phosphorescent light. None of their friends were moving. Peter leapt down the hillside to Mina's side, checking her breathing and pulse. She was alive but not responding. He quickly checked Lonn and Edge who were both in similar condition.

Ian huffed his way up the hill and stood on its peak, flabbergasted by what he saw... the miles-long crater, the other-worldly lights, the alien craft.

"By the stars!" he exhaled.

Fixated on the strange metallic vessel, Ian scrambled down the hillside toward the crater, ignoring his stricken colleagues and the Lieutenant.

"Ian, bring me some water and the med kit!" Peter shouted. "Our friends need our help!"

Ian didn't respond. He picked his way down, transfixed by the remains of the craft and the strange greenish light. His shoe slipped in the scree and he cursed. He fell, tumbling several yards down the opposite face into darkness.

"Ian, can you hear me? Are you alright?" Peter yelled from the other side.

Ian picked himself up from a fissure he had fallen into. He started to dust himself off but went still. "Lieutenant, I think you'll want to see this..." he called hoarsely, coughing. Before him, sprawled on the ground in the midst of rubble was a giant metal man.

Ian searched for his flashlight, clicked it on, and panned his electric torch over the creature. Its skin was silver with a pearly sheen that seemed to swirl around its metallic body. It lacked a face or any distinguishing features beyond sheer mass.

Ian went to one knee to investigate closer. He bent down to touch the creature's shell, passing his fingertips gingerly over the cool metal. "Inconceivable..." Ian breathed.

"What is it? Are you OK?" Peter called.

Ian looked up dragging his eyes away from the mysterious steel giant.

"I think I found the pilot. He... it... appears unconscious..." A green sparkle began to emanate from pinpricks in the creature's body.

"What's this?" he whispered.

The green glow coursed up and down the massive frame, swirling around the creature's torso, arms, and legs. This was technology beyond Ian's comprehension.

"What are you?" he marveled.

In response, the creature's eyes winked to life in two harsh emerald gashes. It turned its head to glare at the scientist. Ian's awe melted into fear. He tried to scramble away but the creature caught his arm in one giant, surprisingly fast, steel hand. Ian futilely tried to pry his arm away but the automaton held him tight. It regarded him with its evil green eyes.

"Get off me!" Ian shouted desperately, squirming.

"Ian, what's wrong?" Peter yelled.

"Get off me!" Ian pleaded, frantically clawing at the robot's metal fist.

Never blinking, unfeeling, the hard green eyes burrowed into Ian's soul, the emerald light from the creature's body swallowing him whole, burning a hot, bright green. As the light enveloped him, Ian screamed.

"Ian!" Peter yelled. "Ian, what's happening over there?" He looked up as a dazzling green corona from the opposite side of the hill blinded him, forcing him to shield his eyes and blink rapidly. The light lessened and Peter's eyes adjusted to the sudden brightness. In its center stood the silhouette of a massive man-shaped object, slowly rising. The light flared sharply and died. Only the soft green glow from the ruined alien disc lit the hillside.

Peter got up from the ground where he was tending to Mina, Edge, and Lonn. The three were only just beginning to stir.

RUMBLE. STOMP. RUMBLE.

Peter watched in awe as an iron nightmare crest the top of the hill. It was some kind of metal creature... an automaton. In its massive arms, it carried Ian's unconscious body. He took a step forward trying to protect his friends. The Iron Golem's eyes blazed a wicked green as it stomped toward him, leaving a deep, giant square footprint in the soft ground of the hill.

Peter gasped at the Monster's approach, the sheer size of the thing.

"Oh my..."

Chapter 2: Blaine

"GAWD..." Blaine Davis wailed sleepily as she rolled over in bed and hit the snooze button dispelling the evil singsong of her smartphone alarm.

Morning was not Blaine's strong suit, particularly this morning, the last Monday of August and the first day of a brand new school year, seventh grade to be exact. She rolled over and looked at the clock on her phone. 6:37 A.M.

"You are an evil monster!" she scolded her small black phone as she jammed a pillow over her head.

Blaine was twelve, going on thirteen, and dead tired. She'd stayed up late the night before painting and gabbing with her best friend, Shelley Merry, and generally dreading the coming dawn. School. The end of summer, the end of carefree days, warm breezes, and walks on the endless Oregon beach with friends... and more importantly, the end of days devoid of Algebra, Civil War facts, and the Capitals of Eastern Europe.

Oh boy! Blaine thought, stuffing a second pillow over the first in a vain attempt to shield herself from the light filtering thru her bedroom window. She lay there for another few minutes before the tell-tale chime of her alarm chirped ominously again. This time she picked it up and dismissed the alarm for good. She rose to a sitting position, wiped the sleep out of her eyes, and took off her headband that kept her spiky black web of hair in place during the night.

It was now 6:43 A.M. She had exactly 22 minutes to get ready, scarf down some breakfast, and hit the car with her power-suit clad mom and older sister, Vickie, for the ride to school. Vickie would no doubt be in full ra-ra mode as the newly-elected cheerleading captain for their Junior High. Dad would probably be nowhere to be seen, out of the house even at this ungodly hour for his long commute to nearby Portland.

Blaine slouched out of bed, scratched her belly, and let out a long yawn. Her bedroom was the stereotypical bedlam of a 12 year old girl. Dominating the room was her dollhouse-shaped bunk bed. The bed had seemed like a dream gift seven years ago but had since transformed into a nightmare curse with the onset of puberty. She did her best to hide the cartoonish purple shutters and bright pink and white facade. A combination of carefully placed snack wrappers, week-old clothing, and an eclectic blend of bumper stickers hid the bright pastel colors of a simpler phase of girlhood.

Now the dollhouse bed, turned derelict boarding house, blended in well with the collection of art supplies, posters, young adult books, and matching sticker strewn ironic-princess armoire that completed the room.

Blaine kicked a pile of clean laundry out of her way and plodded to her nearby bathroom which she shared with her sister. On the way, her gun-metal gray British Short Hair cat, Matteo, made a morning appearance to check on her. Matteo's bright blue eyes and chubby cheeks looked up at Blaine expectantly.

"What, no one feed you yet, Fat Boyfriend?" Blaine asked, scratching her favorite pet under the chin. Matteo purred. "I'll be down in a couple minutes. Keep that belly of yours in check, mister."

She got up and slid the door open to her bathroom. "Oh, not so bright!" she wailed as she entered the brightly-lit water closet that connected her room with her sister's. Matteo sashayed thru the door, wrapping around Vickie's legs as she was already up and well on her way to being ready for school.

"Good morning, sunshine," Vickie chirped. She was applying the finishing touches to her long blonde hair. "Nice to see you joining the land of the living!"

Blaine picked up her toothbrush and squeezed on some organic toothpaste her mother insisted they use.

"*Ugh...*" Blaine huffed as she brought the icky white paste to her nose and sniffed. "How can you make mint taste bad?" Putting on a sour face, she stuck the goo-covered bristles inside her mouth and started to brush.

Vickie looked at her wreck of a sister and shook her head. She finished her hair and bent down to give Matteo a greeting, picking him up in both hands and holding the now visibly uncomfortable cat a few inches in front of her face.

"And how are you, Prince Fatty?"

Matteo gave out a low mewl vainly attempting to wriggle away. Vickie put the hapless feline back down and went back to her morning primping.

"There, the perfect back to school look!" she declared with a smile.

Blaine spit out her toothpaste, slurped some water into her mouth with both hands, and gargled. "Well, don't you look like a vision, sister dearest!" Blaine teased.

"Well, Sleeping Beauty," Vickie cautioned as she left the bathroom. "The tower strikes midnight in 15 minutes. Better be ready or your Fairy God Mother will be ticked!"

"Thanks genius," Blaine retorted, picking up her brush. She started to work last night's knots out of her dark tangle of hair. "If you are going to use fairy tales to teach me a lesson, at least get your stories straight, Dork-er-ella!"

Vickie popped her head back thru the door, stuck out her tongue, and then waved sweetly as she ducked back to catch some breakfast downstairs.

"Disney's lawyers will be calling!" Blaine shouted.

She smiled. While Blaine loved her sister, they couldn't be more different. Blaine was adopted for one. While they cared for and watched out for one another, they looked nothing alike. And more importantly they acted nothing alike.

Vickie, a year older than Blaine, was Miss Popularity at school. She was co-captain of the Junior High Cheer Squad, treasurer of the Eighth Grade Student Council and ran Cross Country year-round, because she read in Teen Vogue running was an excellent way to keep your body fat at 8%. Where Vickie was tanned and blonde with long golden locks, Blaine was pale with unruly, medium-length raven hair and brown eyes. Blaine was the artist's soul of the Davis family. Ever since she had come to live with them seven years ago, she was quiet and reserved. Her loves were sculpting, drawing and, in particular, painting.

Her parents, Nick and Chelsie Davis, were more like Vickie. The Davises were the classic power couple who wanted it all: beautiful house on the Oregon Coast, two perfect kids, two busy jobs, and enough revolving debt from their high end lifestyle to scare a Third World dictator. Nick worked in technology and Chelsie in real estate. Both were consumed by their jobs, fitness regimens, and the local social scene. They tried to be there for their kids but given Blaine was the quieter of the two, and less involved in traditional activities, she didn't see as much of her folks. While she knew her parents would be there in a pinch, Blaine couldn't help but feel invisible in the house.

She finished corralling the worst of the knots in her spiky curls. She did one more quick check in the mirror and walked back to her room to get dressed. Matteo eyed her from an opposite corner.

"So, what will it be for the first day of school, Matteo?" Blaine announced, surveying the melee of clothing scattered in piles throughout the room. "I'm thinking light and comfortable."

The Oregon Coast was in its late summer glory with sunny skies, an ever-present ocean breeze, and pleasant temperatures. Blaine found a pair of skinny jeans, a black and white Hollister t-shirt, and a tie-died scarf she threaded thru her slim waistline for a splash of color. She kicked around and found her Chuck Taylors and slid them on. She walked to her mirror in a corner of her room.

"Hmmm... fashionable with just the right note of attitude. What do you think, Matteo?" The chubby feline purred and went back to his personal hygiene, burying his face between his legs.

"Good look, Fat Boy," she teased. Pleased with her ensemble, Blaine left her room and descended the nearby stairs.

"Five minutes!" her harried mother announced as Blaine entered their airy kitchen. Mom was in a business suit scurrying this way and that stuffing papers, computer chords, and various electronics into her work bag. "Make sure you get some protein for the first day of school!"

"OK Mom, I'm on it," Blaine replied.

She walked to the pantry, grabbed some cereal and milk and sat down next to Vickie at the kitchen counter. Her sister was checking her phone for the latest morning tweets from her eighth grade BFFs nibbling on the last vestiges of a ham and cheese croissant. A half-empty glass of skim milk set at her side.

"Who did you get for home room this year?" Vickie asked, putting down her phone.

"New teacher," Blaine shrugged between bites. "Ms. Poe."

"What does Ms. Poe teach?"

"Literary Arts. I have her for homeroom and then English class for fourth period."

"Good luck with the newbie," Vickie answered, resuming her phone obsession.

Blaine stared out the wide bay windows opposite their kitchen counter island. The Davises had a beautiful colonial house on a small cliff overlooking the Oregon coast. Autumn's Hallow, the town they called home, was a cute county hub nestled in the coastal forests, dairy farms, and beaches of western Oregon. While Blaine was no fan of mornings, she always loved the view from their kitchen in the summer. Soon enough, the Oregon rainy season would begin, which meant dull and dreary from fall thru spring.

"OK girls, phones down and grab your bags," Mom announced, rattling her keys as she picked them up from the counter. "I put $5 in each of your bags for lunch. Double-check to make sure you have all of your school supplies packed away."

"OK Mom," the girls replied in unison. Blaine went into the adjoining mudroom, grabbed her things and followed her Mom and Vickie to their awaiting silver station wagon. She got in the back seat and clicked in as her mom pulled out of the driveway.

They left their small clutch of houses hugging the beachside cliffs and passed the local five and dime store, mom & pop gas station, and post office. Mom turned onto the main road and drove thru a short stretch of green rolling farms through a landscape dotted with small lakes and meandering rivers. Vickie was focused on her phone. Her mom turned on the radio to NPR.

"In national news, conspiracy theorists swamped the nation's capital to protest the mysterious explosions which racked an army installation north of Las Vegas weeks ago. A Senate panel reconvenes today to investigate the matter. Several protestors are claiming the complex houses the mysterious Area 51, the government's purported alien research facilities. Conspiracy theorists and local government representatives claim the explosions represent a concern for the rapidly growing Las Vegas metropolitan area and want more transparency from the Pentagon that has so far proven tight-lipped. In Sports..."

Boring, Blaine thought. She stared out the backseat window. They passed her least favorite sight on the drive into town, a dark and imposing manor house set several acres back from the road, the old Grimm Manor. It was a creepy looking Victorian hotel abandoned over a hundred years ago. Several years back, the dilapidated complex had been bought, renovated, and expanded and was now the Grimm Academy for Boys, a boarding school for the rich, privileged, and inconvenient. Despite the upgrades and fancy new facilities, the place still looked more like a haunted house than a fancy prep school. It gave Blaine the heebie-jeebies.

"I wonder who their famous graduates are... Freddy Kruger and Michael Meyers?" she muttered with a shiver

Their car passed the Grimm Academy grounds and after a short drive thru farms and forest they entered the outskirts of town. Ahead was Autumn's Hallow High School followed by the Junior High. Mrs. Davis pulled the car into the drop off zone.

"OK girls," she announced, turning to the backseat to give her daughters one final inspection, "have a great day at school! Vickie, I'll pick you up at 5:00 after cheer practice and Blaine, I arranged with Mrs. Merry for you to walk home with Shelley. OK! Love you! Have fun!"

"Bye, Mom," the two sisters said in unison as they left the car.

"TTYL, Blaine," Vickie picked up her bag and ran to a gaggle of smartly dressed teen girls standing on the steps leading to the front entrance way. Behind them, a flag of the school mascot, the Yowling Sasquatch, waved in the wind.

Vickie and her BFFs shared a round of hugs, fashion complements and giggles. Wary boys entering school in one's and two's gave the troop of debutantes a wide, cautious berth.

Blaine smiled at her hopeless sister, hoisted her bag, and walked into school.

The front entry hall was buzzing with first-day energy. Clueless sixth graders with blank stares and oblivious frowns walked this way and that trying to get their bearings. Experienced seventh and eighth graders went on auto-pilot pausing only to high-five friends they hadn't seen enough of over the summer holiday. Hall monitors shouted instructions over the commotion as they tried to herd the crush of students.

Blaine walked thru the confusion to her locker. She smiled at a few people but was naturally shy.

"Hi Blaine!" She looked around and saw Kevin Wallis approaching, grinning over a stack of books held precariously in front of him. Kevin was short, bookish, and truth be told a little bit of a geek, but a sweet one Blaine had always thought. He was wire thin, had wavy red hair, a rosy complexion with freckles and wore an oversized retainer that caused him to lisp.

"How was your summer?" he finished his greeting. He paused. "Is Shelley with you?"

Shelley Merry was Blaine's best friend and the object of Kevin's boyish infatuation since third grade. While Shelley was brilliant, a real ace at anything mathematical, she was clueless socially, particularly in the realm of boys.

"Hey Kevin," Blaine rattled off her responses catching Kevin quickly up on her summer activities. "No, I haven't seen Shelley. I bet she's already at homeroom. How was your break?"

"It was great!" Kevin replied enthusiastically, adjusting his books as a group of passing eighth grade boys ran into him and jostled his delicately balanced load. "My dad and I went to a comic convention! I got this cool new game called Gothic! You've got to check it out. Best... Thing... *Ever*!"

"Loot at my phone!" Kevin added, shifting his book stack as he fumbled for his cell phone. Kevin's books wobbled, tilted, and finally spilled to the floor. Cooler kids walked by shaking their heads, while Blaine looked on shyly.

"Butterfingers," he cursed softly as he bent to retrieve his stuff.

"Here, check out the phone, it's a new app called the Gothipedia," he explained. "Shows you all the characters you can play with... epic!"

Epic would not have been the word Blaine used to describe the game. She flicked thru a couple cut scenes showing a selection of comic book-style monsters battling one another, including a Chewbacca knock-off with a bad case of five o'clock monster shadow in a throw-down with a sun deprived flying dude in an old-fashioned tuxedo. Completing the mood, were creepy castles, scary gargoyles, and mad scientist laboratories with far too many fire-code violations for comfort.

"That's pretty cool," Blaine lied, handing back Kevin's phone.

"I can't wait to play with Dash and the gang at lunch!" Kevin replied proudly.

Daschle Gaunt was Kevin's best friend and a fellow geek albeit a strange one because he was a bit of a jock.

First bell rang... "Alright kids!" A nearby hall monitor announced. "Be in class in two minutes! Two minutes!"

"Well, Kevin, I think my classroom is right over there," Blaine said, indicating a door down the hall with a sign reading 'Ms. Bellamy Poe'. "I'll see you around."

"You bet!" Kevin answered, dropping two books as he struggled up from the floor.

Blaine bent down, picked them up and stacked them on top of Kevin's pile. "See you, Kev. If I see Shelley, I'll tell her you said 'hi'."

Kevin smiled and bolted away to find his own homeroom, with a breadcrumb trail of lost pencils, school supplies, and notebooks left in his wake. Blaine turned and girded herself for another nine month grind of droning teachers, mindless lectures, and the greatest of tortures, PE.

Seventh grade... this was sure to be the most boring year of her life, she thought.

Boy, was she wrong.

Chapter 3: Blaine

Homeroom in seventh grade was more a gathering point than an actual class. Blaine walked into the three-quarter full class and scanned for a seat. She found one next to her best friend, Shelley Merry. Shelley was tall and slender with mocha skin and curly, soft brown hair with blonde highlights. She wore a neon green t-shirt with Barbie saying "Math is Hard... Not!", black skinny jeans and white sneakers.

"Hey, brace face!" Blaine greeted.

Shelly gave her a bright smile, revealing her new braces. She was wearing her mottled-brown glasses that matched the hue of her deep brown eyes and despite the bookish look, still came off looking pretty. Shelly brushed aside a loose strand of hair that had fallen from her bangs.

"Hi, Blaine. Gotta head next door to the high school for first period. My dad told me I got placed in advanced math. Hey, saved a seat for you!" She patted the empty desk next to her. "The new English teacher hasn't come in yet."

Blaine put down her bag and took a seat next to her friend. Several students were mulling in the front of the classroom as final bell trilled when a hand appeared at the door, grasping the frame. The hand was pale white and adorned with a large blood-red ruby ring, cast in gold. The mysterious hand moved to the light switch, flicked it on and off rapidly, and then rested the switch at off.

All eyes were on the door as a shadow entered the classroom, wrapped in what looked like a cape. The specter moved across the front row, peering over a wrap in front of its face, its dark eyes staring down any kid unlucky enough to be caught standing after first bell. Several students backed away and found their seats in a nervous screech of chairs. The shadow moved to the light of the overhead projector and revealed a woman with long black hair. She lowered her arms and swiveled her head to survey the room revealing a pale, young, and beautiful face lit from below by the whirring projector.

"I am Ms. Bellamy Poe," the woman announced in a clear voice that had a tinge of some nameless European accent, "your new teacher." She clapped her hands and the lights flickered back on overhead.

"How'd she do that?" Blaine whispered.

"I don't know, some gizmo from the Home Shopping Network?" Shelley replied softly.

Bellamy Poe was, in a word, beautiful. Her face was young, no more than late 20s, and pale white as if carved from alabaster, accented by a small yellow gold nose ring. She had bright blue eyes, almost luminescent like a cat's, and ruby red lips that matched the ring on her right hand. She had long black hair that went to the small of her back that almost hid her gold bangle-earrings. She was dressed like a gypsy with brightly colored scarves wrapped about her neck and waist, with a tight black top, and a multi-colored loose-fitting skirt.

Ms. Poe finished her survey of the room and Blaine could almost swear she settled her gaze directly on her, causing her to shift uncomfortably in her seat.

"Now, let's meet each of you," she said, and allowed a creep of a smile to purse her lips. "If you are here, please say so when I call you. Nelson Applewood…"

Nelson raised his hand and said "here."

"Emily Brewster... Jason Chase... Blaine Davis."

"Here," Blaine raised her hand. Ms. Poe paused, looking Blaine in the eyes causing her to fidget uncomfortably in her seat. After a moment, she moved on, "Marshall Feldman?"

"Do you know her?" Shelley leaned over. "Because she seems to know you."

Blaine shrugged, "No, but a little creepy. Can't wait for fourth period English."

Shelly smiled and whispered, "Well, she seems OK. The clapping thing was cool!"

Ms. Poe finished checking the roll call, shuffled a few papers in front of the projector and said, "And now the morning announcements."

On cue, the school PA system cut in. A man coughed into the microphone and said, "Testing, testing. Yes, Edna, it works... where are my notes?"

The PA cut off for a moment and, with a squeal, resumed. "Good morning students and welcome back to Autumn's Hallow Junior High! This is Principal Marlowe. Today we are on a shortened schedule to accommodate our back-to-school assembly at the end of day. Joining us will be four guests from nearby Grimm Academy so I expect everyone to be on your best behavior! If you have any questions on your schedule, please ask your homeroom teacher or..."

Mr. Marlowe droned on with other start of term updates. Blaine looked around the classroom and noted most kids either spaced out, still unused to the early morning start, or horsing around with friends. She stifled a yawn. Her typical wake-up time in the summer was closer to 10 a.m., not this unholy 7 a.m. business. She looked to the front of the room. Ms. Poe was surveying the class. She saw Blaine's attention shift and gave her a nod. Blaine's eyes widened in surprise and she quickly averted her gaze. What was it with this teacher?

"Have a great day and welcome back to another year of learning and adventure," Mr. Marlowe finished as the PA system clicked off with a hiss of out-of-date electronics.

"OK, class, first period bell is about to ring. Ms. Merry and Ms. Davis, please see me before you leave."

First bell trilled denoting the five minute countdown between periods. With a screech of chairs and a collective rustle of bags, the students emptied their seats and got ready to head to their next class.

Shelley and Blaine move forward to their teacher's desk and stood in front of it as Ms. Poe arranged a few papers. She looked up and smiled. "Hello you two," she said. "We'll have lots of time to get to know one another. I was hoping you could accompany each other to your next class. Shelley, you have geometry in the high school and Blaine you have art in the Annex on the way. Best to travel in groups. Are you each familiar with the high school?"

"Sure thing, Ms. Poe. I took Advanced Algebra there last year. Come on Blaine, I can show you the way." Blaine nodded and they walked off. She could sense that Ms. Poe was staring at her through the walls as she left the classroom.

"She's weird."

"You think everything new is weird," Shelley replied. "I think she's nice. It's great to have a young teacher for a change. Maybe she'll understand us better."

"I still think there is something fishy about her. Where do you think she's from?"

"I dunno. Somewhere in England? She teaches English, after all."

Blaine, winced. "Right, Shell, only people from England can teach English. I can't wait until Julius Caesar comes to teach us about History in 6th bell. And who do you think we'll have for PE today, Shaquille O'Neil or Tiger Woods?" Shelley was about to object but let it drop.

The two walked thru middle school hallways to the cafeteria wing that was shared with the high school. They walked thru the empty lunch room occupied only by the creepy new handyman, Mr. Igor. Blaine wasn't sure if it was *EEE*-gor or *EYE*-gor, as if either was better. The old custodian was operating a floor polisher, humming away in a far corner. He watched the two girls walk thru the other half of the cafeteria suspiciously, his native state. He had large buggy eyes, wrinkly pale skin, a wispy patch of oily grey hair, and stood slightly hunched in his olive coveralls.

"Hey, there's the new janitor," Blaine noted. "Man, talk about rising straight from the crypt..."

"Don't tease the poor guy. He's brand new. He's probably someone's dad!"

"I'm in Sophomore Geometry and I'm such a goodie-two-shoes," Blaine mocked her friend. "But for us mortals, having the caretaker straight out of Hogwarts as your new janitor is a little creepy!"

Shelley smiled and stole a glance at the solitary figure scowling across the way, "Well, he does look *super* creepy, but don't let him hear me say that!" The two giggled and walked thru the opposite bank of doors into the High School Annex.

*****

"Bye Shell," Blaine called from the door of the art studio a few doors down, "See you at 4th period."

Blaine entered the hodge-podge art studio. The room consisted of paint splotched work tables brimming with supplies. On the sides of the room were rows of shelves, chipped wood cabinets, and sinks. The shelves above the cabinets were adorned with a collection of old pieces of student art, oddly-shaped pottery vases and forgotten papier-mâché projects.

Art was Blaine's favorite class. She took a deep breath and soaked in the smell of chalk, old paint, and glue that clung to the studio. She walked in and took a seat near a girl she knew. They smiled at each other as first period bell rung. The other twenty kids in class found their seats as the teacher, Mrs. Chow, called them to attention.

"Good morning, everyone!" Mrs. Chow greeted with a warm smile. "I hope everyone had a great summer and is enjoying this glorious morning."

The students responded with a resounding murmur of indifference.

"That's the spirit! Now, before we get into our project, I want to do a quick roll call to make sure everyone is in the right place." She picked up a clipboard with a list of names and started to check them. She went thru the list and people either called "Here!" or raised their hands meekly.

Halfway down the list she said, "Drake Harker?" A tall dark-haired boy raised his hand and said, "Over here, Mrs. Chow."

"New to our school?" the teacher noted warmly. "Class, let's all make sure Mr. Harker feels welcome to Autumn's Hallow." She continued down her list.

Blaine looked over at the new boy. He had dark straight hair with long bangs that covered much of his forehead and eyebrows. His skin was a shade of olive that seemed to sparkle and soak up the sun from the classroom windows. His eyes were bright blue and while he seemed to smile easily, he had the look of an old soul, someone who had been around the block a few times and felt completely comfortable with himself. He was dressed smartly with a tight-fitting sweater vest, white t-shirt, and dark jeans, each well-pressed and cut.

Blaine wasn't usually boy crazy like her sister, Vickie, but she had to admit the new kid had a look. Even though he was new, he was talking easily with fellow students seated near him, his manner friendly and cool. As she checked him out, Drake looked in Blaine's direction and gave her a quick smile. Blaine tried to look away, hoping the smile had been intended for the peeling, papier-mâché bust of George Washington on the shelf behind her. *Smooth, Blaine*, she chided herself. *Real smooth.*

Mrs. Chow finished the roll call and put her clipboard to the side. "OK, class, onto our first assignment. Since we only have a half hour today and it's our first day back, I wanted to do a quick, fun exercise to get your creative juices flowing. On the tables are paints, brushes, sponges, and whatever you need to craft a memorial to your summers. Use this as a chance to show your creativity! Use brushes, fingers, sponges, you name it. The goal is to capture the colorful essence of summer!

You have 25 minutes and then we will hang up our works and clean up."

Her near miss with Drake Harker forgotten, Blaine donned her art smock and let herself go in her painting. She decided to capture a memory from her family trip to San Francisco, creating a scene from a wharf-side café in Tiburon. She combined yellows, browns, and reds to capture the tall spires and swoops of the Golden Gate Bridge and its reflection in the sparkling waters of the San Francisco Bay. On the sides stood the green and brown cliffs of Marin County and in the distance, the hazy greys and whites of San Francisco's skyscrapers in the summer.

Blaine wasn't shy about getting dirty and frequently used her fingers to create the right smudge or color combination. After 25 minutes she felt she had a pretty good approximation of a warm and carefree summer afternoon. She set aside her work to dry and went about cleaning up her workspace. First up, her forearms and hands were covered elbow to fingernails in paint. She got up from her stool and walked over to a nearby sink.

Using one elbow, she wedged up the faucet arm and waited a moment for the water to warm. Once satisfied, she put her arms under and started to rinse. The last thing she needed was grief from Vickie for having paint wedged under her fingernails. She scrubbed vigorously, watching the paint and suds disappear down the drain and looked down to inspect her arms.

Her eyes widened in shock. Where the center of her palm should be to just above her wrist, all she could see was a silver-lined hole. Underneath was the dull grey sink and the remnants of painty suds draining. Panic building, she moved her hand to her face and inspected her stricken palm. She turned her palm over and saw the top of her hand, knuckles and skin intact. She turned her hand over again and peered thru the silver-lined hole where she could see the brown cabinet on the wall opposite.

Oh, my God, I washed off my hand! she shrieked in her mind. She couldn't rip her eyes from her palm. She moved it up and down and the hole persisted, punctuated by a faint shimmering effect, blurring the see-thru image. *Get a grip on yourself,* she thought. *This is all in your mind, close your eyes and count to five.* Fighting to stay in control, she did so, clenching her eyes tight and holding her hand close to her chest. *One, two, three, four...*

"Hey, is something wrong?" A voice, a young male one, asked behind her. Blaine turned slowly, eyes still shut tight. She opened them slowly. In front of her was the new boy, Drake Harker, a kind look on his face. Blaine stared at him blankly, eyes blinking rapidly, her stricken right hand still balled up in a fist so tight you could form diamonds from coal in it.

"Is it your hand?" Drake asked. He reached down and took her hand in his own. As if, of its own accord, her fist obeyed and slowly opened.

"Oh, I see," he said, inspecting it briefly. "You're having a tough time getting the silver paint off. I had that problem with mine too." Blaine dwelled on Drake's dreamy blue eyes for a beat or two, and then understanding registered. She pulled her hand away and looked down in horror. Her palm was completely normal again. She triple-checked, flipping her hand over repeatedly to check both sides. The only problem was a smudge of silvery paint underneath her thumb.

"The glitter is great, but the oil-based stuff is tough to clean up." He paused, "Hey, you OK?"

Blaine looked up at Drake, shock still registering in her eyes.

"Oh, sorry about grabbing your hand. My mom says I need to respect people's personal space better. I'm Drake, by the way, and you are?"

Blaine stared at Drake dumbly, blinking, mouth agape. He stood in front of her with a warm smile creasing his eyes. "Blaine," she replied, shrinking back to her work area, "and sorry, I'm mental... err, I mean I need to clean my desk."

"No problem," Drake replied, walking up to the sink and watching Blaine back away, tipping over a can of drying brushes in the process. "Nice to meet you, Mental Blaine!"

He smiled. She feigned a chuckle, fumbling with the toppled can of brushes, and turned to walk swiftly back to her desk.

What just happened? she thought on multiple levels, checking her hand as second period bell trilled.

Chapter 4: Blaine

Blaine was troubled the rest of the morning, rubbing her hand and staring at it. "What is happening to me?" she repeated. "Am I seeing things again?" she fretted. "Are the bad memories coming back?"

A terrible fear gripped her, taking her back to the troubled days shortly after her biological parents had died. She was only four but could still remember snippets of that terrible time. It happened in New York City. A hotel room in a tall grey tower, storm clouds outside, a nanny, a police officer with a sad face.

"Plane crash," the policeman had said, "lost over stormy waters... terrible... no survivors... bodies not found."

She remembered the funeral, standing there alone in a child-sized black dress, holding her doll by one arm staring at two empty caskets. She had no living relatives, her parents who moved frequently had no close friends, and she had no city or home to call her own. She was small, scared, and alone.

What followed was a series of foster homes and visits with doctors and therapists. Blaine's coping mechanism was to imagine things, vivid stories, and imaginary friends. Usually they were friendly but sometimes they were dark, conjuring terrible nightmares and inconsolable screaming fits even during the day. It had made her a difficult fit with many families. The more she moved, the worse the visions had become.

Slowly though she recovered and the waking nightmares faded away, replaced by her painting and drawings. What had been a curse, Blaine transformed into a gift. And one day a woman, she couldn't remember the details of her face other than her eyes, the deepest blue, came to the orphanage she was staying in. She was almost six years old.

"Hi, what's your name?" the woman had asked.

"Blaine."

"Blaine what?"

"Blaine Stoker."

"And how old are you?"

"I'm five and three quarters!"

The woman smiled. "Well, Blaine Stoker who's five and three quarters, how would you like to come with me to a new home?" the woman asked.

"Where?" the girl said, innocently sucking on the end of her long dark ponytail.

"A beautiful place," the woman replied, "it's a town by the beach with forests and mountains and farms far away from any scary dreams or bad people. Does that sound nice?"

The little girl looked down at her feet. "Can I bring my dolly?" she asked. Blaine remembered the woman's smile and how it lit up her radiant sapphire eyes.

"Of course, honey. You can bring anything you want." The woman bent down and put her hand on the little girl's head. "There is a loving family who can't wait to meet you and your dolly. Would you like to come?"

"OK... but can we get ice cream on the way?"

"Yes, dear."

That was when she moved in with Nick and Chelsea Davis and met her new big sister, Vickie. Her new parents had tried for years to have another child with no success, all medical options exhausted. They pined for a second little girl and when they got the chance, embraced Blaine as their own. She remembered moving into their beautiful house and her breath being taken away by the big dollhouse bed in her very own bedroom, the first she could ever remember having.

Blaine hadn't had another bad dream since... until today.

"Ms. Davis, is everything alright?" Ms. Poe asked, during fourth period Literary Arts.

"What?" Blaine asked, blinking.

"You seem distracted, dear."

"Oh, no. I'm fine Ms. Poe. Thank you," she said, blushing.

Ms. Poe nodded and resumed her instruction. "Mr. Gaunt, what are your thoughts on the poem we just read?"

Daschle Gaunt, 'Dash' to his friends, sat in the last row of class next to his buddy, Kevin Wallis. He was a tall and rangy boy, with shaggy blonde hair, and a deep tan from playing sports outside. He had been doodling in the margins of his notebook, having just completed a mean triple Ollie with a stick figure skateboarder. He looked up with confusion that quickly turned into panic. Class participation was not his strong suit.

"Uh, I don't know?" he offered.

Kevin shook his head in sympathy while a couple kids near them sniggered.

"An honest, if incomplete, analysis. More time focusing on poetry, Mr. Gaunt, and less on artwork, if you please."

Fifth bell rang. Ms. Poe watched Blaine with concern. Blaine bowed her head, too shy to approach her new teacher. She left for the lunch room and decided to put the events of this morning behind her. Some things were too personal to talk about, even with best friends.

Shelley walked up beside her. "She's cool."

"Who?" Blaine asked.

"Ms. Poe. She's so real. It's like she's seen and done things and not just read about them."

"Yeah," Blaine said, absent-mindedly.

"Are you OK, Blaine?"

Blaine turned and smiled at her. "Yeah Shell, I'm OK. Thanks for asking."

"Hey Shelley!" It was Kevin Wallis, hustling up from behind them with Daschle Gaunt in tow. "You guys going to lunch?"

"Yes, Kevin," Shelley replied, with a quick smile. "You guys want to join us?"

"Sure! You OK with that, Dash?"

"Dude," Dash shook his head, "the guys are waiting for us. We've got a Gothic match! Oh, 'sup Blaine, Shelley." The girls greeted Dash.

"Oh yeah," Kevin replied, crestfallen. He perked up quickly. "Well, maybe some other time! See you guys!"

"Bye Kevin," Blaine called, as the two boys walked away. She turned to Shelley, perking up, a mischievous grin crossing her face. "You know he has a crush on you."

"He *SO* does not!" Shelley replied, blushing slightly.

"For a math whiz, you are clueless Shell," Blaine replied, shrugging her bag up her shoulder.

Shelley opened her mouth to disagree but just shrugged and smiled. The two girls shared a good laugh as they joined a group of students walking towards the lunch room. *It was good to have friends,* Blaine thought.

*****

The lunch room was a crush of seventh and eighth graders, dashing around with lunch bags and trays of cafeteria food, gabbing in flocks around circular tables with colorful chairs. Blaine felt like pizza, so proceeded to the opposite end of the hall. On the way, she saw Vickie huddled with her coven of friends. Vickie looked up, whispered to her gal pals and walked straight over to her sister.

"Have you met the new boy yet?" she asked excitedly. "Drake Harker?" Vickie sighed, looking upward dreamily.

"Yeah," Blaine replied. "he's in my art class. Why?"

"He is to die for! My friends and I swear we have seen him in a movie before or maybe it was TV. Do you recognize him? Did you get a chance to talk to him?"

"Only for a second," Blaine shrugged, unconsciously rubbing her right hand. "He seemed nice."

"Nice? He is like a little slice of Beverly Hills walking thru the school, Blaine. Mark my words, I will be getting to know him better. If you see him, I want to know everything you do. OK? Sister promise?" she finished sweetly.

Vickie rejoined her friends in a chorus of giggles as they surveyed the room for topics of conversation.

Blaine rolled her eyes. She was glad her sister didn't have any concerns weighing her down. Blaine was holding enough baggage for both Davis sisters.

*****

Final bell rang and the teachers instructed everyone to make their way to school assembly. Blaine and Shelley followed the crush of students into the gymnasium.

The crowd of sixth, seventh and eighth grade kids were buzzing with late afternoon energy at the coming release from school. Everyone was eager to escape to the warm sunshine of a late August afternoon. In front of the home team bleachers, the eighth grade pep band was playing an approximation of school fight songs, worse for wear after a long summer with little practice.

Blaine and Shelley entered the bleachers from the mezzanine above the gym and looked around for seats. It was crowded. Halfway down, Kevin Wallis sat with his group of friends and caught their eye. He waved to them, indicating they still had room in their section. The girls made their way down the aisle, avoiding the odd paper airplane or origami ninja throwing star being chucked about.

As Blaine walked, she saw Vickie in one of the upper rows. She and her friends were surrounding a dark-haired boy who had several of the better known eighth graders sitting with him. The boy looked up, it was Drake Harker.

He seemed to take notice of Blaine, making eye contact with her and smiling. Blaine averted her eyes and bumped into a large seventh grade boy wearing an oversize football jersey trying to exit his aisle.

"Oh sorry," she apologized.

"Watch where you're walking, art nerd!" he growled.

"Hey Paul, why don't you stuff it?" called a voice from behind Blaine.

The XXL bully looked up from Blaine threateningly, but then smiled.

"Ah, didn't mean to offend your girlfriend, Dash-trash," Paul responded. He allowed Blaine to pass him without further harassment.

Daschle Gaunt stood behind Blaine, wearing his own yellow and brown school football jersey over his regular clothes. He had a grim face that creased into a grin as he shook his head at his teammate.

"Not a girlfriend," he said, high-fiving Paul, "but you wouldn't know what that is anyway, so why bother explaining?"

"Funny," Paul replied, playfully pushing his friend into Blaine who looked back, a little annoyed. She didn't like being in the middle of so many male hormones.

"Why don't you hang out with us for the assembly?" Paul offered. "Coach wants us all to sit together for school spirit events."

"Can't, I promised Kevin and the guys I'd hang with them before practice," Dash shrugged, continuing down a few aisles.

"Gaunt, you are hopeless," the other waved him off, teasing. "Have fun playing with your cards and elves!"

"Yeah, see you at practice. Don't eat any sixth graders!" Dash said, catching up to Blaine. "Sorry about Paul." He followed her to Shelley, Kevin and the rest of Kevin's crew. "He gets moody when he hasn't eaten enough protein, usually a lost child or small forest creature does the trick."

She looked back at him and shook her head. *Boys were strange*, she thought. She sat next to Shelly without further comment, stewing on her own concerns.

Dash took a seat between Kevin and two other boys, Walter and Mike. The three were playing the group's new favorite game, Gothic. Between them, they had four plastic figurines, a deck of cards, and Kevin's and Walter's smartphones setting on the metal bleacher. The three-inch plastic figurines were of gory-looking monsters in battle poses set on top of round bases depicting some form of horror movie scene.

There were four characters: The Wolf Man, Count Dracula, The Invisible Man and Frankenstein's Monster. Kevin had the Wolf Man and Walter the Invisible Man and each proceeded to put their character on their smartphone screen facing each other. The smart chips in each of the figures talked to their corresponding phones and started the Gothic software with a flourish of creepy sound effects.

"Wolf Man vs. Invisible Man!" their phones intoned in a narrator's voice straight from the underworld.

"OK," Kevin announced, pressing a big red button on his screen. "Wolf Man gets first strike and I use 'Howl of Torture!' on you."

His phone blared a long baying sound as Walter's phone let out a corresponding "Ughh!" and battle damage sound effect.

The evil Crypt-Keeper voice on Kevin's phone announced, "Invisible Man, loose a turn!" followed by a sinister laugh and a sound effect of a heavy door creaking shut with a bang.

"Now to finish you!" Kevin pronounced happily as Mike egged him on. "I'm putting all my action points in this one, Walt! Swarm of Claws, super attack!"

Kevin's phone lit up under the figure and its eyes glowed bright blue as a series of swiping sound effects and snarls came from its speaker. Walter's phone trembled. The figurine's clear hands and head lit in a white glow and Walter's phone announced "Miss! Aura of Invisibility. Invisible Man counters!"

A loud "Heeyah!" sound escaped Walter's phone and Kevin's shrieked a giant dog yelp followed by a shudder as the narrator on Walter's phone solemnly announced "Critical wounds! Wolf Man is at Death's Door"

"That's not fair!" Kevin protested.

"Hey, you're the one who wanted to attack the Invisible Man with an oversize Chihuahua!" Walter countered, looking at his figure gleefully.

The PA in the gym crackled and Principal Marlowe called the assembly to order. After a brief set of comments he introduced a thin, hard-looking older man in an immaculate blue suit. It was the head master of nearby Grimm Academy. Behind him sat three boys sitting perfectly rigid, each a mirror image of the other - snow white hair, tall, athletic, fair-skinned.

The old headmaster approached the microphone. Dark sunglasses hid his eyes and deep wrinkles creased his face. He wore a grim, sour expression and was hunched over.

"Dude, that guy looks Yoda-old and Emperor-evil," Dash commented.

"Watch out for blue lightning," Kevin snickered.

"Good afternoon. I am Van Guiles, the headmaster of Grimm Academy," his voice strong and dry. "While I have been with Grimm only a few weeks, it is clear we're an elite institution of learning, available only to a privileged few. Our students and faculty are the fastest, the brightest, the most gifted. Our school is a beacon to others."

"Wow, the Emperor is really humble about his Death Star," Blaine murmured. Dash grinned. Chicks who could hang with Star Wars humor were alright in his book.

"I'm pleased to announce we will be opening the gates to our academy to many of you in the coming weeks. We want to get to know our neighbors, share our facilities, and understand your backgrounds."

"As part of this exchange program, we will also send students to your school. Allow me to introduce Heinz, Frederick and Carlos." The three boys stood and looked out at the crowd, standing tall and still. Guiles indicated for them to retake their seats. They did so in unison.

"Talk about the *Brothers Grimm...*" Kevin muttered.

"I hope you will welcome these three fine boys to your school, much like we look forward to getting to know each of you."

He smiled, a malevolent grin crept up the side of his sunglasses, an unnatural feature on his skeletal face, and turned the proceedings back to the principal.

"Sign me up for Dr. Crypt Keeper's tomb of learning!" Dash exclaimed, as Principal Marlowe resumed his place at the podium.

"Ditto," Kevin added, "that Grimm Academy is scary. It gives me the shivers whenever we drive by."

Blaine shuddered. *Grimm Academy, invisible hands, bad memories... great, keep talking guys.*

"I think it's fantastic we're getting to know the kids there," Shelley replied. "You hardly ever see anyone attending the school. They always stay walled up in that big mansion like it's some kind of prison."

"I'm afraid of what the inmates will be like," Dash grunted. "We play them this week for the opening game. First time ever. We'll see what those rich boys are made of."

"Well, I'm going to ask Principal Marlowe more about the program. It would be good to find out what their school has to offer."

Principal Marlowe wrapped up his comments and released the kids for the day. Guiles and the Brothers Grimm exited out the side entrance.

"Hey Dash, do you have time for one more round of Gothic before football practice?" Kevin asked, as the group of kids got up with the crowd.

"You bet, Kev. I want to give that Vampire a try!"

"No way, he will take down my Wolf Man!" Kevin countered, punching his larger friend in the shoulder.

Dorks, was all Blaine could think shaking her head. She exited with Shelley and headed to her house for the afternoon. Hopefully staying busy with friends would keep the dark memories at bay.

*****

Guiles dismissed Heinz, Frederick, and Carlos and entered the back seat of a black SUV with dark-tinted windows.

"Drive," he commanded, closing the door. His phone rang as the car pulled away.

"Guiles," he said into the speaker.

"Master," a familiar voice on the other end of the line breathed.

Guiles voice shifted, taking on his natural tones. There was no need for ruses with his chief lieutenant. "What progress have we made identifying the heirs?"

"We know the woman has brought them together in this town and has been hiding them for some time. We have not identified all yet, but we know one is the girl from New York."

"Whose parents we killed eight years ago?" Guiles, aka von Frankenstein mused. "The Stoker child, correct?"

"Yes, the woman had the child hidden and moved frequently, but we know who she is now. Should I have her brought to you and her family disposed of?"

"No, not until we have identified the others. But hurry, I grow weary of this game. I do not want to stoop to sponsoring open houses to find our quarry."

"Yes, Master."

Von Frankenstein stopped to consider. "Let the boys out to hunt tonight. See if they can get some information from the locals. Worst case, they will have some sport. Best case, we find something useful."

"Yes, Master."

"Do we have news of Harker?" von Frankenstein sneered at the mere mention of the name.

"She is here but remains hidden. She plans a trap for us. We believe she will use the heirs as bait."

"Her husband and their whelp?"

"We know them to be aiding her. The old man is being watched closely. The boy we have not yet identified, but I suspect a student at the school."

"Good, if you identify her or her son, deal with them decisively."

"Master?"

"What?" the Doctor snapped.

"Tempest's heir is here."

Von Frankenstein paused. His niece's heir, his flesh and blood. "Inform me when you identify my great-grandniece. I will deal with this matter *personally*."

"Yes, Master."

Von Frankenstein hung up as the SUV pulled into the gates of Grimm Academy. Things were coming together. Soon he would have his prey. And no one could help them.

*****

Blaine got home from Shelley's later that evening. It had been good to spend time with her friend but the events from this morning and subsequent memories still weighed on her mind.

"Hi Blaine," her mom called.

Blaine walked into the kitchen and saw Matteo up on the kitchen counter and her mom leaning over a magazine, reading. On the back lawn, Vickie was practicing cheer routines while her father was firing up the barbecue on the patio, home early for a change from work. Blaine walked up to her mother and gave her a big hug, squeezing tight.

"Well, what was that for?" her mother asked, smiling.

"Nothing, just thank you for being there for me."

"Blaine, we'll always be there for you."

"I know, Mom. I know… Wanna head out back?"

Her mother nodded, joining her. She walked outside to share news from her first day back at school and spend some time with those she loved. Invisible hands and bad memories of dark times, at least for now, forgotten.

Chapter 5: Mina

Roswell, New Mexico… 7 days after the incident.

"I can't believe they are going to take those finds and not tell us anything!" Mina fumed, as she chopped vegetables on a cutting board on her wobbly, make-shift kitchen table.

"Easy there, killer," Peter replied, hovering over a piping-hot sauce dish cooking on the cramped gas stove. "While you're fuming about Army Intelligence, could you pass me the oregano?"

"This is a once in a lifetime… heck once in anyone's lifetime opportunity!" she said, passing him the jar of dried spices. "An Alien spacecraft and a giant Martian! And we, the people who found it, are told nothing?"

"Mina, listen. This is the Army and the government. You should feel lucky they aren't taking you away too," he said, shaking spices into the bubbling pot.

"I'm glad none of you got hurt!" Peter continued, stirring the sauce and giving it a quick taste. "That was scary stuff out there. You didn't see that robot crest the hill and just stand there!"

"Ahhh… my brave, handsome, fighter pilot got scared?" Mina teased.

Peter grinned. "Let's just have a nice dinner tonight and bring it up again with Major Carlisle tomorrow. He's a reasonable CO and the Intel guys aren't packing up and leaving for Groom's Lake for another three days."

He put the spoon down with a satisfied smile. "Come on over and give this a try. It's Mother Murphy's secret recipe!"

"Don't try to play cute with me, soldier boy," she said, putting her knife down on the cutting board. "I'll give your Mom's sauce a try, but don't think I'm going to drop this subject!"

Mina's quarters were a small four-room dorm in the base complex of the Roswell Observatory. Over her eight months rotation she had made some personal touches to give the cabin a warm and cozy feel but space was still tight, particularly in her small kitchenette off the main living room. Despite having some room to move, Peter remained standing where he had been cooking, liking the close proximity to his girlfriend.

"Cozy," he smiled, giving her a small squeeze around the waist. "Tell me what you think of my Mom's special recipe?" He offered her a wooden spoon laden with a dab of sauce. Mina blew to cool it down and took a tentative taste.

"OK, so you can cook," she replied, leaning back into Peter. She closed her eyes as he held her and he looked out the kitchen window. Outside, the night was dry and clear with stars in the sky and a full bright moon covering everything with a faint blue hue.

"I'm still upset," she said, frustration clearly expressed in her voice. "How long until the pasta is ready?"

"Another ten or twenty minutes. I started the other burner to get the pasta going." Both burners were burning hot and bright blue on the stove. A big pot of water waited on the side to be placed to boil. He paused and turned his head. "Do you hear that?" Outside, a howl cut through the air. It sounded close. Mina unwrapped herself from Peter as he moved to the window in the living room.

"Did Angie and Lonn get a new dog?" Mina asked. The howl renewed, this time closer, louder.

"That doesn't sound like a dog," Peter paused. "Too big, that's a wolf. Never heard one so close to town before."

The phone rang and Peter answered. "Hello. Yes, this is Peter. Angie? Calm down. Talk slower. I can't understand. Lonn? He's acting strangely? He's outside howling? At the moon? Hold on, Angie. Hold on, I'll be right over. Just down the block at Mina's. Yes. Yes… be right there." Peter put the phone in its cradle and went to get his coat off the couch.

Without looking, he called back to Mina, "I've got to go down to the Cheney's quarters. Something's wrong with Lonn. Angie says he has been agitated all evening but once the full moon rose, he's going bonkers. Will you be… Mina, your hand!"

Peter had turned around and was staring at Mina who remained in the kitchen. Mina looked at her right hand. It was resting on the red hot grill of the spare burner, blue flames surrounding her fingers. A strange grey and black smoke enveloped her entire lower arm licking over her skin and clothing in undulating wisps that evaporated as they climbed.

She screamed and quickly lifted her arm away, cradling it to her body. Peter rushed over to aid her. "Let me see your arm!" he ordered.

Mina gave him a stricken look, uncovered her arm and duly offered it to Peter for inspection. The grey and black smoke was dissipating with only a few tendrils remaining. The strange mist seemed to be emanating directly from her skin. Peter lifted her hand tenderly inspecting it for what he feared would be horrible burns. Nothing. Her skin was as pale and perfect as ever. Peter and Mina looked up and stared at each other in amazement.

"What just happened?" Mina whispered.

Peter didn't get a chance to reply as another howl cut thru the night, this time from right outside.

Chapter 6: Dash

Dash headed out of final assembly with Kevin and played a quick game of Gothic. His new Count Dracula figure was victorious over Kevin's all bark, no bite Wolf Man. After showing his hapless friend who was boss of the beasts, Dash jogged down to the locker rooms abutting the gym to don his football gear.

Daschle Gaunt was a tall boy of twelve who was growing as his Grandmother frequently said "like a weed." Over the summer, he sprouted four inches and was now one of the tallest kids in his class. His sandy-colored hair was thick and shaggy with a permanent surfer dude look, immune to the charms of a comb. His skin had a rich summer tan, the result of participating in whatever pick-up sports games he could find.

While he'd loved sport his entire life, his recent growth spurt put him into a new league of ability. Over the summer, he had not only grown but had gotten faster and started to put a little muscle on his frame. Football was his particular passion and he played both inside linebacker and halfback, a rarity for a seventh grader on a combination seventh and eighth grade team. While he was nervous with the new responsibility of being a starter, he was eager to show his coach what he could do.

Dash greeted his friends in the locker room, found his cubby, and put on his jersey and dusty cleats. He jogged out to practice with a clutch of his teammates. After warm-ups, the team split in groups with defensive drills kicking off the day.

"Dash, over here with the defensive line. We need a runner!" his assistant coach ordered.

The line coach blew his whistle "OK, boys. Let's get in a line. We're going to start with a tackle drill. Dash is going to be our runner. Each of you will start out on your backs facing me. When I blow the whistle, you will get up, turn around, and try to make contact with Dash who is running the ball. Wrap him up and then let him go. No full tackles! Ready?"

The coach blew his whistle again and everyone got in line. Dash stood about ten yards in front of the linemen and when coach blew his whistle, he did a quick cut to the left or right of the players. The first two went well. The linemen got up and tried to get him. One wasn't nearly quick enough and Dash managed to get past him easily. The second was older and a little faster but only managed to get a hand grasping his jersey.

"Ok, boys, I want to see some improvement!" Coach instructed. "Dash is fast but we need you guys to be quicker! Joe, you're next!"

Oh boy, Dash thought, *Joe Olaf...*

Joe rumbled forward and lay down on the ground, tension exuding from his body. While Joe was big, he was also nimble with fast reflexes in short runs. Dash was pretty sure he would get caught on this one. The coach blew his whistle and Dash ran right. Joe got up fast but not fast enough. He managed to get a hand on Dash's leg but Dash was able to run by him.

"Give me another shot, Coach!" Joe called, as Dash ran back. "I stumbled getting up."

"OK Olaf. You game, Gaunt?" Dash's confidence was higher now. He nodded, still puffing from his last sprint. The players got in position and Coach tweeted his whistle. Olaf anticipated the coach's signal, getting a split-second head start on Dash. Dash ran left but Joe barreled down on him and hit him hard. Joe wrapped him up and instead of stopping, pummeled Dash into the ground.

The coach tweeted his whistle repeatedly. "That's enough, Olaf! I said wrap and release!"

"Sorry, Coach," Joe lied, with a wicked snicker. He got up and pushed down on Dash who was still on the ground.

"Gaunt, you OK?" Coach asked, hovering over him. The hit had hurt physically but more importantly dented his pride. Dash got up slowly.

"Yeah, Coach, I'm fine. Let's get back to drilling. I can handle it."

They went thru the drills again. Dash was a little wobbly after his hit from Joe but still managed to get past most of the other players. They cycled thru everyone and it was Olaf's turn again. The coach trilled his whistle. Again, Joe cheated and pile-drived Dash into the ground.

"That's enough, Olaf!" Coach warned. "One more and you are benched!"

Dash's face was on the ground. He could taste grass and dirt pressed up between his face mask. He was tired of Joe Olaf and his bullying and cheating. Suddenly, anger started to overcome his embarrassment. He spit out the dirt from his mouth and pushed himself up.

"It's OK, Coach," Dash said, standing up and dusting himself off. "In fact, I want another try against Olaf. Let's see if he can take me down three times!"

"You sure, Gaunt? That was a heckuva hit."

Dash replied with a grunt and a head nod. Joe smiled, cracked his knuckles, and got back into position for the drill. The other linemen egged him on, hoping to see him give a good cracking to the nimble, young runner who had eluded them for most of practice.

Dash got into position and looked up at the coach and Olaf. As the coach brought the whistle to his mouth, time felt like it slowed down. Dash's eyesight narrowed, his senses became sharper. He saw the breeze blowing the dark green blades of grass separating him and Joe. He could smell the dirt in his face mask, the sweat from the other players, and the leathery scent from the ball he carried. He imagined he could see inside those who surrounded him with x-ray vision, their veins pulsing with each beat of their heart, their muscles tightening and unclenching as they shifted and moved. The feeling was exhilarating.

Coach blew the whistle and Dash reacted. Instead of running left or right, Dash chose to surprise Joe. He dashed directly up the middle, right at the lumbering giant, as he got up from his crouch. Feeling every fiber of muscle firing in tune, Dash exploded from his stance and ran directly at Joe who was now halfway up.

One step, two steps, three steps. Joe was now up and looking for his prey. Dash could see surprise register in Olaf's eyes turning to an evil sneer as he realized the runner was coming right at him, a foolish move. Joe tensed and got into a tackling position, preparing to bowl into the smaller runner again, punishing him for his challenge.

Four steps, five steps, six steps, contact. Dash lowered his shoulder and ran right into Joe who was uncoiling into a tackle position, trying to ram his shoulder into

Dash's mid-section and wrap his arms around his chest. Dash let out a low growl, felt his eyes widen and his leg muscles explode with new found strength. Time remained in slow motion. As they made contact, Joe's sneer evaporated into a look of confusion and then shock. Power coursed thru Dash, power he didn't know he had. Joe was unable to wrap his arms around Dash's surging form, his legs and body buckled as Dash plowed straight through him. Dash let out a roar as he steamed thru the lineman.

Joe let out a grunt and a gasp as he fell backward, his momentum stopped and reversed. It took seconds, but to Dash it felt like a lifetime. Time renewed its normal cadence and Dash slowed down to a jog. He stopped and turned.

On the ground lay the crumpled Joe laying on his back trying to stir. The other linemen and the coach were staring at Dash with looks of surprise. What had been a fast but young runner was now a locomotive in human form.

"Holy cow, Gaunt!" Coach broke the silence. "Where did that come from?!?"

One of the other players was trying to help Joe get up but fell over him as the big guy fell back onto his elbows shaking his head, dazed.

Dash jogged slowly back. "Sorry Coach, I was just tired of Joe cheating. Is he OK?"

Olaf looked up still dazed at Coach and said, "*Aunt Betty*?"

Coach put his arms around Joe and helped him to his feet, handing him over to two linemen. "Take him to the trainer." He turned to Gaunt and said, "He just got his bell rung. Go back with the linebackers, Gaunt." Dash nodded and jogged to the other side of the field. *Wow,* he thought smiling, *I didn't know I had that in me.*

The rest of practice went without incident with Joe Olaf and the other defensive linemen giving Dash a wide berth.

*****

Football practice ended and Dash was showered and dressed by 5:00 P.M. He said goodbye to a couple of buddies getting into waiting parents' cars, hoisted his book bag, and started to walk home. He was feeling hungry after practice and decided to take a detour, swinging thru Main Street to grab a snack. Sundown wouldn't be for another few hours and Dash enjoyed the cool ocean breeze and the warm late day sun as he walked on the bike path down the main road.

Dash approached the city center which was a dense selection of two and three-story brick and wood buildings clustered over a couple city blocks. The obligatory Fudge Shoppe was followed by the Arts and Crafts store, featuring 1,001 ways to make art with seashells followed by a selection of small bars, cafes, restaurants, and shops. Dash stopped in front of the Salty Dog Provision Co. and opened the creaky metal screen door. A bell tinkled above as he entered.

An old woman sat behind a nearby counter, stocked top to floor with a collection of sweets and candy bars, reading the local newspaper. Dash approached and read the front page headline *"Bear or Sasquatch? Local Man Comes Face To Face With Bigfoot"* followed by a picture of a man in a trucker's cap and bathrobe standing beside a crushed garbage can outside his home.

The store consisted of three rows of mostly food and tourist items with a few aged refrigerators in back cooling sodas, milk, and the like. As Dash walked up, the lady peered over her paper.

"Why, Daschle Gaunt," she greeted, setting her paper aside, "how is your grandmother doing? Been a while since I saw either of you in church!"

"She's fine," Dash lied. His grandmother had been sick for several months and infrequently left their small single-wide home in the hills above town.

"Tell her Rose would appreciate a visit from time to time!" the shopkeeper replied. "Now, what can I get you, dear?"

"Two pieces of beef jerky, please," Dash answered, eyeing two large hunks in a jar by the cash register. "And maybe a couple nickel pieces of taffy... licorice and strawberry." Rose smiled and went about getting the items.

"Have you heard from your mother lately?" she asked, fishing out jerky chunks.

"No," Dash answered tersely. Dash hadn't seen his mother in almost two years. She left him with his grandmother at Christmas in 5th grade and hadn't been heard from since.

"Sorry to hear that, hon," Rose replied, humming to herself. "Did you see the article in the paper? Says some dentist up in one of those fancy new subdivisions saw Bigfoot clawing thru his trash." She pointed to the paper and the front page article. "If you ask me he's been inhaling too much of his own laughing gas," she scoffed.

Dash smiled politely as she put the jerky and four pieces of candy into a small brown paper bag and pressed a few buttons on the old mechanical cash register. "That will be $2.50."

Dash fished out the remainder of his lunch money and handed over, mostly in spare change. Rose passed over the bag and Dash grabbed the jerky and took a big chew. "Thanks," he replied, between muffled bites.

"No problem," Rose replied. "Come again! And watch out for Sasquatch! Or worst still, that crazy dentist!"

Dash walked outside and finished his first piece of jerky. He took the other piece and put the taffy into his pocket, crumpling up the paper bag and throwing it into a half-empty wastebasket. Sated after a long day and hard practice, he set off for home in the forested hills overlooking town. As he passed an alley which snaked behind several businesses, he heard someone say "Hey, give me back my figure!"

"Kevin?" Dash said aloud. He stopped chewing and cocked his head to hear better.

Nothing.

He had definitely heard something down the side street and could swear it was his best friend's voice. Dash decided to take a quick look. He walked into the brick-lined alley, stuffing more of his jerky into his mouth and finishing it quickly. A set of old tires lay against one wall while trash cans and old cardboard boxes lined the back of the art store opposite. Dash's feet crunched on the dusty gravel of the unfinished alley pavement. He called out, "Kevin?"

"Dash!" came a call back up ahead, to the right. It was definitely his friend.

Dash moved forward cautiously and put his bag down near the lip of the alley entrance where he had heard his friend call. He turned the corner to see Kevin being held by the collar by three eerily similar-looking boys. Dash recognized Heinz, Frederick, and Carlos, the Brothers Grimm from school assembly earlier in the day, surrounding Kevin. Heinz was forcing Kevin to stand on his tiptoes. He held aloft Kevin's Wolf Man figurine, taunting him with it over his head. The other boys looked on with bullying smiles.

"What's going on?" Dash declared, as he took it all in. "Kevin, you OK?"

"No," Kevin squeaked before Heinz pushed him away. Kevin crumpled in a pile on the opposite end of the alley. He stirred slowly, nursing a sore elbow.

Heinz stepped forward while the other two Brothers Grimm flanked him on either side. He sniffed at the air with a mean leer spreading across his otherwise perfect, blonde face. "It smells like wet dog," he said, stepping closer to Dash and making a distasteful expression. "I can't stand wet, stinky animals."

"Listen," Dash replied, tensing himself as the other two approached, "we don't want any trouble. Why don't you give Kevin back his stuff?"

"You mean this toy?" Heinz replied. He dropped it on the ground and crushed it with the heel of his sneaker with a satisfying crunch.

"Hey, that's a collector's edition!" Kevin yelped from the side.

Heinz ignored the hapless Kevin. He and the other two boys menaced forward, forming a triangle around Dash. "I think it's time we taught you a lesson, mutt."

Carlos and Frederick moved to grab Dash's arms but Dash was too quick. He ducked Carlos, lowered his shoulder and bowled into Frederick, knocking him off-balance. Frederick tried to grapple with Dash and keep him pinned to the gravelly pavement while his compatriots moved in. Dash got up quickly, ripping his grey sweatshirt. Carlos took a swing at Dash who ducked, pushed Carlos over, and moved to the left, directly in front of Heinz.

"Hello, mutt," Heinz grinned and pulled back his arm to punch Dash in the face.

Dash reacted instinctively. Heinz threw a powerful roundhouse directly at his face. Dash ducked, feeling the whoosh of air from Heinz's fist as it rushed just past his left ear. With a rush of energy, he uncoiled his body, connecting with a right hook squarely on Heinz's exposed chin. Heinz's lower face dissolved into Dash's fist, exploding into a swarming cloud of a thousand buzzing pieces. Dash's fist rushed right through the swarm. Dash recovered his balance and stepped back in horror.

The buzzing grey cloud expanded into a swarm around Heinz's head. The cloud undulated like an angry hive of bees, buzzing and moving as if it were a living nightmare. Heinz stood tall and turned his head to look down at Dash through the swirling veil, contempt and loathing oozing from his cold blue eyes. His face was destroyed as if the lower half of a mask that surrounded his head exploded. Over his eyes, nose, and upper cheek, Heinz's face was still perfect. But his lower jaw was in tatters.

A chill shuddered thru Dash as he looked at Heinz. Where perfect skin and bone structure had once been, lay a picture of ruin. Heinz's jaw appeared grey and rotting, his lips a sooty black and his skin flaking away in puffs of ash, revealing disintegrating charcoal bone.

Whatever Heinz appeared on the outside was only there to conceal some horrible creature underneath.

Heinz stepped into the buzzing cloud and raised his ruined chin. The swarm moved around his head, expanding and contracting in unison, congealing around him. The tiny pieces knit together forming the outlines of a honeycombed jawbone which hardened and turned molten silver, expanding over and concealing the zombie face beneath. The strange molten substance swirled and expanded, filling the gaps of bone, muscle, and flesh resolving into a strong, square chin and perfectly formed, lightly-tanned skin. Heinz's face was just like new, the horror beneath concealed.

What the heck is going on here! Dash's mind screamed, his body frozen in place by the shock of what he had just seen.

Heinz turned his now perfect face and looked at Dash with contempt. He smiled devilishly, adjusting his reformed jaw with a crack.

"My turn," Heinz hissed. Before Dash could react, Heinz grabbed him by the shoulders, swung him around, and threw him into a set of trash bins. The bins scattered as Dash was flung helplessly into their midst. He hit the ground hard.

The Brothers Grimm stalked Dash from across the alley. Dash got up in a woozy crouch, eyeing the look-alikes. He was tired after a tough football practice and outnumbered three to one by preppy bullies he had never met. To make matters worse, one or more of them was some kind of zombie-bot or else Dash had been hit harder than he thought. Either way, this was not going to end well.

"Time to take your beating, dog boy. Next time you should be put on a…" Heinz was cut off by the guttural high-pitched battle-cry of Kevin and the rumbling of wheels of a medium-sized plastic dumpster the smaller boy was pushing with all his might from the back of the alley. The Brothers Grimm looked up with alarm, but too late. Kevin rammed the dumpster into the three boys who were knocked against the opposite wall into a trash bin filled with rotting vegetables and buzzing flies.

"Dash, are you okay?" Kevin said, running over to his friend and helping him up.

"Yeah, thanks Kevin," Dash coughed, as he rose on wobbly legs. "Dude, we need to get out of here. These guys are serious trouble."

Kevin grinned, adrenaline still pumping thru his young body, and looked back at the Brothers Grimm. Heinz, Frederick, and Carlos were struggling to push back the brown plastic dumpster and extract themselves from the week-old vegetable and fruit rinds from the overturned compost barrel.

"That's for the Wolf Man, you dweebs!" he yelled, as he and Dash booked out of the alley.

Heinz pushed the dumpster angrily away, smashing it against the opposite wall. He rose from the ground and picked out an orange peel from his erstwhile perfectly-combed hair. He walked to the opposite side of the alley as his two companions got up and started to clean themselves off. He watched the fleeing figures of Dash and Kevin as they made a turn onto Main Street. He noticed the discarded backpack Dash had dropped, picked it up, opened the main zipper, and selected a text book from inside.

"Daschle Gaunt" the name tag on the inside front cover read. Heinz smiled as he dropped the book and walked back to his friends with the bag. Clearly, they had found one of the heirs. Time to report back, but first they would have a bit of fun.

Chapter 7: Dash

Dash and Kevin sprinted down Main Street, cut up a side road, and continued to run until their sides ached and lungs screamed for oxygen.

"Dash, we gotta... stop... for a second," Kevin wheezed, slowing down and leaning against a chain-link fence in front of a small rental house. Dash stopped and walked back to his friend. He craned his neck looking behind them.

"Ok... just for... a second," he replied, breathing heavily himself. "I want to put some distance between us and those Grimm goons. Did you see what that kid's face did when I hit him?"

Kevin's face was a blank. "What are you talking about?" Kevin shrugged, still huffing and puffing.

"It exploded! It was like... well I don't know what it was like! It exploded into a thousand little pieces and then reformed right in front of me."

"You mean one of those guys is a Terminator?" Kevin mock shouted. "Which one of us is Sarah Connor? Are they the good kind of Terminator, who just shoots you in the kneecaps, or the really bad ones that throw you out of a flying helicopter?"

"Stop it. I know what I saw."

"Dash, I think you got hit harder than you think," Kevin said, finally catching his breath. "That doesn't happen."

"Well, I know what I saw. It was like he was wearing a suit and it exploded when I punched him. He was all grey and decaying underneath..."

"So they are Zombie Terminators? That would be a really cool comic book."

Dash punched Kevin in the shoulder. "You're welcome, by the way."

"Thanks," Kevin replied sheepishly, "man, I don't know what would have happened if you hadn't shown up."

"Let's keep moving," Dash helped his friend up from his crouch, looking over his shoulder for pursuit. "Walk and talk. We can figure things out at my house." He stopped and covered his face with his hands, a look of despair hitting him. He cussed loudly.

"What's wrong now?" Kevin asked, looking around rapidly. "Are they coming?"

"No, but I forgot my backpack back in the alley. My Gran is going to kill me!"

"Do you want to double back and get it?" Kevin asked cautiously.

"Not with those psychos on the loose. Better to lay low." He started to walk up the road which began a gradual ascent from the shore area.

"I'll run by the alley before school," Dash continued. "I didn't have any homework tonight anyway... at least any that I planned to do." He flashed Kevin a wolfish smile and the two pressed on.

"So if we want to avoid town, what's the best way home?" Kevin asked.

Kevin lived in a new planned community in the woods overlooking town a few streets down from the trailer park in which Dash shared a small pre-fab home with his grandmother. The tree-covered hills that surrounded Autumn's Hallow and much of the northern Oregon Coast were steep with few access roads.

Already, the boys were passing fewer and fewer houses, just few blocks out of the city center, as the land rolled into dairy farms, and farms into dense coastal forest.

"We'll have to cut through Old Man Murphy's scrapyard," Dash shrugged. "No big deal. I do it all the time."

"You mean no big deal if he or his dog doesn't see you."

"The old guy keeps Chuckles tied up," Dash reassured his friend. "Besides, they are both ancient. I think that Dog is older than the town. It'll be fine."

The two walked up the narrow, two-lane road. On one side, a fence hugged the street with cows grazing close by. On the other side, a small collection of houses gave way to a fallow field that turned into woods an acre or so in. The road began to climb to the hills in the distance.

"What's the story with you and Shelley? You like her, don't you?"

Kevin looked down, blushing. "Is it that obvious?"

"Kev, you have been my best friend since I pushed that kid off you who was sitting on your face in Kindergarten. Remember him, Stevie Dufus, the one who used to eat all the blue crayons? I think I'd know if you liked someone."

"Oh yeah, Stevie…" Kevin looked up, giving a sheepish smile. "Yeah, I like her. But I don't think she knows I exist."

"Oh, I think she knows you exist," Dash answered, grinning broadly. "Besides, who could resist the sophistication and charm of the world renowned ladies' man, Kevin Wallis?"

Kevin shoved his friend in the back. "Stop it, Dash. I've liked Shelley since third grade. I just can't figure out how to talk to her. She's... complicated."

"I'm no expert but I think that describes all girls." Dash replied. "I think the first thing you need to do is get her alone. She always seems to be attached at the hip with her friend, Blaine Davis. That girl is weird."

Dash wouldn't admit it but weird had an odd definition for a twelve year old boy. In truth, he thought Blaine was cute and maybe even cool. So *weird* better defined the curious and new feelings he had for her, rather than the girl herself.

"Would you help me?" Kevin asked, perking up. "Get her alone. Give me back up. Talk to her friend.... You... you could be my Wing Commander?"

"You mean wing man," Dash replied, shaking his head. "Yeah, sure Kevin. That's a great idea. You talk to Shelley while I talk to the quiet, oddball friend." In truth, Dash did think it was a good idea. He was just as scared as his friend to do it.

"Come on, Dash!" Kevin urged.

Dash relented, "We'll see. Hey, there's the front entrance to Old Man Murphy's."

They rounded a bend in the road which ended abruptly a few hundred meters ahead at a rusty chain link fence with a large gate and gnarled barbed wire across the top. An old corroded sign on the gate read "*Murphy's Scrap Services – Turn Your Scrap into Scratch*" with dollar signs and exclamation points following the tagline. A small byline at the bottom read "*Established 1947*".

On the other side was a sprawling yard of piles of metal trash, industrial rubbish, a mound of discarded kitchen appliances, densely packed shoulder high rows of balding rubber tires, and old sheet metal stacked on greying wood pallets. Completing the picture were old cars and trucks in varying states of disrepair and neglect, some stripped to the chassis on concrete blocks, others with fronts and sides crushed in from a bygone accident. The yard went on for several acres, with woods closing in on either side, backing up into a cliff that rose above the valley floor. Several hundred yards from the gates and to the left, a grey two-story house and a large, shabby work shed sat with what appeared to be the only working mechanical item in the yard, an old Ford pick-up, its blue and white nose sticking out of the shed entrance where it was parked.

Kevin and Dash approached the gates, which were locked together by a loose-fitting chain and pad lock that had a *"CLOSED"* sign affixed to it. The gates were creaking in the early evening coastal wind with a large gap between each. Kevin sniffed and scrunched up his nose. The place smelled like rust and rot, not very inviting.

"Ok, so we squeeze through the gates, cut thru the rows of tires, and find the gap in the fence over by the refrigerators." Dash looked at his friend. "There's a path on the other side that leads up to an old lumber truck road that will take us home."

"Are you sure about the dog?" Kevin asked cautiously. "I'm allergic."

"Kevin, quit being such a wimp and squeeze through. I'll follow." Dash grabbed the rusty metal gates and pushed them apart until the slack chain binding them together tightened. Kevin squeezed through the opening and Dash followed, ducking under the chain.

Once on the other side, the boys peered around. There was still an hour or so of sunshine left in the late summer evening but the angle of the sun in the west created long shadows from the large piles of scrap and rubbish scattered across the yard. It had been several weeks since the area had seen rain so the lot was dusty and dry. Parched, cracked earth and long, spindly dried weeds accentuated the mounds of discarded refrigerators, fifty year old ovens, and abandoned vehicles.

Dash looked toward the house and servicing shed a couple hundred yards away. No movement.

"Looks like Murphy and Chuckles aren't around. Let's cut through those rows of old tires and head to the back fence. There's a gap we can squeeze through that's close to the logger road."

Kevin nodded and followed his taller friend, who walked across the empty expanse of dirt and gravel to the discarded tire section. The crunching of their sneakers and the swaying of nearby trees in the early evening breeze were the only sounds coming from the lifeless scrapyard. They rounded the tall rows of tires to head to the far corner of the fence line. Still no one in sight.

"So far, so good," Dash smiled at his nervous buddy.

"In the movies that's usually when the floor gives out…" Kevin grumbled.

As if on cue, the boys heard shuffling footsteps and an old gravelly voice grumbling. Dash put his hand to Kevin's chest to silently command him to stop. He stood still, trying to focus on the location of the noise. It was coming from a nearby row of tires and, worse yet, was getting closer.

"Dash, that's someone coming!" Kevin whispered urgently.

"What? Did you hear that Chuckles?" The voice asked. It was in the row directly behind them!

"Kevin, shut up!" Dash whispered, squeezing his friend's shoulder.

"Who's there?" The old voice piped up again. "If you don't fess up, I'm going to set my dog loose to have a snack!"

Dash looked behind them and saw a large black and tan dog with a big, square, jowly head round a row of tires. It was Old Man Murphy's Rottweiler, Chuckles. The dog was huge, with a foaming mouth in the hot afternoon sun, big muscular shoulders, bright brown eyes and floppy ears that perked up when he caught whiff of Dash and Kevin. Chuckles assumed guard dog mode, raising his haunches, and let out a low growl as he focused his attention on the two boys. He paced forward.

"Kevin," Dash said, slowly pushing Kevin forward and readying his body for a sprint, "when I say go, we book it for the fence. You go straight and I'll try to lure the jowls of death to chase me."

They looked at the dog advancing toward them as it lowered its stance and its growl intensified.

"Chuckles, what is it boy?" the voice from behind the tires asked. It was close.

"When you find the gap, go through. It's right by a bunch of refrigerators, you can't miss it." Dash gulped. "I'll be right behind you."

The dog was close now, just a few yards away. "Nice psycho poochie..." Dash whispered to the approaching animal. He gripped Kevin hard and gave him a big shove. "Go!"

Kevin scrambled away, his momentum aided by his friend's push. He almost lost his balance but quickly found his footing and ran as fast as his legs could carry him. Dash wasn't far behind except where Kevin ran straight, Dash veered left down a nearby intersection in the rows of tires. The dog snapped his head up as the two boys sprinted away and with only a split second hesitation took off in chase. Dash's plan worked for all of three seconds, when instead of following him, Chuckles took off after Kevin. Kevin looked back with terror as the growling dog bore down on him. Dash could swear he heard him call out for his mommy.

Dash had no choice but to follow. He pivoted and sprinted after Kevin and the pursuing Chuckles. Kevin had about 20 yards on the dog but Chuckles moved fast and was chewing up the difference. Dash poured on the speed, roaring at Chuckles to shift his attention from his hapless friend. Chuckles, panting hard, spittle flying everywhere, continued to bear down on Kevin, who ran like a screaming, panicked lunatic.

Dash had one chance to save his friend from being the giant dog's next chew toy. He slid to a stop, grabbed a decent-sized stone from the ground, and chucked it at the Rottweiler as hard as he could. The rock's aim was true and caught the huffing and puffing guard dog in the back haunch. Chuckles yelped, skidding mid-stride and turned to face Dash. He growled with fresh venom, forgetting the smaller boy, and faced down Dash. Kevin ran on.

"OK Gaunt, what's the plan now?" Dash thought, as Chuckles paced forward, stalking his new prey. Chuckles started to circle the boy, his growl low and fierce. Dash had nowhere left to run. The dog was swifter than him and would bear down on him fast. His only option was to take Chuckles head on and hope for the best. He stared at the dog, his mind racing.

Dash and Chuckles locked eyes with one another as the dog's growl intensified. Dash stared back, his heart pumping fast and adrenaline flowing. Dash couldn't avert his gaze from the circling canine. Involuntarily, he felt a guttural sensation build in the pit of his chest. The hair on his arms and neck raised and his lips curled as a growl spilled out of his mouth. At first it was low and quiet but slowly built into a mean and angry snarl.

GRRRRR!!!

In response, Chuckles snapped at the air and barked a few short gnarly warnings. Dash's face twisted and his snarl became louder, angrier. Chuckles' eyes widened and he backed away, his growl dampening. Dash snapped at the retreating dog, losing all control of his behavior to this strange animal. He felt a different sound build in him. Of their own accord his lips rounded, his throat opened and a rush of air escaped his chest that turned into a low howl like that of a wolf. The sound was low and pure but picked up power as he lifted his chin and bayed loudly.

AAAAOOO!!!

That was all Chuckles could take. At the sound of Dash's howl, the Rottweiler flattened his ears, turned his head, and rushed away, letting out a low yelp.

Old Man Murphy rounded the bend in the tires, limping on a knotty cane, in time to see his one hundred pound guard dog turn tail and run from a skinny twelve year old boy.

"Confound it! Get back here you geriatric excuse for a guard dog," he snapped. He eyed Dash from down the row of tires. He was an ancient-looking man with pure snow-white hair and wrinkly skin. He wore grease stained denim coveralls, dusty brown boots, and a grease smudged red and white trucker's cap that read "*Murphy's*" on its front.

"You!" he continued. "You stay right there!"

Having somehow touched his inner-canine, and miraculously escaping Chuckles unscathed, Dash had no intention of lingering for an interrogation from a grouchy, old, garbage man. He turned tail and ran for the refrigerator pile hiding the gap in the fence that Kevin had sprinted off to.

"Hey!" Murphy shouted after him. "Get back here!"

Dash made it to the gap and immediately squeezed through. He found Kevin waiting, staring thru the metal mesh of the fence.

"How the heck did you get that dog to run away?" Kevin gushed, as Dash got up and dusted himself off.

"I have no idea, but I want to get the heck out of here before that sucker changes his mind. Let's boogie."

"First Zombie Terminators and now King of the Beasts," Kevin replied, following his friend thru the scrub brush that separated the fence from the nearby logger road. "Maybe there is something going on with you, Gaunt."

Dash shook his head and kept pressing on. They walked for a few minutes. The loggers-run meandered upward thru thick, knotty pine trees. An owl hooted in the distance with the coming evening, as the sky above began to darken.

"Dash, are there any wild animals we need to worry about out here?" Kevin asked, breaking the silence between them. "My Mom was talking about a bunch of bear sightings recently. And in the paper this morning, my Dad said some guy down the block claims to have seen Bigfoot!"

Dash shook his head, remembering the comments from Rose in the convenience store. "After a day like today, I wouldn't be surprised if a pack of rabid squirrels attacked us," Dash huffed, as he climbed the steep, rocky road. "But no, I don't think we have anything to worry about. Besides you know what they say about bears?"

"What?"

"You don't need to be faster than the bear, just faster than your friend."

"That's comforting to hear from our school's starting halfback. Great… one more thing to worry about, fending off wild bears and Bigfoot."

Dash kept walking. Kevin was right, there were lots of things to worry about, and even bigger mysteries to ponder. But first things first, he thought, I need to face my Granny and tell her about my lost book bag.

Dash shivered. He would have preferred a bear attack.

Chapter 8: Dash

Granny was sick in bed when Dash got home.

The trek up the logger's run had been uneventful, with no sign of pursuit from the old man and his dog or the three creeps from Grimm Academy. It had actually been a nice break from an otherwise crazy day. On top of the typical first day of school madness Dash had levelled a starting linemen, got into a fight with three kids he'd never met, and experienced more strangeness than he thought possible in a lifetime from dissolving faces to a snarl-a-thon with an out-of-control guard dog.

He wished he had someone to talk to about it. Despite being a comics and fantasy fiction fan-boy, Kevin insisted it was all in Dash's head. There was no other explanation. Besides, by the time they crested the rutted, twisty logging road to the paved state highway that connected the upper neighborhoods with town, the hour had grown late. The sun was ducking under the coastline and the first hints of night were creeping in over the hills and mountains to the east.

Kevin checked his mobile phone. Three texts, all from his Mom. Each escalated upon the last regarding the consequences of not getting home to supper... *now*.

"Sorry, Dash," Kevin explained, as they passed a side road which led into a well-groomed subdivision. "I gotta get home. Walk to school tomorrow?"

"Nah," Dash replied waving to his friend as he walked on, "I need to head down the hill early. See if I can find my backpack back in that alley. I'll see you at second period." Kevin waved goodbye and hustled up the lane to his home.

Dash hiked another block down the road and turned into a small subdivision with a sign out front that read *"PLEASANT ACRES"*. In truth, Pleasant Acres was closer to a modified trailer park than a formal neighborhood. While folks in the rambling, pine tree-lined streets kept their places well-tended, the homes were mostly modest and manufactured. In a few spots, a trailer or RV sat in an open lot where a home should otherwise sit. Kids ran around playing in the early evening on scooters or bikes. Dash walked down the main street and turned up his cul-de-sac. At the end sat his Granny's place, a single wide pre-fab home, a little worse for wear. While Granny put the pressure on Dash to keep the yard trimmed and the flowerbeds tended, the place had seen better days.

Unfortunately, Granny was feeling ill and already went to bed leaving a note for Dash. She was feeling sick more and more, Dash noted. It worried him. Since his Mom had left, Granny was all he had.

On the plus side, he was able to duck any questions about the whereabouts of his bag or school work. He grabbed some fried chicken from the fridge along with a tall glass of milk, watched TV, and decided to hit the sack early. He had to get up first thing the next morning to find his backpack. Besides, he was beat and still confused after today's excitement. He rolled out his bed from their convertible living room couch, got his pillow from the closet, and lay down, resting his head and staring at the night sky thru the family room window. The night was cloudless with a crescent moon bright overhead that peeked over the surrounding pine trees. It took a long time for sleep to come, visions of boys with evaporating faces and snarling dogs plagued his dreams.

*****

Dash awoke with a start the next morning as light streamed from the skylight above his bed. He looked at the DVD player under their old TV set: 6:15 A.M.

Good, he thought. *I can grab a quick shower, some cereal, and hustle down to that alley to get my stuff before school.*

He got up and got ready for the day, putting on some jeans and an old green and white t-shirt, scarfed down breakfast, then set off. The morning was crisp with dew settling over everything. The neighborhood was still sleepy. He walked to the entrance to Pleasant Acres and decided to take the Main Road to town. He didn't want another close shave with Mr. Murphy and Chuckles.

The walk was downhill and largely free of cars this time of day. It helped to clear his thoughts after a troubled night's sleep. Something was happening to him and he was pretty sure it went beyond the standard puberty drama their Middle School Health teacher would drone on about. This was more than bad BO and body hair sprouting in odd places. Maybe he was going mental, but Dash could not shake the image of that boy's face dissolving. He was positive that it had not been the result of too many hormones or a knock to the head. It had most definitely happened… no matter what Kevin said.

He also couldn't explain the changes he had felt when he went up against Olaf, the three Grimm goons, or Murphy's crazy guard dog. He'd felt energized, powerful, even wild, like some kind of animal spirit had been freed within him. He shook his head. *Animal spirits*, he thought, *that is crazy talk, Ke-mo sah-be.*

The slope of the street started to lessen as it bended down into a pasture. Up ahead was the main road and the modest skyline of downtown Autumn's Hallow. Dash checked his watch, 6:52. He would have just enough time to swing by the alley and hunt down his book bag. He picked up his pace and walked through a few side lanes, finding the alley between the book store and the art shop.

No book bag. Dash cursed loudly. He searched, opening trash cans and moving recycling bins around. He looked up the side alley where he had confronted the Brothers Grimm and scoured one end of it to the other. Still no book bag.

He left the alley and tried the shops nearby. Maybe someone had taken out the trash and found his stuff. No one was open except for Mulroney's Café, and the young woman working there with the purple tinged hair and pierced eyebrow hadn't seen any sign of a stray book bag.

Dash left the café, cussed under his breath, and kicked a rock down the block forlornly. He slunk his shoulders in defeat and walked the three blocks to school, knowing he was in for a scolding from his teachers and, more importantly, Granny for losing his new backpack, his school supplies, and half his text books.

He entered the front door of the Junior High just as first period bell rang, the last stragglers running in and to their classrooms. Dash made his way to first period, Pre-Algebra. Before he got to the classroom door a voice called out from down the hall. "Truant!"

Dash looked up. A thin, bedraggled figure was limping down the hall pushing a mop and janitor's bucket. It was Igor, the new school janitor.

"Caught ya!" Igor huffed, as he approached. He looked Dash up and down. "What's your name?"

"Dash, Daschle Gaunt," Dash replied, cautiously eyeing the strange raggedy man. "I was just going into math class…"

Igor was thin and bony with a crooked back and shoulders that caused him to hunch over his mop and bucket. His hair was greasy grey and hung about him shoulder length. One eye seemed to be bigger than the other, focusing on Dash while the other seemed to roll around on its own accord. He sneered, revealing uneven teeth, several missing, and others covered in grey metal and gold. At the sound of Dash's name his expression twisted into a cold smile that scrunched up his wrinkly face, closing his wild eye.

"Oh, the Gaunt boy, is it!" he said, poking Dash in the chest with his free hand. "You are wanted in the Principal's office."

"For being two minutes late?" Dash exclaimed, his mouth agape. "I was just…"

Igor laughed a wheezy cackle. "Seems you're a wanted man. Announced it on the P.A., they did, at morning announcements. Now, get off with you!" Igor hobbled off, then turned around after half a hall length and yelled "*Get!*"

Dash sighed and a rush of worry engulfed him. What would Principle Marlowe want to talk to him about? He turned and walked up the hall toward the front office. As he walked, fear turned into a sliver of hope. *Maybe they found my book bag,* he thought, but his gut told him to expect otherwise.

Dash hurried toward the main entryway and the front office, past the awards cases. The front office of Autumn's Hallow Middle School was cold and medicinal feeling, like so many school front offices. A few magazines, mostly touting book drives or school supplies, sat on the waiting chairs and tables. Dash walked in as two sixth grade girls were leaving for class. He approached the front desk where an older woman sat behind a counter with a visitor's notebook, a paper calendar, and a small nondescript plastic, green, potted plant set.

"Oh, hello dear," the woman behind the desk said sweetly. She had a kind look on her round face. "What can I do for you?"

"Hi, I was told I was called down to the Principal's office," Dash said, shyly. "I'm Daschle Gaunt."

The kindly woman's face turned stern and disapproving. "Oh, hello Mr. Gaunt. Principal Marlowe will be right out to see you. Please wait at the seat by his door."

She pointed to an old wooden chair outside of the Principal's office in a corner.

Dash sighed and slunk over to the chair, taking a seat. The secretary ignored him, returning to her paperwork. She had a radio on her desk with the volume turned low. After an ad for a local lawn care service, the DJ came on.

"And now, back to the news." The DJ announced, in his small-market radio voice. *"Local man, Dr. Larry Phelps, had a close encounter of the hairy kind two nights ago... or so he claims. Dr. Phelps, a respected*

local dentist in Autumn's Hallow, claims he came face-to-face with local celebrity monster, Bigfoot, outside his home in the upscale suburb of Dresden Manor. While Dr. Phelps was unable to provide photographic evidence, he did have three crushed garbage cans to show for his trouble. You should take a selfie next time, Doc! Local authorities are urging calm, saying it's unlikely we are suffering from a Sasquatch infestation. They are also advising residents to be on the look-out for bears who are the likely culprits of Dr. Phelps trash troubles. Seems all the new development we have been experiencing in town is starting to crash on Yogi the Bear and his friends' turf. Hey, hey, Boo-Boo-Boy! In other news..."

Dash looked up as the door to Mr. Marlowe's office opened, revealing the roly-poly figure of the Principal. "Come in Daschle," Mr. Marlowe said, opening the door wide for Dash to pass.

Dash got up, confused and even more nervous. He entered the Principal's office and saw four other people waiting inside. Dr. Guiles, the headmaster from Grimm Academy, stood beside Principal Marlowe's wooden desk with a hard expression. In front of him sat Heinz, Frederick, and Carlos. They looked worse for wear since the last time Dash had seen them. Heinz had a crutch propped against the chair next to him and a brace around his ankle. Frederick had a swollen purple bruise around one eye and Carlos had his left arm in a sling. Each boy had a pouty face like someone had stolen their favorite lollipop from them.

Dash entered the room, cautiously taking in the occupants. Principal Marlowe closed the door behind him and walked behind his desk, sitting in his large leather swivel chair. It creaked with his weight.

"Well young man, what do you have to say for yourself?" Mr. Marlowe asked, after settling in his seat.

"Err… I'm sorry I was tardy for Math class?" Dash stammered.

"Principal Marlowe, this is waste of time!" Dr. Guiles cut in. "This scoundrel obviously will not admit what he did to these three young boys, these guests at your school."

"This ruffian lured these three students into an alleyway and he and his gang of thugs proceeded to beat them!"

"What do you mean me and my friends jumped these three goons?" Dash asked, staring back and forth at Guiles and Marlowe. He pointed at Heinz, Frederick, and Carlos. "Those psychos were trying to beat up my friend, Kevin. It was totally the other way around. We were lucky to get away from them!"

"Ah, see! He already admits one of his accomplices." Guiles fumed. He turned on Dash bending his tall frame to bring his angry expression within inches of Dash's face. "Why did you harm these students? Who else besides this ruffian, Kevin, was with you?" He walked around the desk and gripped Heinz by the shoulder, hoisting him to his feet. It was all Heinz could do to grab his crutch in time. Frederick and Carlos followed suit, not wanting to suffer their Headmaster's wrath. "Come, Heinz, Carlos, Frederick. Let's go."

He turned to Principal Marlowe. "You and I shall discuss later the future of this exchange program. For now my students will be staying at *MY* school." He looked at Dash with an expression of hate curling his lips. He slammed the door and left.

Principal Marlowe rubbed his temples and slumped on his desk. After a moment he peered at Dash. "Were you in a fight with those three boys?" he asked, looking Dash in the eye.

"Yes... but they started it," Dash quickly replied. "And no way were those injuries from me or Kevin. They are bullies, Mr. Marlowe!"

Principal Marlowe put up his hand and waved Dash to stop. "It's your word against theirs, Daschle," Mr. Marlowe replied, a look of sympathy on his face. "And while I am inclined to believe your version of events, particularly after that outburst from their headmaster, we need to be fair... and think of the greater good."

He leaned back in his seat. "Fighting is serious, even in self-defense as you claim it was. I'm going to have to place you in a one day in-school suspension. We'll do it this Thursday. You will sit outside my office all day and do your school work here, monitored by myself and Mrs. Edna at the front desk. Consider this a warning. If I hear about one more altercation, more serious remedies will be required."

Dash sighed and looked down nodding his head. "What about football, this weekend is our season opening game. Can I play?" he asked, with a hint of desperation. This would be his first shot as starting halfback for the Jr. High team.

"That will be between you and your coach, Dash. Now, get back to class and try hard to keep your nose clean. No more fighting."

"Yes, sir," Dash grumbled, turning around and proceeding to the door.

"Oh, Mr. Gaunt, one more thing," Mr. Marlowe called, turning and picking something up from behind his desk. He presented Dash with a blue, camouflage-patterned backpack. "This was found and turned in to lost and found last night. I believe it belongs to you. Found in an alley by a shopkeeper."

Dash walked back and picked up his bag, relief spreading through him that at least one mess had been resolved. He hefted it on his shoulder. He walked out of Principal Marlowe's office and through the door leading out of the front office lobby. He stopped in the common area near the school entrance to check his things before heading back to math class. His books and school supplies were all there. He opened his Algebra book to make sure everything was intact.

Someone had scribbled all over the inside covers and many of the pages of the book. Crude language and coarse phrases were paired with ugly scribbles and violent pictures. On the back cover, a large sketch of a wolf's head had been drawn in heavy black pencil. The wolf's eyes were crossed out and his tongue lolled hopelessly from its mouth. Under the head, someone had drawn in red ink a big red pool making it look like the animal's head had been severed, underneath it read: *"We're coming for you, dog boy!"*

Dash shivered. He tried to erase the sketches and words in the book but could only remove about three quarters of the graphite and ink. Try as he might, a shadow of what had been written remained, a permanent reminder of his encounter the previous evening. He considered going back to the Principal and showing him what the boys had done, but thought better of it. What could Mr. Marlowe do? Dash would still get his punishment and it wasn't like that whack-job, Dr. Guiles, was going to be on his side. He stashed his math textbook, resolving to continue cleaning it next period, picked up his bag and headed to class. It already felt like a long day and he wasn't even finished with first period yet.

*****

Despite the bumpy beginning, the rest of the day went smoothly. Classes were a blur. Dash commiserated with Kevin over his punishment and showed him how the Grimm boys had defaced his math book. They caught up again after seventh bell, sitting together on the floor next to their lockers.

"What's up with their fascination with dead dogs?" Kevin asked, looking at one particularly graphic depiction of a crudely drawn stick man beheading a rough approximation of a stick wiener dog.

"I dunno," Dash pondered, trying again to erase the many other pieces of artwork the Brothers Grimm had left for him with the nub of a pink eraser. "They seem to pick a stalker theme and stick with it."

"Someone should call PETA," Kevin whistled. "These boys should not be allowed to adopt any pets."

"Thanks, I'll get right on that."

"So, their headmaster is a psycho too?"

"It sure seemed like it," Dash replied, scrubbing his book margin furiously and blowing away the eraser shavings. "Man, this stuff is never going to come out."

"Well, watch your back, man. Aren't you playing those guys this week for the home opener football game?"

"Thanks for reminding me. After their headmaster's threats, I'll have their whole team gunning for me. That is, if I play. I still have to tell coach I got in trouble for fighting."

Kevin gave his friend a sympathetic look. "Here comes Shelley and her buddy, Blaine," Kevin whispered urgently. He tried to slick back his hair and straighten his posture. "Act cool!"

"Right, cool…" Dash said, not bothering to look up.

"Hey Shelley!" Kevin greeted.

"Hi, Kevin," Shelley replied, as she walked past him and Dash.

"What are you doing Dash?" Blaine asked, stopping to look at the two friends seated in the empty hall.

"Art criticism. Where are you guys going?"

"I've gotta go home," Blaine replied. "My mom is coming to pick me up after I drop off my things."

"I've got band practice," Shelley said, walking to her nearby locker and inputting her combination. "Don't you have football or something? You're on the team, right?"

"Yeah," Dash said, getting up from his cross-legged position and dusting off his jeans of all the pink eraser bits, "just heading down now. Kevin, you coming?"

"Oh, sure. Maybe we'll see you guys later!"

"Bye Kevin, Dash!" The girls replied, as the two boys walked away.

Dash said goodbye to Kevin, promising to catch up with him later, and went down to the gym locker area. He stopped at the coach's office and confessed to the altercation the previous evening and the punishment he had been given. Coach acted grave and advised him on the proper conduct outside of school hours, but let him off with a warning. Dash was relieved, but only temporarily so.

His biggest worry was facing Granny when he got home and informing her. Granny may be getting older and was often sick, but she was a strict disciplinarian. Dash feared his home punishment would be far worse than whatever his coach or Principal Marlowe could dole out.

Practice was hard. The coaching staff was drilling them fiercely in advance of their home opening game. While Grimm was a much smaller school, they were an elite, private institution that offered plum scholarships to athletes of all ages. Because of their differences in student size, this was the first year the two schools had agreed to play each other. But none of the coaching staff were fooled. Grimm had won the State Championship in their division three out of the last eight years. They would be ready to show their bigger, public school neighbors who was top banana in this town.

Dash hit the showers, cleaned up, got dressed, and walked out the back entrance to the paths that led up to the upper suburbs. Coach took them long today, so it was later than normal and the first purple hints of nightfall were beginning to color the cloudy sky. A few other students were milling around, waiting for parents to pick them up, horsing around. The band also stayed late and was just breaking up from practice.

Dash hunched his book bag and set off for the path. Behind him someone called, "Dash!" He turned. It was Shelley Merry.

"Hi, Shelley," he waved, "band get out late too?"

"Yeah," Shelley said walking up to him, "Middle School is going to be part of the halftime show at the opening game on Friday. Extra practice since everyone is still pretty rusty. Do you go home this way too?"

"Yeah, my house is up the hill. Where's yours?"

"Same way. Mind if I tag along? It's getting kinda late."

Dash smiled. "Sure, come on."

"Where's your friend, Kevin?" Shelley asked, walking alongside Dash.

"He went home after school, I think. I'll let him know you were asking about him," Dash teased, turning to grin at Shelley.

She blushed. "Oh, he's sweet. Sorry, I only ever see you two together."

"Yeah, he's a good guy." They walked on in the awkward silence of a seventh grade boy and girl, not used to talking to members of the opposite gender.

Dash broke the ice. "So which neighborhood do you live in?" he asked, as they hiked up the woodland path. The trees surrounded them closely and the late-day clouds were causing the sky to darken quicker than normal. In the gathering darkness, the familiar trail they walked was rapidly becoming creepy with long strange shadows crisscrossing the path.

"Oh, Dresden Manor."

"That's the same as Kevin."

"Yeah, we just moved there. We live next to the Phelps."

"Isn't that the guy who said King Kong attacked his trash cans or something?" Dash said, remembering the radio broadcast from the school office.

"Bigfoot," Shelley confirmed, "yeah, my dad thinks they were just raccoons, or maybe a black bear. He says Dr. Phelps keeps a canister of laughing gas in his garage and sometimes acts a little crazy." She twirled her finger around her ear for emphasis. Shelley paused and peered around the dark woods nervously. The trees and undergrowth were quiet. "You don't think we have anything to worry about out here, do you?"

"That's funny," Dash grinned, "Kevin asked me the same thing yesterday..."

CRACK!

"What was that?" he asked. He stopped and cocked his head to listen.

"Quit joking around, Dash," Shelley said seriously, turning to face him.

Dash remained still, listening.

"I'm not falling for it," she continued, putting her hands on her hips and looking at him sternly.

SNAP!

In the woods behind them the sound of a large stick breaking pierced the woods, then everything was silent. The early evening hum of insects and animal life went still. Only dark woods and the soft rustle of leaves and branches could be heard.

"What was that?" Shelley asked, moving closer to Dash.

"Shhhh..." Dash said, peering in the direction of the sound from the undergrowth. He stared hard into the surrounding shrubs and trees unnerved by the lack of noise.

Another crack broke the silence, this one closer, followed by a stomp that shook the ground around them. Dash started to walk backward, away from the mysterious sounds approaching. Shelley followed, hovering against his shoulder closely.

Another giant footstep shook the ground and a nearby set of branches rustled violently. "Shelley, we should get going," Dash quickened his pace uphill, still straining to peer into the surrounding underbrush and darkening woods. Shelley nodded, holding her breath.

"RAAWRRRR!" A low, moaning growl rippled from the darkness beside them.

"Run!" Dash yelled. Shelley didn't need to be told twice. She gripped her book bag and clarinet case and ran up the trail, Dash close on her heels. Fear and adrenaline carried their legs as fast as they could go.

Behind them, a giant foot emerged from the darkness creating a deep gouge in the dirt. The creature it belonged to let out another long, low moan and lumbered after them in pursuit. This was no bear!

Chapter 9: Mina

Grooms Lake, Nevada… three weeks after the incident.

"We want to welcome you to the Grooms Lake Army Air Corps Station," Colonel Dickinson announced, walking the group of researchers and their families to their new facilities. "This is a new base in the Army's Research & Development division. While the terrain in these parts may seem uninviting, I think you will find the staff and accommodations more than to your liking."

Colonel Dickinson paused with a smile. Outside the windows of the gleaming R&D lab, the terrain was flat and barren. Salt flats spanned in either direction with only the occasional odd rock formation or sand dune breaking the horizon. It was like looking out a rocket ship portal onto Mars.

Mina thought it was an oddly appropriate location to have moved their research team, considering recent events.

"I want to introduce my executive officer, Major Lance Belcher, who will proceed with the briefing," the Colonel finished, inviting another man with a broad orange mustache to speak.

Major Belcher stepped forward in his Army khakis and nodded to Mina, Lieutenant Murphy, who had relocated as the group's Army liaison, and the rest of the Roswell team: Lonn Cheney, his wife and daughter, Edgewick Stoker and his family, and Ian van Helsing and a lovely young twenty-something girl, Tempest van Helsing, Ian's niece.

"Thank you, sir, and welcome to our team of Roswell researchers or as we have officially designated your unit, The Monster Squad," he said, tipping his head in the direction of the back of the lab.

Standing in the back beyond the rows of lab benches and workstations was a ten foot tall gleaming silver robot, faceless and thick. This giant metal man was the one Ian encountered after the crash three weeks ago. It and the heavily damaged alien craft remained a mystery for the Army and the team from Roswell since that fateful day.

The robot stood tall, silent, and unmoving. Since it had scanned Ian moments after the crash landing of the mysterious UFO, it had yet to communicate with anyone. In fact, it would only respond to Ian and, oddly, his niece, Tempest, and even then only to simple commands like "stay" and "come." Edge teased Ian about inheriting a giant alien golden retriever. Ian, always sensitive, did not appreciate the jibes. Since their encounter in the Roswell desert, he had been consumed with probing the metal man's secrets, particularly since the odd events that had affected his teammates over the last few weeks.

"Your new lab space will be here in Area 51 of the Grooms Lake facility. I realize your briefing materials referenced Area 50, but we have recently converted that section of the base to a storage facility for some rare antiquities from a..." Major Belcher referred to a clipboard at his side. "Dr. Jones," he continued. "Area 51 will be your new home and contains the best facilities that the Army has to offer. I think you'll find it is uniquely suited to your distinctive areas of research."

The team turned to admire the new lab space. In addition to the standard work benches and lab desks, the lab held several unique assets. First was the punch card terminal which accessed the base's state-of-the-art super computer, the Zeus Mark III. The second was the array of testing equipment designed to assess the team's special talents. These included a set of gym bars, a high speed treadmill, and an odd collection of electrical equipment, tesla coils and mirrors set up in a maze.

Edge walked up to one of the mirrors, rolled up his sleeve and placed his hand in front of the reflective surface. Slowly his skin began to shimmer and blended in with the silver gloss of the mirror as if by magic.

"I can't wait to have a go with these!" he smiled with a wink.

Major Belcher stopped in mid-speech and stared at Edge in surprise.

Colonel Dickinson stepped forward.

"I'd read the reports and seen the pictures but this is truly remarkable," he said, looking at Edge's arm. It appeared to be wrapped in the reflective silver of the mirror like a Chameleon's skin.

"Are you all affected in this way?" the Colonel asked, looking at the others.

"Only Edge, Mina and myself, Colonel," Lonn replied, holding his wife by the shoulder. "We don't know why we were affected but we hope your facility can help us find out."

"Yes," Mina continued, "Edge can manipulate his appearance. His skin blends with his surroundings rendering him invisible. Lonn's powers are unpredictable."

She paused remembering the night two weeks ago when Lonn had torn a hole in his home's wall and was found baying at the moon on a two-story roof. No one knew how he had gotten up there but it appeared he had either jumped or climbed the sheer walls with his hands and feet. It had taken Peter and two base guards to get him down. "But they appear to impact his strength and speed giving him super human capabilities."

"Not to mention super-canine body odor," Edge deadpanned.

Lonn shook his head and grunted.

"And my powers," Mina paused rubbing her right arm absently, "we are still trying to sort those out but it seems I am..."

"Invulnerable," Edge interrupted, his arm changing back to normal color as he removed it from the set of nearby mirrors, "she is ruddy Super Girl."

Edge took a comic book from his seven year old boy's hands, Action Comic #1. On the cover was a man in blue and red with a cape and a giant S on his chest, a new hero called Superman. He handed it to the Colonel who eyed it briefly, nodding.

"And what about you?" Major Belcher asked, pointing in Ian's direction.

Ian squirmed uncomfortably in his jacket. His niece smiled sweetly but he scrunched his face in disappointment.

"I was not affected in that way. The others encountered the alien craft first and were somehow changed based on their experience. I found the creature. My gift, if you can call it that, is that the robot appears bound to me."

"And to me for some reason," Tempest chimed in. "Come here, Frank!"

The robot's electric green eyes lit up on its blank silver face and the automaton moved forward. It took two steps before Ian barked, "Creature, stop!"

Ian looked at Tempest, frustration painting his face, "Tempest, please. The robot is not a play thing. And stop calling it Frank!"

"Come now, lad," Edge said, walking over to the giant robot and giving it a pat on the back, "I think Frank is a perfect name for this gargantuan. Frankenstein... Hey, that would make you Dr. Frankenstein!"

"Dr. Stoker, please," Ian snapped.

"Oh, sorry, Dr. von Frankenstein," Edge teased, with a grin.

He walked over to rejoin the larger group and addressed Major Belcher and Colonel Dickinson. "Anyway, what's the plan for us, lads?" he asked. "We've up and moved our families to this mysterious place and not entirely by choice, mind you. What does the US government have in store for us?"

"Yes," Lonn pressed, "and where is the alien craft? Studying that will be critical for our research."

"All your questions will be answered in due time," Colonel Dickinson replied. "We have a staff here dedicated to helping us understand what has happened to you and your team, Professor Cheney."

"The equipment in these labs will help us to study your powers and hopefully understand how to fix them or at least harness them. Understanding the creature and the ship it arrived in is a top priority of which we will keep each of you assessed. Rest assured, the alien craft is being stored close-by and is the focus of research by top men in the US Government. We will leave study of the creature to you and your team, particularly given its special affinity to Dr. van Helsing."

Colonel Dickinson surveyed the group of researchers and their families before continuing, "Each of you is special. Your powers and the experience with what can only be described as alien technology that gave them to you requires special study and utmost secrecy."

"This team... *your* team will help us understand this technology and if possible locate further evidence of it. We have the assistance of the British and the French governments in scouring the globe to find more evidence and you will be among the first responders, if we find any."

"In the meantime, Grooms Lake and the facilities and staff here in Area 51 are at your disposal. Each of you is an honored guest of the United States Government. And we treat our guest's right."

The Colonel turned to Peter. "Lieutenant Murphy, I'm going to rely on you to work with Major Belcher to get these folks settled and this lab up and running. Your mission is to make sure this team and their families are comfortable, secure, productive and most importantly, safe. Are we clear?"

"Yes sir. Crystal clear, Colonel."

"Good, then I am going to turn it over to your capable hands." He turned to address the others once more, "Lieutenant Murphy and Major Belcher will take it from here. Again, I want to personally welcome the Army's newest specialized research unit, the Monster Squad, to Area 51."

"Dismissed," the colonel barked, and left.

Chapter 10: Shelley

Shelley and Dash sprinted up the hillside as the evening darkness shrouded the woodland path. Up ahead they could make out the winking lights of a housing development thru the undergrowth. Shelley tripped on a root and lost her balance. Her clarinet case went flying.

Dash skidded to a stop and hurried back, giving her a hand.

"Are you okay?"

"I think so," Shelley replied, scanning the ground, "but I can't find my clarinet."

BOOM!

Bushes shuddered 50 yards downhill as the creature pursuing them lumbered up the path in close pursuit.

"Come on!" Dash urged. "We're almost to your neighborhood. We can double back and get your clarinet later."

Shelley hitched her backpack onto her shoulders and ran the remaining length of the path as fast as her long legs could carry her. She and Dash exited into a neatly trimmed cul-de-sac to a small park with a bench, play area, and community BBQ. An overhead lamp lit the street on a nearby pole.

They paused to catch their breath near a pair of teeter-totters inside the cone of phosphorescent light. A small pug dog, who had escaped from his yard, was nosing around the bench. He looked at them curiously, cocking his head. The undergrowth from the woods began to rustle. The pug twitched his head back to the path they had exited and began to growl.

"We better get going," Dash said, backing away from the park. "That thing is still following us."

"My house is up the street," Shelley agreed. "We can get help there." She started to move forward as the bushes surrounding the path's mouth shook ominously.

The pug's haunches rose and he began to bark excitedly. He growled and yapped, approaching the path like he was ten times his actual lap dog size. The bushes twitched again.

Shelley stopped and turned back to the furiously barking animal. "Hercules! Come here!" she yelled.

"They named that runt Hercules?" Dash murmured.

Shelley ignored him trying to get the pint sized pooch to follow.

"Hercules, come here boy… Get away from that path! We have to get out of here."

Hercules was having none of it. He amped up his barking and was closing in on the darkness surrounding the entrance. The hair on his back was standing straight up.

The bushes shook again and Shelley heard a low moaning from the woods and a series of stomps. She didn't hesitate. She raced back to the barking Pug and scooped him up. Hercules was in a lather, barking and growling at the woods, struggling to break free of Shelley and attack whatever was waiting inside.

Shelley, expecting the worst, shut her eyes and flinched, visions of a giant bear with huge steely claws flashing thru her mind.

She waited.

Nothing. Instead, she saw bushes shaking further down the path and the stomping that had been pursuing them for the last handful of heart-pounding minutes grew faint.

Dash came running up beside her. "Holy cow! That was awesome!" he gushed.

"What? Are we alive?" Shelley said, peeking open her eyes, still trembling.

"What do you mean?!" Dash said, clapping her on the back and giving Hercules a giant noogie. "You and your super dog scared away whatever that thing was. Look, it's running back down the hill!"

Shelley slowly put down Hercules who, now that the mysterious presence in the woods was gone, sniffed happily at her legs and sneezed in the freshly-mown park grass. She stood up and looked to the woods. The ominous rustling of undergrowth and clomping sounds of their pursuer were gone. The underbrush was again still and the late summer sounds of animal life and buzzing insects were returning to normal.

She peered into the dim path entrance and saw a faint greenish glow. "What is that?" she said, moving a few hesitant steps closer.

"Is something still there?" Dash asked, warily coming alongside her.

"No, do you see that glow? It looks like it is all over the woods."

Curiosity got the best of her and Shelley moved forward into the darkness surrounding the head of the wooded trail.

"Shelley, wait! That thing might still be lurking close by." A few seconds passed, with Dash tensing up at each tick of the clock.

"Dash, you should come and see this." Dash stepped forward, forgetting the hero pug which was now meandering back to the play area. He walked into the deep shadows of the wooded path. Under the trees it was nearly dark. It took a moment for his eyes to adjust and he walked hesitantly forward, rounding a nearby bend. He stopped as he saw Shelley standing in a clearing, his mouth agape.

"I know, pretty amazing, huh?" Shelley said, as he entered.

The clearing glowed a soft metallic green, like someone had taken a glow in the dark can of paint and splashed it on the trees, the bushes, even the dirt on the path. Dash brushed by a nearby glowing branch and saw a puff of dust shake loose. The dust sparkled like a thousand little emeralds and wafted toward the ground, leaving the branch bare of the strange substance. Dash rubbed his finger against a glowing tree trunk and saw a thick film of shiny powder cake his fingertips. He quickly rubbed his fingers on his jeans, leaving a faint sparkling streak of lime.

"What is it?" he asked.

"I think it came from whatever was chasing us. It goes on for a ways down the path. It looks like the glow is temporary though. The light is already fading."

"What the heck kind of animal was after us?" Dash asked, looking around. "With this pixie dust covering everything, it's like a leprechaun exploded."

"I don't think it was a bear, I'm not even sure if it was an animal." She bent down to retrieve a glowing box on the ground. It was her clarinet case, covered in the strange phosphorescent dust. Next to it was a giant rectangular indentation in the dirt, an oversized footprint.

"Look at this," she said, pointing to the square footprint. It was as big as a large shoe box in dimension and the impression went several inches into the ground, as if something very heavy had made it.

"There are others down the path," she said, pointing.

Dash bent down to get a closer look. "What do you think it could be?"

"I don't know," Shelley replied, picking up her case and wiping the powder caking it into a lunch sack she took from her bag, "but I'll take this down to the biology lab at school. They have a digital microscope which might be able to tell us what this is made of."

"Do you think it's dangerous?" Dash said, alarmed. He was brushing off his pants where the faint glow of his finger smudge was slowly fading.

"I don't know, but I think we better get home and clean up," Shelley said, brushing the last bits off her clarinet case. "I'll ask my Dad what he thinks. We should contact the police to tell them that something large is on the loose."

"Maybe your dentist neighbor isn't so crazy after all?" Dash replied, as they left the clearing.

"Maybe not," Shelley agreed.

*****

"Bye Dash!" Shelley called from her front door.

Dash had walked her up the street to her house, but needed to get home to check in with Granny as it was growing late. The clouds were starting to look like rain and she would be worried. He told Shelley he'd catch up with her tomorrow. He also promised to ask around to see if anyone else had run-ins in the woods recently.

Shelley walked into her house and shut the door. She saw Dad was home already from the car in the driveway.

"Shelley, is that you?" a deep male voice called from upstairs.

"Yeah, dad," Shelley replied, dropping her bag at the base of the stairs. She made sure to retrieve her lunch bag with the glowing forest path samples inside.

"I'll be down in a minute to whip up dinner. Just got home myself."

"OK!"

She walked from the front hall into the kitchen. On the way she passed a picture of an attractive red-haired woman in a white naval officer's uniform. Shelley touched her hand to the picture and whispered "Hi, Mom," as she passed into the kitchen.

Shelley's mother was on assignment with the Navy in the Middle East and had been away for a number of months. It was just her and her father holding down the fort at home. Her father was nice but Shelley missed her mom. She would try to get in contact with her to share what had happened.

Shelley's father bounded down the back stairwell in running shorts and a t-shirt.

"Was that a boy I saw you with, Miss Shelton Tempest Davis?" her father asked, in mock-seriousness.

"Yes, Dad, and please don't use my full name," Shelley replied, smiling. Shelley's middle name came from her mother's side, an old family first name from a great grandmother she had never met. She, in particular, cringed at Shelton, the name of her great grandfather on her Dad's side.

"Do I need to get the shotgun out?" he asked, giving Shelley a kiss on the forehead on the way to the refrigerator. "You know I don't want any girl-crazy teenaged boys crowding my front lawn?"

"No, Dad, he's just a friend," Shelley smiled. "But I do need to tell you something. We were chased by something up the path from school."

"Something?" her father looked concerned, putting some vegetables down on a cutting board. "What was it?"

"Look at this," she said, offering her lunch bag to her father as evidence.

Mr. Merry walked around their kitchen island and retrieved the bag. He opened it and shrugged. "It looks like you put dirt in your lunch bag, honey."

"What?" Shelley replied, looking in the bag. The dust she had collected stopped glowing and was now dormant, dirty grey, and clumped together like dry clay.

"Is this boy asking you to try pills? Wear any stickers of dancing bears?" Her father asked suspiciously. "Are you OK? Seeing things that aren't there?"

Shelley shook her head. "No, Daddy," she replied, putting the lunch bag aside. "He's not shady and yes, I'm OK. But I know what I saw. Something huge was chasing us up the hill and then disappeared and what was left was a bunch of strange glowing dust surrounding the forest. That's what I collected in my bag!"

"Uh huh," her father replied, starting to chop vegetables. "You go into the woods with a strange boy I have never met, come home late, and then claim you saw an invisible monster in a forest lit up like a glow stick and brought home fairy dust which looks like dirt and you don't expect me to act suspicious?"

Shelley looked at her father and started to feel a tear well up. "I know what I saw!"

"I know you think you saw something, sweetheart," Mr. Merry said, stopping his cutting. "I just worry about you, and to be honest what you are saying is a little hard to believe."

"Will you come to the woods and look? I swear there was something after us."

"After dinner I will check it out. In the meantime, why don't you go upstairs and clean-up for supper. I'll have things ready in ten minutes."

"OK," Shelley murmured. She got up and took her lunch bag with her. "Mom would have believed me," she muttered, as she stomped up the back stairwell.

"What was that, honey?"

"Nothing," she replied.

*****

The next morning Shelley got up early to get ready for school. She wanted to get to the biology lab before first bell to check on the samples from the previous night.

True to his word, her dad went down to the clearing with a flashlight but it had begun to rain with the onset of evening. While there were tracks, the square shape and depth of the indentations had gone away, and if any of the strange dust was left, it had washed away or was indecipherable from the clay soil of the forest. Shelley's father dialed the police to inform them of a possible bear sighting but they had little to tell the Merry family in turn.

Shelley had gone to bed frustrated with her father who was much more interested in learning about Dash, the strange boy who was hanging out with his daughter, than the mystery in the woods. More importantly, she had been unable to get in contact with her mom. She sent her an email and text message but her mother was Naval Intelligence and frequently out of touch for days on end. Shelley was on her own to sort out this mystery.

Shelley said goodbye to her dad and donned her rain jacket. The morning was dreary and unseasonably chilly from the steady rain. The rain still fell in a light mist. Not wanting to repeat her experience in the woods with Dash, Shelley opted to take her bike to school. The way was longer down the winding state road but it was all downhill and wouldn't take much time.

Shelley got to school without event and locked her ten-speed in a bike rack near the main entrance. It was 7:05 which gave her 30 minutes before first bell. She stopped by her locker to drop off her coat and extra books and with her first period math book, her laptop, and lunch bag walked to the science corridor. The hall was empty and the lights were off.

She entered the bio lab and found a seat at a nearby microscope station. She set her computer down, powered it up, and plugged in a digital microscope in a USB slot. The microscope flickered to life and the computer auto-opened a program that showed the display from the high-powered lens of the scope. Shelley removed a piece of analysis glass from a tray and carefully tapped a few specs of the dried dust from the woods onto the clear plate, just like her instructor at this summer's science camp had shown her. She carefully inserted the plate under the lens. Shelley smiled to herself, thinking that being a nerd occasionally had its privileges.

The view under the lens was blurry and she clicked her mouse a few times to adjust the image. At first, all she saw was a bunch of grey globs smeared on a glass plate. She clicked again changing the magnification to a higher setting, zeroing in on one of the globs. The picture became more interesting.

What was a grey blob at the first level of magnification appeared to be a strange mass of overlapping hexagonal patterns. The image on the screen looked like an infinite series of Lego blocks, stuck together in a complex honeycomb. In one section of the screen, Shelley saw a faint green glow. She highlighted this section with her mouse and clicked zoom again.

"Wow…" Shelley mouthed, looking at her screen and leaning in. At 500X magnification, Shelley saw faint movement inside the blown-up helix. The Legos now looked more distinct. They were no longer blocks but groups of smaller dots bunched together. A few of the dots gave off a strange greenish glow and moved fitfully inside their block.

Shelley zoomed in on one dot and put the microscope to its highest setting, which was 1,000X. The dot became larger on the screen but was still small, like looking at a car from a landing airplane. The dot now appeared to be a tiny, metallic bug. The creature was made of some kind of metal, with circuitry covering its body and faint green pulses traversing the wires. Thin green gossamer wings extended from its top in four directions and dozens of tiny legs moved fitfully under its body. Shelley couldn't tell if it had a head but noted several rods that extended from its body like antennae.

The strange microscopic creature was on its last legs. The lights on its exterior were fading, its legs flailing.

Slowly, the creature's light extinguished and its legs and wings folded in on itself, mimicking the other dots surrounding it.

"What are you doing in there?"

Shelley nearly screamed in fright at the surprise. She gasped and looked up from her screen and saw the bony face of Mr. Igor peering in from the doorway to the lab, mop in hand, one beady eye opened wide, staring at her.

"Oh, Mr. Igor, I, I…" she said, sitting straight up and closing her laptop screen.

"Yeah," he growled, taking a step into the lab, "you trying to steal that expensive piece of equipment, Missy?"

"No," Shelley looked down at the microscope. "I'm doing a school project. Well, really an assignment I started over the summer." Shelley wasn't sure why her impulse was to lie but she didn't trust Mr. Igor. He certainly didn't trust her or any of the students for that matter.

Igor limped into the room, leaning on his mop for support, one shoulder hunched above the other. He eyed her suspiciously. "Whose computer is that?"

"It's mine… from home." Shelley said, picking up her things. "I was just wrapping up."

"Does Mr. Connelly know you're in here using his equipment?" He watched her carefully. "That doohickey looks expensive." He finished pointing at the digital microscope Shelley had plugged into her PC.

"I didn't get a chance to talk to him yet," Shelley replied, stowing her laptop and lunch bag into her bag. "But I will first thing third period." She backed away from the creepy janitor and around another work station toward the door.

"Make sure you do. Now, get to your first period. I don't want to see anymore truants!"

"Yes sir," Shelley stammered, leaving.

Igor watched her back out of the room and hustle down the science hall. Once he was satisfied she was out of view, the strange janitor looked at the microscope. He flicked open the latches to the analysis plate with a practiced ease and examined the sample. He brought a cell phone out from his coveralls and clicked speed dial, waiting a moment for the other end to pick up.

"Master," he intoned, his gruff voice shifting to a sophisticated Eastern European accent. He eyed the sample plate. "The girl you spoke of... she knows. I believe we have found another of the heirs."

*****

Shelley scurried down the hall from the strange custodian, reeling from what she had witnessed. Whatever she had seen under that microscope was beyond anything she had read. What could that creature have been? Was it some tiny machine? An artificial life? Something else entirely? The possibilities swirled in her head.

She rounded a corner, looking back to make sure Igor wasn't following, and bumped into someone coming round the opposite bend, causing him to drop the books he had been holding.

"Hey!" a young male voice shouted, and then paused. "Shelley?" It was Kevin Wallis.

"Kevin!" she said, bending down to help him with his things. "Thank goodness it's you. Have you seen Blaine or Dash?"

"No. Are you okay? You look like you've seen a ghost?"

"You don't know the half of it," Shelley said, handing him his Earth Sciences text.

"Anything I can help you with?" Kevin asked, rebalancing his books.

"Not unless you know a lot about tiny microscopic robot creatures," Shelley replied, looking around nervously.

"Oh, you mean like nanobots?"

"Nano-whats?"

"Nanobots, nanotechnology, tiny robots made at a subatomic level. They can manipulate matter, give the wielder nearly magical abilities, and render all but the most sophisticated technology powerless. You don't read comic books do you?" He gave her a critical look, as if reappraising her.

Shelley gave him a similar look. A light bulb flashed in her brain. "No, Kevin, I don't. But I think you might be on to something."

She led him to a nearby alcove with a study table. Kevin was delighted. It was the first time he'd been this close and this alone with his long-time crush.

"Tell me about nanobots," she instructed, taking out her laptop and firing it up.

"Well, geez, what do you want to know?" Kevin replied, moving to her computer and clicking on the browser. "Nanotechnology is everywhere online. Do you want the real stuff or the comic book version?"

"Real stuff," Shelley instructed, hovering over Kevin's shoulder.

He looked back at her and with a goofy grin started to type.

"9,555,000 results," Kevin announced, after finishing his search query, "looks like there is a lot. Let's click this one."

Kevin read from the site:

"Nanotechnology is an emerging science, studying machines built at a molecular level in some cases as small as a strand of DNA. Applications for the technology are varied: construction, materials, medicine, and weaponry. Nanotechnology can make items appear invisible, make loose cloth bullet proof, or create useful or sometimes dangerous chemical reactions depending on the application. Scientists believe it can be used to treat DNA at a molecular level curing disease, creating new organisms, or changing existing cells altogether."

"Is this what you wanted?" Kevin asked.

"Yeah, scroll down and see what nanotechnology is being used for today," Shelley instructed, scanning the page while Kevin read.

"Most applications are still primitive, relative to the promise of the technology. Scientists believe full commercialization of nanotech requires another 10 to 15 years development. Most non-government applications are simulations on a computer. One cause for concern in the use of nanotech is a theoretical phenomenon called Grey Goo, inorganic matter left over from nanotech activity."

"Do they provide an example of grey goo?" Shelley asked, interested. It sounded similar to what she was seeing with the samples she took from the woods.

"Nah, since all this stuff is still just theory, it looks like it is all just speculation," Kevin replied, shutting the laptop lid. "It sounds really cool, though. In my comic books, SHEILD uses nanotech to render the Incredible

Hulk powerless and that guy is gamma radiation powered! Why are you interested in this stuff, anyway?"

"Long story and you probably wouldn't believe me," Shelley replied, stowing away her laptop again.

"I will believe anything you ever tell me," Kevin uttered with a look of total seriousness on his face, just as first bell rang.

Shelley paused and smiled as she looked at the stony faced boy.

"I'll tell you later. Why don't you, Dash, Blaine, and I huddle over lunch?"

"Ok!" Kevin answered, brightly. "I'll make sure Dash is there. See you after fourth period!"

"Ok, Kevin," Shelley replied, gripped his shoulder, and smiled warmly, "and thanks for believing in me."

As she walked away, Kevin stood there grinning stupidly as Shelley hurried down the hall toward Geometry. He put his hand on his shoulder where Shelley had held him.

"*She touched me,*" he mouthed.

Chapter 11: Shelley

"Hey Shelley! Missed you at start of school!" Blaine greeted her friend, as Shelley arrived in fourth period Literary Arts.

"Hey Blaine," Shelley greeted, as she quickly scooted to her buddy. "You weren't online last night. You're not going to believe what's happening."

"Try me," Blaine invited, lifting up her book bag from a seat next to her. "Saved you a seat." Shelley sat down and dived right in, giving a rat-a-tat summary of the previous 24 hours, starting from the end of band practice thru her encounter with Igor and web search with Kevin.

"Whatever was following us, it wasn't natural. And I don't think it was the first time it got near my neighborhood! My wacky neighbor swears he saw something huge flattening his garbage cans... which are right next to our house!"

"What do you think?" Shelley finished.

"My hand magically disappeared and then reappeared," Blaine blurted.

"Hold on, *what*?" Shelley replied, confused. "What does this have to do with a monster in my backyard?"

"It happened Monday and I thought I was going crazy but then you started to talk about monsters and glowing green Autobots," Blaine replied, quickly.

"Nanobots," Shelley corrected.

"Whatever," Blaine shook her head, "my point is strange stuff has been happening to you at the same time weird things are happening to me. It can't be coincidence."

"Didn't you just say these ink blots...?" Blaine continued.

"Nanobots."

"Argh!" Blaine said, frustrated. "These *nanobots* could make things invisible?"

"Yes," Shelley replied, leaning in conspiratorially. "So you think these things are related?"

"What things?"

Blaine and Shelley both looked up. Standing in front of them was their Literary Arts teacher, Ms. Bellamy Poe.

"Is there something you'd like to share with the class? Fourth bell has rung but you two seem to be engaged in an intense discussion."

"It's nothing, Ms. Poe," Shelley said, shrinking in her seat.

Blaine looked up and away from her teacher, lifting up her English book futilely in front of her face and smiling.

"Hmmm..." Ms. Poe answered. She gave each of them a long look, followed by a knowing smirk, and walked away.

The balance of class went quickly with lunch bell ringing at 11:50. The kids got up from their seats and made a rush for the door.

"Ms. Merry! Ms. Davis! A word," Ms. Poe called, as Blaine and Shelley tried to make a break for the door. Dash and Kevin were waiting expectantly in the hall.

Shelley and Blaine walked over to the front desk where Ms. Poe sat.

"Ladies. I want you both to know if you are having any problems, any changes you are seeing, anything *strange*, I'm always here to lend a helpful ear. Is there anything you'd like to tell me about?"

Shelley and Blaine looked at each other and shrugged. "No, Ms. Poe."

"Nothing strange, Ms. Poe."

"I see. Well, know you have a friend in Literary Arts." She got up from behind her desk and held out her hand, inviting the girls toward the door. "I see Mr. Wallis and Mr. Gaunt are waiting for you in the hall. I won't hold you from your lunches further."

Blaine and Shelley turned without a word and exited, thanking their strange new teacher as they left. Neither stopped to ask how Ms. Poe knew Dash and Kevin were waiting outside, skulking around a corner, unseen.

*****

"Wow!" was all Kevin could manage after Shelley, Blaine, and Dash shared their stories from the previous two days. They were in a corner of the busy lunch room away from other tables.

He turned to Blaine. "So, can you make your hand disappear at will?"

"I don't know," she responded, rubbing her right hand. "To be honest, I've been trying to forget it happened." Blaine lifted her hand for her friends to see and stared at it hard, concentrating. Nothing happened.

"Come on, keep trying," Kevin whispered.

Blaine closed her eyes and focused with all her might. She pressed her hands on the table and, after a moment, opened her eyes and said, "It's just not working."

She paused.

"What?" she asked. Her three friends were staring at her, mouths agape. Blaine looked down at her hand. It, along with her arm, wasn't there. She looked down at her other arm and body. All gone. She screeched her chair back in shock and almost screamed.

"Whoa," Kevin said, with a big stupid grin. "You're the Invisible Woman. In my game, Gothic, you're like a seriously rare figure. I think you're only for sale in South Korea."

"Kevin…" Dash admonished, shaking his head. "Blaine, are you alright? Are you still there?"

Blaine was curled in a ball in her chair, invisible hands covering her invisible eyes, which were welling up with tears.

"Blaine?" Shelley asked.

"Yes, I'm still here," Blaine whispered, miserably. She looked down at her invisible body. "What is happening to me?"

"I don't know, but it is incredible," Shelley replied, "your clothes and everything are… gone."

"Did anybody see?" Blaine asked, urgently lifting her head up to look around.

Dash scanned the busy cafeteria. "I don't think so. It doesn't look like anyone is staring."

"How are you making your clothes disappear too?" Kevin asked.

"I don't know, Kevin! I don't know how I'm making my hand disappear, let alone my sneakers!"

"Blaine, take your jacket off and see what happens," Shelley suggested. "Just set it on the table."

Blaine glared at Kevin one last time, resentful that he thought her condition was so cool. Blaine had a hunch he wouldn't be so excited if *his* body parts started disappearing.

The other kids could hear a rustling from Blaine's chair as she removed her black denim jacket and laid it on the table next to her tray. At first, the jacket remained invisible but slowly it reappeared, the shroud of invisibility melting away in a silvery sheen.

"Holy frijoles," Dash breathed. "That is amazing."

All four had their eyes glued to the now visible designer jacket. They missed Vickie, Blaine's sister, approaching.

"Hey, have you guys seen my sister?" she asked, bubbly as ever.

Shelley, Kevin, and Dash looked up in unison, alarm on their faces. "No, definitely not!" Kevin gushed.

"No clue, Vickie," Shelley repeated.

Dash just shrugged helplessly. Blaine sat stone silent in her seat.

"Then why is her jacket sitting next to a tray with a half-eaten piece of pizza?"

"Oh, you mean have we *seen* Blaine," Shelley replied. "Yes, she just got up to go to her locker. She should be back in a few minutes."

"Be a pal and tell her I'm looking for her, OK Shell? I forgot my lunch money this morning and was hoping to borrow a few dollars. If not, I'm sure my new boyfriend, Drake, will be happy to take care of it."

She pointed back to the cool kids section of the eighth grade tables. Drake Harker sat there with a coven of Vickie's girlfriends and a cross-section of boys. Drake noticed her, got up, and walked over.

"Hey Vickie," he said, flashing a gleaming white smile, "who are your friends?"

"Hi Drake. Thanks for coming to check on me. These aren't my friends. They're my sister's seventh grade playmates. This is Shelley and these two are..."

"Dash and Kevin," Dash said, nodding at the other boy.

"Where's Blaine?" he asked, staring straight at the apparently empty chair Blaine occupied. Blaine cringed, praying no one would discover her.

"She went to get something from her locker," Shelley cut in.

"Oh, tell her I said 'hi' when she pops back." He turned to Blaine's sister and held her hand. "Come on, Vickie. I'll cover you for lunch today," he said, walking away with her.

"I didn't know you knew my sister..." Vickie started, as they walked back into the lunch room crowds.

Drake turned as they left and waved goodbye. "Nice meeting you guys!"

"That was close!" Kevin gushed. "That was like rolling a 19 on a 20 sided die!"

"Kevin!" Blaine hissed. "Stop comparing my situation to a video game!"

"It's actually more an interactive collectible card game..."

"Blaine, let's get you out of here and figure out how to get you back to normal," Shelley advised. "I'll get up and you follow me. Dash and Kevin can take care of our lunch trays and your jacket and meet us over by the gym locker rooms. They should be quiet this time of day."

"OK," Blaine murmured uncertainly. "What if someone runs into me?"

"We'll wait for a lull in the crowd heading to the annex," Shelley offered, scanning the mass of students. "You ready? Let's go."

Shelley got up and Blaine followed closely, careful not to touch anything. Shelley walked quickly. They managed to skirt across the lunch room. Shelley opened the door to the annex wide enough for Blaine to squeeze past. Blaine brushed against Shelley's backpack. Shelley looked in amazement as her bag flickered in a silvery light, becoming momentarily translucent before returning to normal. Blaine could make more than herself invisible!

Shelley joined Blaine in the hall and half-walked, half-jogged to the nearby gymnasium. They took the stairs down to the locker rooms two at a time. Shelley opened the door and heard Blaine hustle through, breathing a sigh of relief as she sat on a nearby bench. The changing area was empty. Shelley peered around to make sure they were alone and hurried back to her friend.

"What's happening to me, Shelley?" Blaine whispered, tears re-emerging.

"I don't know Blainey, but it has to be tied into the other strange things happening to you, me, and Dash," Shelley replied, kneeling down near her closest pal.

"If you concentrate like you did in the lunch room, can you make it stop?" she offered.

"I dunno. Let me try." She closed her eyes and tried hard to envision her hands and body reappearing. Her forehead started to bead in concentration.

"Blaine! It's working!"

Blaine opened her eyes and looked in a full-length mirror opposite her. Her jaw dropped as she saw a silvery wave shimmer over the outlines of her body as the see-through cloak that surrounded her washed away. Slowly, her body came back into view, ending with a silvery flash at her fingertips.

"Thank God," Blaine gushed, hugging herself as her body became whole again.

"That is the most incredible thing I've ever seen, Blaine. We need to figure out what's happening to you. Was Monday the first time you experienced something like this?"

"Yes! Geez, do you think I could keep something like this a secret from my best friend? If there's a silver lining, I'm just glad I'm not going bonkers!"

"Dash is being hunted by preppy zombies, you are becoming invisible, and I have some kind of monster camping out in my backyard," Shelley said, leaning her head back on the wall. "And the only lead we have to explain it is tiny glowing green bugs that disappear almost as fast as you can collect them."

"Do you think there's anyone we can turn to for help?"

"I don't know. I think most adults will react the same as my Dad. Do you want to try that trick again, in front of a teacher or a parent?"

"I don't know if I could do it again. And being sent to the funny farm for adopted kids isn't high on my list."

"So, we're on our own until we find some hard evidence," Shelley mused. "We have to understand if this is all connected somehow, which seems obvious but I don't know how."

"Shelley! Blaine! Are you guys here?" It was Dash. He was calling from outside the locker area with Kevin in tow.

"It's the boys," Shelley said, "let's go talk to them about what to do next."

"OK," Blaine said doubtfully, "Do you think this is a result of Taco Tuesday gone bad? Some kind of mass hallucination from expired Government chimichangas?"

Shelley smiled at Blaine's lame if valiant attempt at humor. They walked out of the locker area to join the boys.

*****

The four kids huddled for the balance of the lunch hour and decided the best course of action was to collect more evidence, something that would be impossible for an adult to ignore. Until they did so, they resolved to keep things to themselves and lie low.

Kevin would work with Shelley on researching the mysterious glowing green nanobots. Dash and Blaine would focus on more information about the mysterious creature in the woods. All four promised to alert the others if they saw any trace of the Brothers Grimm. The three Grimm look-alikes had been missing in action since their irate Headmaster stormed out of school with them the day before.

The rest of the day passed by, with each of them eager to get onto their chosen task. Shelley caught up with Kevin following band practice and the two rode their bikes to the gated community they shared. Shelley's father had called and said he wouldn't be home until late. She invited Kevin in, as he had stopped at home to retrieve his tablet. The two sat around the kitchen table, each staring at their own screen. Time passed with little to show.

"I can't find anything," Kevin gasped, setting aside his pad and rubbing his tired eyes. "We've been searching for ages and nothing comes up that matches."

"Check this out," Shelley said, turning the laptop screen to Kevin. "It's an alien conspiracy website with a bunch of sketchy content. But check out the video near the top."

Kevin touched the screen and clicked the video. A grainy camera phone feed showed a muddy barnyard with a chicken coop, an old barn and a scrap heap of discarded tractor parts and rusting cars on cinder blocks. The hand holding the camera was shaking with an occasional thumb passing into the frame as the amateur cameraman panned. He focused on a scrawny middle-aged man in coveralls and a red trucker's hat that read *"Warning: I Have Mad Ninja Skills"* standing near a jagged, giant-size hole in the sheet metal of his barn. A caption at the bottom said *August 12th, Slickpoo, Idaho.*

Kevin paused the video. "Hold on, is there really a town called Slickpoo, Idaho?"

"Just watch," Shelley said, shaking her head. "And yes, there is. I checked it out."

The man in the funny hat began to narrate, pointing at the hole in the barn:

"This here is where the feller busted thru my barn! Varmint must have been ten or twelve feet tall, he was. Yessiree. Didn't get a good look at him though, being dark and all. But I did get a good look at my chickens!"

The camera swiveled to a nearby chicken coop of knotty wires and double-stacked wood chicken houses. The narrator walked into the frame, shotgun in hand.

"I yelled at that sonumagun to 'git off my property and unhand my poultry'! Thing just stared at me dumb-like."

The narrator paused, staring into the camera, mouth agape. "So, I did what anyone would do. Shot him. Square in the chest."

He hefted his gun. "But gol durn it if he didn't turn and run! Left a big hole in my chicken coop and big hoof prints all around my yard!" The camera panned around the yard showing a trail of rectangular foot prints trailing to the corn fields beyond. The narrator poked his head in the frame for a close-up.

"And that weren't the strangest thing! He made my chickens glow... all green like! Like they were little clucking Martians!"

He stepped back from the camera and rested his shotgun on his leg. "I tell you what and I'm dead serious, I'm just glad he didn't probe my anus."

The video cut off. Shelley looked at Kevin seriously.

"That was hilarious!" Kevin laughed.

"Kevin, he described everything we saw in the woods. The deep footprints, the glowing green dust, even the size of the thing."

"Did anyone else see anything or do all we have to go on is Cletus from the Simpsons and his glow in the dark chickens?"

Shelley checked the comment count: zero.

"No, but it's a start!"

"Yeah," Kevin replied. He stretched and yawned.

"Shelley, I think I need to get home. It's late."

"Ok, Kevin," Shelley said. She rose to see him out. "I'll see you tomorrow?"

"You bet! Hopefully Dash and Blaine had more luck than we did."

"Yeah, here's hoping."

Chapter 12: Shelley

Dash and Blaine snooped online but hadn't come up with anything more on the mysterious creature besides the local news reports about Shelley's neighbor. Thursday was a series of dead ends as well. Blaine went to the sheriff's office after school to ask about any animal sightings in the woods. No luck. Kevin went to the library to find books on nanotechnology with little to show for his time. Shelley and Dash were slammed with football and band practice, tomorrow being the opening game against Grimm Academy. They helped out where they could but again came up empty.

Today was the day Dash had to serve his in-school suspension. He was stuck all day behind a desk helping Mrs. Edna, the school secretary, with errands.

One company that came up repeatedly in their research was a large multinational conglomerate called Black Labs. They were creating a technology called Black Labs Omni-Building Systems or B.L.O.B.S. for short. BLOBS were microscopic machines which could build anything you could dream of. There were a couple of cool concept videos and presentations from their founder and CEO, Gabriel Black, but not much more details to go on.

"Cool name," Kevin commented to Shelley, as they compared notes on Friday morning with Blaine and Dash, "I always admire a snappy acronym."

"Yeah, but it doesn't really get us any closer to solving our monster mystery." She sighed, "I'm beginning to sound like Velma from Scooby Doo…"

Dash smiled. He was wearing his Yowling Sasquatch football jersey to show his school spirit. His Middle School team would be playing Grimm Academy on Saturday following the varsity game this evening.

"*Zoinks!*" he goofed. "I bet Kevin could solve it for a Scooby Snack!" They all laughed.

First bell rang. They gathered their things and left for class. Shelley and Blaine walked toward the High School. As they passed the front office, the secretary, Mrs. Edna, stuck her head out.

"Ms. Merry! I was just about to call for you on the PA. The Principal would like to see you, dear."

Shelley turned to Blaine with a questioning look. Blaine shrugged in reply.

"OK, Ms. Edna. Bye, Blaine. Catch up with you later."

Shelley followed Ms. Edna who showed her to Principal Marlowe's office. There she saw the Principal sitting behind his desk and to the side stood the gnarled figure of Dr. Guiles, headmaster of Grimm Academy, a cold smile creasing his face under his impenetrable dark glasses.

"Ah, Ms. Davis," Mr. Marlowe greeted, "please come in." He gestured for her to take a seat in front of his desk.

"As you know, we have a student exchange program with Grimm Academy," her principal started.

"Which, despite early setbacks," Dr. Guiles cut in, looking at Marlowe with disdain, "we would like to continue."

"Yes," Mr. Marlowe said, glancing sidelong at Guiles. "Dr. Guiles would like to talk to you about a special science program he is putting together. You know they have done significant renovations at Grimm over the summer. The new science wing is most impressive."

"OK…" Shelley said slowly.

"Your reputation as a stellar student proceeds you, Ms. Davis," Guiles replied. "I have reviewed your file. It appears your prowess in academics goes back several generations in your family. Your mother, who graduated from the Naval Academy, prominent relatives in research and academia all the way back to your Great Grandmother, Tempest van Helsing, a prominent figure at DARPA. You are a natural-born scholar. Science, it seems, is in your genes."

"Thanks," Shelley murmured. She thought it was creepy that Guiles knew so much about her.

"Oh, don't thank me until I extend my offer," said Guiles, waving away her reply. "We would like you to join us at Grimm as an intern to me. In fact, I would like to give you a tour of our facilities tomorrow morning where we can discuss the arrangement. Afterwards, you can enjoy the football match between our two schools. I've no doubt you have friends on the team." Guiles smiled. The wrinkles on his face twisted unnaturally under the dark glasses he always seemed to wear.

"I don't know," she replied, "I'll have to talk it over with my Dad."

Annoyance flashed on his face. Guiles recovered and resumed his forced pleasantness.

"If you are interested, be at our facilities at 9 A.M. sharp. I would be pleased to share with you *all* that our school has to offer."

"And to show you my sincerity, I offer you a gift," he handed her a pearly white rectangular box. On the outside were the logos for Grimm Academy and an iScroll, manufactured by Black Labs.

"An interactive brochure for our school. I'm sure you will find it informative."

"Thanks," she replied, cautiously taking the box.

"Alright, Shelley," Mr. Marlowe smiled warmly, "that will be all." He got up and showed her to the door. "I encourage you to consider Dr. Guiles' offer. It's a rare opportunity."

Shelley walked out of the office and into the main entry area. Final bell had rung and she was alone. She opened the white box. Inside, nestled in fancy velvet, was a rolled up sheath of clear plastic. Shelley took it out and unrolled it. The sheet was about 8 inches diagonal. On its top was an etched B that was pulsing faint blue. Shelley touched the logo and felt the sheath go rigid and the clear plastic flicker into a dark screen. It was a tablet! The screen lit and shifted to a simple interface with a few rows of icons, most relating to information about Grimm Academy. There were maps of the school, school history, and videos. Shelley browsed the screens and then pressed the logo at the top to power down the device. The sheath went limp again and rolled into a scroll.

'Wow,' Shelley thought, *'Guiles is creepy but he sported cool swag!'* She decided to explore the device later when she reconnected with her friends. For now, she had to get to class.

*****

"Check this out!" Shelley said, as she sat between Blaine and Dash in Literary Arts. She handed them the iScroll.

"Cool," Dash said. "I've read about these things. It's got a new kind of flexible display that bends like paper. Where did you get it?"

"Dr. Guiles from Grimm Academy. The creep wants me to become his intern as part of the new exchange program."

Dash's expression darkened. "He's bad news, Shell. He and his robo students are up to something and it's no good."

"Yeah, and that Grimm place is like *Saddam Hussein's School For Aspiring Bloodthirsty Potentates*," Blaine added. "I have to pass it every day on the way to school and it never fails to give me the shivers."

"That's kinda what I was thinking," Shelley replied. "He knew all about me too, my mom, even my great grandmother, and I've never even met her."

She paused and examined the iScroll. "I also think it's more than a coincidence he gave me a fancy computer from the same company that seems to be behind all the coolest advances in nanotechnology. I did a little digging between classes, and Black Labs is a big contributor to Grimm Academy. They sponsored the summer expansion of their Science Wing. And guess who is the father of your buddies - Heinz, Frederick and Carlos? Gabriel Black, the founder of Black Labs."

"Did you find out anything about Guiles?" Dash asked.

"Before he was became headmaster of Grimm, there is nothing on him. No news articles, no search results, not even a Facebook page. It's like the guy didn't exist."

The kids all paused to think.

"Are you going to go to the Academy?" Blaine asked.

"Heck no! He can have his fancy tablet back."

Dash leaned forward, a serious expression on his face. "It could be a good way to find out some information. Other than a video of some crazy chicken man and a couple of news articles, we don't have much to go on besides waiting for Bigfoot to pop up in your backyard or one of those psycho Grimm dudes to take a shot at me again."

"I dunno…" Shelley paused. She did not like the idea of going.

"Hey guys!" Kevin greeted, taking a seat next to them. "Oooo… is that an iScroll? Those aren't supposed to be on sale for months!" He picked it up and turned it on.

"Sweet… the new version of Gothic is supposed to be epic on this. It renders the characters in 3D with the optional glasses. Where did you get it?" The gang filled Kevin in.

"So you are going to go and check it out, right Shelley? It's the best lead we've had! Sinister headmaster, mutant zombie kids, shady corporate benefactor… all signs point to Grimm." Shelley still had her doubts.

"We can all go with you, Shelley," Blaine offered. "The high school game is here at Autumn's Hallow but the Middle School game is played at Grimm. You won't be alone." Shelley smiled at her friend.

"Right," Kevin agreed enthusiastically. "We will be your wingmen!"

"And whose wing will you be protecting, Mr. Wallis?" It was Ms. Poe. She had walked up while the four were talking.

"Uh, no one?" Kevin replied, with a sheepish grin.

"Thank you, Mr. Wallis. Good morning class! Please turn to page 54 and let's resume yesterday's lesson."

Shelley had difficulty focusing on the short story they had been assigned the previous evening. Her thoughts went to the iScroll tucked in her bag and the strange series of events over the past week. Kevin was right. All signs were pointing to Grimm Academy and they needed answers. This would be her best shot to get an up-close look of the grounds and understand more about the mysterious Dr. Van Guiles.

By the end of class, she resolved that she would go. She was nervous but she would do it.

Fifth bell rang. All the kids got up to leave for lunch. Ms. Poe stopped Shelley as she was leaving. "I heard thru the grapevine you had a meeting this morning with Dr. Van Guiles from Grimm Academy."

"Yes..." Shelley answered, slowly.

Ms. Poe smiled a mischievous twinkle in her eyes. "I am familiar with Van Guiles, Shelley. We have a history of sorts. He is a man with a long but mysterious past."

"How do you know him?" Shelley asked, stepping closer.

"It's complicated. Another time, perhaps."

"He seems super creepy," Shelley blurted, blushing.

Ms. Poe smiled. "Perhaps he is more the man he seems than I give him credit for," she chuckled. Her expression became serious. "Shelley, I've seen you and your friends talking. Are you sure there's nothing you'd like to discuss? I might be able to help."

Shelley was tempted to lay it out for her teacher, but she thought of Dash, Kevin, and Blaine and the agreement they had. No adults until they had something more solid to go on.

"No, Ms. Poe, everything is fine."

Ms. Poe regarded her for a moment, sizing her up. "Alright then. I can see you are a responsible young lady. Remember if you need anything, I'm always here to help. Enjoy the football game tonight."

Shelley nodded and started to leave the room. As she did so, she nearly ran into a tall well-dressed boy entering the classroom.

"Hi, Shelley," Drake Harker greeted her, flashing his trademark bright white smile.

"Drake. Hi. I was just leaving."

"No problem," Drake stepped aside for her. "Did you ever manage to see Blaine again?"

Shelley stared at him for a moment. Was he implying a double meaning?

"Yeah, she's fine. She'll be at lunch now."

"Good. Tell her 'hi' for me."

"OK."

"Hi, Ms. Poe, you called for me?" Drake asked, as Shelley left the classroom.

She walked down the hall towards the cafeteria, past groups of students dressed in their school colors and banners pumping the big home opener this evening. Her friends would be waiting for her. She was more determined than ever to learn about Dr. Guiles and what was going on at Grimm Academy. She needed to talk with Blaine, Kevin, and Dash about their plans. Tomorrow would be an important day for the four of them.

*****

The crowds were thick in the Autumn's Hallow High School stadium as the football teams finished their warm ups. This would be the first match-up between the crosstown rivals, the Autumn's Hallow Yowling Sasquatch and Grimm Academy Ravens. Anticipation was high. The Sasquatch were in yellow and brown uniforms, running back and forth and throwing the ball around nervously, awaiting kick off. On the sideline their mascot, an oversize cartoon Bigfoot in a jersey, was pumping up the rowdy home team crowd.

The Ravens wore purple and black and performed calisthenics with military precision. The visitor stands were sparsely populated and muted. The school's gaunt Headmaster sat in a cordoned off section near the middle of the stands, surrounded by a few staff. On the sidelines, a giant black bird, the school's mascot, the Grim Reaper, squawked loudly. Its claws were strapped in place so it wouldn't fly away. The Reaper flapped its huge wings in defiance, twitching its head and beady eyes this way and that.

Shelley arrived at school early for a final rehearsal for the half-time show. The evening was cloudy but the weatherman said it would clear up as the night wore on. You could see glimpses of the full moon thru the clouds above. She walked down the path toward the stadium after receiving a text message from Blaine. She was to meet her, Dash, and Kevin near the home section snack stand. Shelley flashed her student ID and waded thru the milling crowds. She reached the snack bar and spotted her friends.

"Hey guys! Can you believe all these people?"

"Yeah," Dash smiled, "I just hope we get half this crowd at our Junior High game!" Dash paused and put a hand out to steady himself against the snack stand. The moon was poking thru a break in the clouds. Dash could feel the hair on his arms bristle and his vision became cloudy.

"Dash, are you alright buddy?" Kevin asked.

Dash took a deep breath. The clouds moved and obscured the moon overhead. He began to feel better.

"That was weird," Dash said, steadying himself. "Man, for a second there I felt really light-headed. But I'm okay now."

"You sure?" Blaine asked.

Dash nodded his head in the affirmative.

"It must be all the hits you're taking on the football field, you big Neanderthal," Blaine joked, taking him by the arm. "Come on. Let's find some seats before they fill up." The four made their way through the crowd toward the home team stands, greeting other friends as they passed. As they were rounding the track surrounding the field someone ran into Dash, knocking him aside.

He looked up. It was Heinz. He was followed by the other two Brothers Grimm, Frederick and Carlos. All three looked robot perfect as ever.

"Look, Frederick, it's mutt-boy," Heinz scoffed. "Well, Fido, is this your pack?"

Dash scowled. "It looks like you heal up fast," Dash said gritting his teeth. "Forget your fake crutches?"

Heinz gave a wicked grin. "Oh, I hope you didn't get in too much trouble?" he mocked. "It would be such a shame if you couldn't play against us tomorrow."

The clouds parted and the moon shone bright. Dash felt his skin prickle again and adrenaline course thru him.

"Don't worry about me," he growled. "I'll happily rip that face of yours off again."

Heinz's grin evaporated and he approached nose to nose with Dash. "You won't survive to tomorrow, dog breath," Heinz whispered, sticking his finger in Dash's chest, "and neither will your friends."

Frederick and Carlos stalked toward the girls and Kevin, menace on their faces.

Dash felt his hair stand on end down the back of his neck and up his arms. He was having difficulty controlling himself. His vision began to narrow and all he could focus on was Heinz. For an instant, he thought he could see the other boy's heart thumping in his chest as if thru an infra-red camera. His senses were turbo charged. He inhaled, smelling the hotdog stand, the aggression emanating from Heinz, the fear from his friends, and the sweat from the players on the field. The sounds of the crowd magnified and Dash could pick out every individual voice, every crunch of gravel, every laugh, cry, and sneeze.

He moved in a flash, grabbing Heinz's finger from his chest and twisting upward. The other boy gasped and dropped to the ground in pain. Frederick and Carlos looked on in alarm.

"If you touch my friends," Dash snarled, "I will hunt you down personally." The cloud cover returned, obscuring the moon overhead. Dash let go of Heinz's finger and took a step back toward his friends, glaring at the other two Brothers Grimm.

Heinz rose, nursing his finger. "This isn't over, mongrel. I'm going to find you at half-time and we're going to settle this." He turned and headed toward the visitor stands, Carlos and Frederick in tow.

Dash felt his blood begin to cool and his senses return to normal. He shook his head to clear his senses.

"Wow," Blaine said walking next to him, "Remind me not to get on your bad side."

Dash smirked. "I just hope I can back it up. He wasn't kidding about finding me at half-time."

"Dash, you don't have to fight him," Shelley replied. "Don't stoop to his level."

"I won't, but I'm also not going to let him threaten my friends. Come on, let's get some seats. We can talk while we watch the game."

*****

The game was close and the crowd was raucous. There wasn't much opportunity for talking between the friends. At the two minute warning, Shelley left to go join her bandmates for the half-time show. As the clocked ticked down, none of them had come up with a plan for dealing with the Brothers Grimm or tomorrow.

Shelley went to the gathering area near the visiting team's end zone where her band gear and clarinet waited. She donned her jersey and hat. As she prepped, the stands emptied and the teams departed for their locker rooms. The P.A. announced the big half-time show and the marching band leader got everyone in order. Shelley was in one of the last rows.

The sky above was clearing and stars and the moon were poking through. Shelley waited in line for her turn to march on the field.

"*Aaaaoooooo!!!*" She heard a howl in the distance above the sounds of the crowd.

Moments later, Kevin came sprinting to the end zone, dodging under a security guard.

"Shelley!" he huffed.

"Kevin!" Shelley hissed, beginning to march on the field. "I have to perform!"

Kevin ran up next to her as she marched. A couple of her bandmates glanced sidelong at him and he just shrugged it off.

"Shelley, I need your help!" Kevin said, between gulps of air. "Those Grimm creeps are messing with Dash... and they have friends... lots of them!"

"Kevin, I can't," she put her clarinet to her mouth. "I'll be there in a few minutes!"

"We don't have a few minutes," he yelled, grabbing her clarinet. "Dash is out of control. He started howling and snarling and ran off into the woods! The Grimm kids are hunting him down." Shelley stopped and looked at Kevin.

"Where's Blaine?" she asked.

"I don't know!" he pleaded. "She left to get snacks at half-time and I haven't seen her since. We have to go get Dash now! He's in trouble."

Shelley made a snap decision. She ran off the field, dropping her clarinet and jersey on the sideline while grabbing her bag.

"Come on," she replied grimly. "We need to get to the bottom of this." The two sprinted away.

I just hope we can deal with it when we find out, she said under her breath.

Chapter 13: Mina

Area 51, Grooms Lake Nevada... 1 year after the incident

"Welcome back to the happy couple!" Edgewick Stoker greeted. He was dressed in a lab coat and looked up from his testing station, assisted by Tempest van Helsing.

"Thank you, Edge!" Mina blushed.

It was her and Peter's first day back from their honeymoon. They had been gone for several weeks after a small wedding at the base facility.

"And where did you go?" Edge asked, walking up to Mina. He gave her a warm hug and Peter a congratulatory handshake.

"Autumn's Hallow, Oregon, my hometown," Peter explained. "It's beautiful in the summer. Besides, I wanted to give Mina a chance to meet my folks!"

"Mina! Peter! Welcome home!" Lonn greeted, as he entered their lab. He looked as shaggy and hearty as ever. He was followed by the pale, slumped figure of Ian van Helsing. "Look, Ian, the Murphys have returned!"

"Salutations," Ian murmured, barely looking up from his paper work. He shuffled to a nearby desk and faced away from his colleagues.

Mina looked at Ian. The last year had been hard on him. Their colleague had never been warm or personable, quite the opposite of his bubbly niece, Tempest, but over the past several months he had grown increasingly cold and distant.

"Where is your monster, old boy?" Edge asked Ian.

"He is a not a monster, you leprechaun. The automaton is near the ship, undergoing testing."

"It appears the mad scientist is a bit snippy today," Edge joked. "So, when are we going to see little Peters and Minas running around?"

Mina slipped away from Peter and let him carry the conversation with Lonn, Edge and Tempest. She approached Ian. "Hi Ian."

Ian looked up from his papers. The hard edge to his face softened. "Hello Mina," he replied, shifting in his chair uncomfortably.

"We missed you at the wedding. It was a lovely affair."

Ian's sharp expression returned. He buried his nose back in his research folder. "Well, someone had to keep working. The world is on the brink of war. All this needs to amount to something."

Mina had read the headlines. The summer of 1939 was a perilous time. Japan was at China's throat. Germany was bullying Europe and the US was still enfeebled by the lasting effects of the Great Depression. No one wanted another Great War but all signs seemed to point to an inevitable conflict.

Mina stepped forward and sat on the side of Ian's desk. "So, what have you found? Come on, Ian. I know you from school. You were my graduate studies tutor, after all! You're too smart not to have found something about all of this mysterious technology."

Ian looked at her and sighed. "You always were the most gifted student in the class Mina," Ian said, wistfully. "I enjoyed studying with you." He picked up his folder and passed it to her. "Look at this. I think it explains a lot about what is happening to you and the others."

Mina read the folder. Inside were photographs taken from a new piece of equipment in the lab, an electron microscope, and Ian's testing notes. She absorbed the information quickly.

"So, you're saying the robot and the ship are actually composed of billions of tiny machines?" Mina said pointing at a photo of a tiny, bug-like mechanism blown up thousands of times.

"Yes, and that's not all. These machines seem to have chosen you, Lonn and Edge, to bind with uniquely. They are changing you at a molecular level. Your encounter with the ship seemed to use the last of its power reserves. I think something similar happened to me and the robot. It is bound to me and people who share my genes, it seems."

"How is that possible?" Mina asked, looking at her hand. She successfully avoided an incident with her new powers for several weeks, a condition of being able to leave the base for her honeymoon.

"I don't know but the implications are incredible. These machines could be used to manipulate anything. Change animals to monsters, turn a bomb into an apocalypse, men into super beings..."

"Ian, those are horrible things to imagine!"

"Well," Ian stammered, "those are just examples. The point is, these machines are the future. Whoever controls them, will control the world."

"For good or for bad," Mina murmured.

"What are you two up to?" Peter asked, smiling.

"Nothing, honey, Ian was just sharing some of his recent findings."

"Yeah, Edge started showing off." He nodded in Edge's direction. He was currently making his head invisible, frightening one of the newer lab assistants, and laughing with Lonn and Tempest. "It seems the more he uses them, the more powerful they become."

Ian's expression twisted into a scowl again. "If that's all, Mina, I am very busy. Good day to you, and to you, Lieutenant."

Mina and Peter walked off. "I worry about him," Mina mused to her husband.

"So do I," Peter replied, but for different reasons. Ever since Roswell, he didn't trust Ian.

Chapter 14: Kevin

Kevin raced with Shelley thru the crowds. They ran from the field, to the front entrance, and into the grassy area surrounding the stadium. Long shadows from the football field lights crisscrossed the grassy knoll, extending to the nearby wall of trees. Few people were outside and most were up to no good or couples sneaking away for some privacy. Kevin tripped over two surprised seniors attempting a half-time smooch.

"High Schoolers…" he murmured, as he ran past the surprised girl and her irate boyfriend.

"*Aaaoooo!*"

They skid to a stop at a long, low howl from the woods. Inside, they could see bobbing cell phones acting as impromptu flashlights. There were dozens of them running this way and that.

"Which way?" Shelley asked, breathing hard.

A Grimm student came flinging thru the underbrush landing hard on the grass. He fell in a broken heap, skipping across the lawn, landing in the bright glare of the stadium.

Kevin looked closer. It wasn't Heinz, Frederick, or Carlos but the kid looked like he could have been a relative; snow white hair, fair skin, and the same perfectly pressed clothes. Except this one looked broken. His head and legs were pitched at odd angles and he lay still on the ground. A swarm of tiny, odd-looking insects rose up around him glinting metallic in the light.

Shelley gasped as the swarm congealed on the Grimm student and his body contorted. The strange bugs melted onto the boy, reshaping his broken limbs and injuries, while emitting a soft greenish light. The Grimm picked himself up from the ground and looked at Shelley and Kevin with a sneer as a gash on his forehead closed. A final metallic bug flew into his mouth and he bit down, licking his lips. He ran back into the underbrush toward where he had been thrown.

"That way!" Kevin said, pointing at where the mutant Grimm had run off to.

"After you…" Shelley said with a gulp.

"Thanks…" Kevin whispered, running into the woods after the boy, Shelley close on his heels.

Darkness closed on them fast as they entered the woods. The trees were tall and the underbrush was thick. Bright stadium light stabbed thru the branches and trunks but most of the woods were pitch black. Kevin pushed forward, following the trail the Grimm student had paved. He caught sight of him thru a gap in the trees jumping ten feet in the air over a thick bramble patch.

"Holy cow!" Kevin said. "That kid moves like Spiderman!"

"What are they? That Grimm kid is like some kind of monster," Shelley said.

Kevin grabbed his cell phone and punched in some information. "Cyborgs," he replied grimly, as he handed over his phone.

Shelley took it and looked at the screen. Kevin had launched his phone's Gothic app and pulled up an entry from the Gothic Monsterpedia. A 3D picture of a scary half-man, half-machine revolved in the foreground with a table of attributes and brief description to its side.

"Machine augmented humans, usually controlled by a remote source. Very high strength and constitution. Low charisma. Proceed with caution. Best dealt with range weapons, ideally a high grade plasma cannon."

"I forgot my photon torpedoes at home," Shelley quipped, giving back his phone. "Any suggestions?"

"Do you know any friendly, time travelling Terminators?"

From out of the gloom two Grimm students stalked forward. They were perfect reflections of each other. They walked through a bright shaft of stadium light, revealing their harsh jeers and robotic blue eyes.

"You will come with us, heir," the first said to Shelley. The second moved forward to grab her by the shoulder.

Kevin pushed him. "Hey! Leave my friend alone!"

The second boy regarded Kevin with disdain. The Grimm grabbed him by the collar and hoisted him in the air.

"You are the one who evaded the Heinz unit," he said, leering at Kevin who dangled from the ground, struggling against the boy's grip. "You are no heir." He flung Kevin to the side who landed in a nearby bush.

"Kevin!" Shelley shouted, shirking away from the Grimm students.

"You will come with us now, heir," the first Grimm boy said, approaching Kevin and picking him up by the hair. "Or we will break your companion's neck."

Shelley raced forward and tried to tackle the Grimm kid holding Kevin. The second pushed her away. She fell in a heap on the ground near a large tree trunk. She looked up woozily.

"Get her," the first said to his companion.

The second stepped forward.

BOOM!

The trees shook.

BOOM! BOOM! BOOM!

The Grimm student scanned the nearby trees. The earth and lower limbs shook.

"What is that?" the second Grimm asked.

From out of the bushes, a giant metal fist smashed into the Grimm student nearest Shelley and slammed him into in a tree, hitting it at fantastic speed. The student evaporated in a swirling puff of angry, buzzing, metal insects. The insects fell to the ground, dying with a soft green light.

The first Grimm dropped Kevin who looked up to see a giant metal man walk from under the shadows of a nearby fir tree. The Grimm student crouched into a fighting position as the giant robot raised to its full height, towering over him, its harsh emerald eyes glaring down. The Grimm cyborg sneered and launched himself at the robot.

The giant iron creature grabbed the student in midair with one hand and whipped him around, smashing him into a nearby tree. Like his companion, the Grimm exploded into a million tiny pieces. A cloud of glowing lime-hued metal buzzed angrily and then fell helplessly to the ground, turning to a dull grey dust.

Kevin scrambled to Shelley, staring at the giant robot in fright. The creature was huge, easily ten feet tall. Its body was smooth and metallic with large iron fists and feet which carved deep impressions in the soft forest earth. It had no features on its body or face except for two bright green slits that served as eyes.

The creature turned its head and regarded Shelley and Kevin. The harsh green of its eyes softened and the slits angled down to a neutral expression. It turned its body and stood still before them.

"Holy cow!" Kevin muttered.

Shelley got up on her elbows and looked at the glistening steel robot. "What does your phone say about this one, Kevin?" she breathed.

Kevin shakily took his phone from his pocket. He gulped. "Robot," he whispered, "infinite strength, unknown weaknesses, intentions unclear."

Shelley took a long breath. "Nice robot..." she said shakily. She slowly rose. The robot watched her intently. Shelley moved to one side. The golem tracked her with its head but otherwise stood still.

"What's it doing?" Kevin asked.

"I don't know. I don't think it wants to hurt us though."

"Who are you?" Shelley asked, looking the creature up and down.

She bent down as she passed one of the giant footsteps the automaton had left in the dirt.

"Kevin, bring over your phone so I can take a look at this." Kevin walked over, not taking his eyes off the giant metal man. He stopped by Shelley and shone his phone screen on the dirt.

"These footsteps are the same as the ones I saw in the woods with Dash." She approached the iron giant and walked slowly around him. "Kevin, shine your phone on him."

Kevin got up and paced around the creature next to Shelley, shining his phone's flashlight app on the metal man. Its surface was silver, reflecting his phone's light with an opalescent sheen. The robot was square-shouldered and thick but otherwise human-shaped. Its feet ended in wide rectangles attaching to sturdy legs on thick hinges. Where his ears should have been, there were two circular objects which looked like wide silver bolts. Its face was featureless, save for two glowing green eyes that moved dynamically to generate expressions. The eyes were oval and watching Shelley unblinking.

"What's your name?" Shelley asked.

The robot cocked its head to one side. The lights serving as its eyes separated, creating two eyebrows over smaller ovals in a questioning expression.

"Kevin, look, it responds!"

"Great, send it for pizza and let's get out of here!" Kevin muttered, nervously.

"Where are you from?" Shelley asked the robot, stopping in front of it.

The robot looked at her for a moment and then raised one giant hand and pointed southeast. He paused for a moment and raised his arm to the sky. He pointed at a far off point of light and held his pose before looking at Shelley again.

She put her hand hesitantly on the creature's giant metal torso. Cool to the touch.

"Are you from that star?" she asked.

The creature looked at her. It peered back at the sky and pointed to the same far off point of light.

"Wow…" Shelley whispered.

"Aaaooo!"

Another low howl pierced the night, leading deeper into the woods. In the distance, the crowds roared as the football game played on.

"Shelley, we have to find Dash. He's still in trouble and these Grimm goons look like they are swarming all over the place... literally..."

Kevin kicked at a pile of dust that one of the Grimm students had disintegrated into. A couple of the greenish bugs flew fitfully but fell back to the ground, their lights winking out.

"Yuck," Kevin muttered.

Shelley turned back to the metal monster, "We have to go now."

She and Kevin ran toward the distant howling noise. As they left, the robot began to trail them, one large foot rumbling in front of the other.

"Kevin, it's following us," Shelley said, dodging a low-hanging branch.

"I suppose having a giant body guard could come in handy... oomph," he cursed as he tripped on a root sticking up from the ground. "This is going to be rough. Do you think he can carve us a path?"

"Aaaooo!" A second howl echoed in the distance.

Shelley stopped and looked back at the creature. "Mr. Robot, we need to find our friend. Can you lead us to that howling sound?"

The robot turned in the direction of the howl. The bolts on the side of its head extended and rotated in place. The golem stomped thru the forest toward Dash's location, its eyes creating a harsh green glow for the two friends to follow.

Kevin looked at Shelley and shrugged. "It beats stumbling around in the dark."

Shelley blew a strand of hair out of her eyes and chased after Kevin and her new pet robot.

155

*****

They found Dash in a moon-lit clearing surrounded by Grimm cyborgs. High overhead the full moon beamed, painting the clearing in an eerie blue light.

Dash was on the ground with five of the mechanical swarm-powered boys piling on top of him. He growled fiercely and threw the pile of Grimm bots off him in a surge of strength. Another came at him and he dropped, sweeping his body and lower legs out in a vicious kick that sent the cyborg-enhanced boy sprawling. Two more followed from either side. Dash sent them tumbling with a roundhouse kick followed by a nasty upper cut. Puffs of the angry metallic insect swarms scattered off each of the Grimm boys with every kick and punch.

Dash looked around him, sniffing and snarling, as a dozen Grimm boys surrounded him in a wary circle. He let out a loud baying sound, followed by a long howl. His face was contorted in animal rage, his blonde hair mussed across his forehead.

"Holy smoke!" Kevin exclaimed. "Dash has gone full werewolf on these guys!"

"What's happening to him?" Shelley asked.

"I don't know, Shelley, but he needs our help." Kevin strode forward into the clearing. "Hey losers! Mitts off my best friend!"

The Grimms looked at Kevin and four of them broke from the circle, converging on the snarling Dash. They stalked toward Kevin and Shelley. The robot stood behind them, lending light to the clearing with his emerald green eyes. The lead Grimm, the tallest, cracked his knuckles viciously.

"A little help, Shell," Kevin whispered, putting his dukes up.

"Mr. Robot, can you defend us from those creeps?" Shelley asked.

The robot looked down and nodded. It stepped forward in front of Kevin and Shelley and approached the Grimms. The four students looked at each other, a moment of nerves clouding their otherwise perfect faces. The lead indicated for his three companions to fan out and take the robot on all sides. The tall boy looked the creature in the face and snarled, nodding for all four to converge on the iron golem.

The Grimm cyborgs leapt in an attempt to grapple the iron goliath to the ground. The metal man showed surprising agility. It ducked the first cyborg, sending it crashing into a nearby branch, and grabbed two others flying at it from either side. The robot smashed them together in a sickly crunch of glowing green metallic dust. Having dealt with the first three, the metal man stepped forward, crunching a pile of angry lime metal bugs under one giant foot. The taller Grimm stepped back, no longer confident in its strategy. He turned and motioned for two more of his companions to help take down the iron giant.

It was Dash's turn. He struck. He plowed thru the remaining Grimm boys as they divided their attention between him and their new robot adversary. Dash was a flurry of punches, sending swarms of green tinted dust into the air, as he raced from opponent to opponent. When he was done, five more Grimm students lay on the ground in piles of glowing emerald ash.

The tall cyborg and his two companions looked at Dash and the robot warily. They turned and ran, leaping for cover in the surrounding darkness. The giant lumbered into the forest, chasing after them.

Dash stared at Kevin and Shelley, breathing hard, with sweat pouring from his forehead. He had a wild, angry look in his eyes and snarled as he regarded his friends. Overhead, clouds obscured the full moon and the clearing darkened. Dash shook his head.

"*Kevin... Shelley...*" he breathed. He took a step forward and collapsed to the ground.

"Dash!" Kevin yelled rushing forward to aid his friend, Shelley close on his heels. Kevin reached Dash first and cradled his head. Dash looked up and blinked.

"What... what's going on? What's happening to me?"

"I don't know," Kevin answered, helping to prop his friend up. "I was going to ask you the same thing."

Dash sat up and shook the cobwebs out of his head. He looked at Kevin and Shelley. "The last thing I remember, we were behind the stands at half-time waiting for Blaine to come back from the snack stand. Heinz came up to us with his friends from Grimm Academy, and then... I blacked out."

"Dash, you went loco," Kevin replied, a look of worry on his face, "Heinz pushed you and you went Justice League on him. His buddies rushed us, you had a wild look on your face, howled, and bolted for the woods."

"What?" Dash asked blankly. "I howled?"

"And once you bolted for the woods, Kevin came and grabbed me to find you."

"Where are those Grimm kids now?"

Kevin looked around the clearing at the slowly dying piles of glowing green metallic dust. "Like I said, you went all Wolverine on them... literally."

Dash looked around the clearing at the piles of buzzing green metal bugs slowly winking out. He whistled and took a deep breath.

"They aren't just preppy kids with chips on their shoulders," Shelley said. "Something's going on here, Dash, and I think it has to do with the dust we found in the woods."

Dash remembered his encounter with Heinz, Frederick, and Carlos, the swarming mass that surrounded and repaired Heinz's ruined face and the strange glowing dust in the woods. The answers started to click into place.

"You mean the kids at Grimm Academy are some of kind of nanotech zombies?" he said, staring at a nearby buzzing green pile.

"Actually cyborgs," Kevin countered.

"At least some of them. Let's get out of here. There's more of them in the woods and I don't know how long the robot is going to hang out with us," Shelley replied.

"Did you say robot?" Dash asked, blinking.

"Yeah, about that…"

The giant metal man stomped thru the dark woods behind them. He stared down at Dash with his unblinking, glowing green eyes.

"*Whoa*…" Dash whispered. "What the heck is that?"

"That, I think, is our monster from the woods."

"Come on," Kevin said, helping his friend up. "We can explain on the way. For now, Shelley's right, we need to get out of here."

Dash rose, his eyes glued to the giant metal man standing guard behind Shelley. "OK, but you are going to need to fill in the details, Kev. This is crazy."

"Yeah, I know." Kevin dusted off his friend. "Come on, let's get going." They started to walk from the clearing the robot following.

"Before you fill me in on the whole story, tell me," Dash stopped and looked at Shelley and Kevin, "where's Blaine?"

Chapter 15: Blaine

Blaine waved goodbye to Kevin and Dash to get a head start on the rush to the snack line. There were only a few seconds before half-time and the Sasquatch and Ravens were tied 17-17. The crowd was rowdy with the parents and students in high spirits cheering on the home team.

Blaine exited the stands just as the buzzer blared over the loud speakers. The announcer hyped the upcoming half-time show featuring the Autumn's Hallow High School marching band. Blaine was eager to get back to Kevin and Dash to watch Shelley in her half-time debut. She and the other members of the Middle School band would be marching in the show.

She got to the stand just as a line was starting to form. Blaine quickly got to the front and bought popcorn and a drink for herself and two candy bars for the boys. She thanked the mom attending the stand and turned around, wading thru the growing line. She popped out onto the track.

"Hello there, little girl," Igor greeted her, standing behind him were Frederick and Carlos, two of the Brothers Grimm.

Blaine glanced at the stooped handyman and hurried toward the stands. Igor limped alongside her while Frederick and Carlos blocked her path.

"I wouldn't bother trying to find your friends. They have already been dealt with."

He grabbed Blaine by the shoulder and she jerked away. "Get off me," she barked.

"Come with me quietly and you will not be harmed," Igor warned. "My Master wishes to speak with you, Blaine Stoker."

Blaine gasped. How did this jerk know her old name? "Who are you?" she asked, backing away. "What do you want from me?"

"You are an heir," Igor replied, stepping forward, he was no longer limping, "and you will come with me."

He reached for her and she screamed, throwing her drinking cup at him. Igor jerked back, drenched.

"*Diet...*" He snarled, his face dripping with brown, syrupy liquid. "Disgusting..."

Igor's face twisted with rage. "My patience is at an end, heir."

"What's the problem here?" An Autumn Hallow police officer stepped forward, confronting Igor.

Blaine looked at the policeman with relief flooding her face. *Thank goodness*, she breathed, *help had arrived.*

The cop inserted himself between Blaine and Igor. Igor sighed loudly and made a sour face. "I don't have time for this. Enough with these games." He reached under his coat and before the policeman could react, pulled out a black Taser. In one fluid motion, he jammed the blue sparking prods into the officer's midsection and sent the man tumbling to the ground. The onlookers surrounding stepped back in alarm.

"Get the girl, while I deal with this oaf," Igor kicked the cop over with one boot. Frederick and Carlos stepped toward Blaine. Behind them, three boys from school grabbed them and said "Hey, stay away from her!" Frederick and Carlos turned, grabbed the arms of the boys and twisted them down to their knees. The third boy turned and ran. Blaine didn't wait for more help to come. She bolted for the stands.

"Get her!" Igor roared.

Blaine dodged thru the crowds of people milling around the track. On the field, the marching band was playing, adding to the commotion. She dashed toward the back of the stands to find a place to hide. Frederick and Carlos released the boys and sprinted in pursuit. A wave of half-time revelers washed over the track, slowing them down.

Blaine bolted over a low chain-link fence and toward the back of the stands. She weaved her way thru the iron girders holding up the seats and curled up behind a large concrete footer. She looked back the way she had come checking if the coast was clear. Frederick and Carlos ran into view in the grassy area outside. She ducked behind the concrete block and tried to think.

Only one option. "Please work," she whispered frantically, "please, please work." She imagined the silvery glow washing over her, cloaking her entire body.

Slowly, her fingers began to disintegrate from view, the soft silvery sheen washing over her. Something was wrong, the shimmer flickered and she could see a faint outline of her arms and body. She screwed up her face in concentration and tried again. No luck. Faint flickers rolled over her body. She was transparent but like a ghost with a wispy outline. She hefted a rock and watched it turn shadowy and ghost-like, matching her hand. It was tougher to see but still visible.

"Come on, *work*!" She gritted her teeth and concentrated harder. As she did, she shifted and her foot kicked a nearby can.

"Frederick! Come here!" Carlos whispered coarsely. He was close.

Blaine squeezed her eyes closed, forcing her breathing down. She heard Carlos and Frederick's shoes crunch in the gravel as people stomped in the stands above. Half-time was almost over.

"Work, work, work..." but her concentration was fractured. She kept imagining the two Grimm Brothers finding her and couldn't focus on imagining her hand fully invisible.

"Come here, pretty girl!" Frederick called. "We won't hurt you."

Carlos chuckled next to him. "Yes, come out and you will be fine. We are friends!"

She heard the Brothers Grimm crunching sneakers growing nearer. The announcer on the stadium P.A. announced half-time would be ending in two minutes. Blaine held her breath. She looked at the rock in her hand and gripped it tight. As she did the silvery glow surrounding it intensified and flexed in a wave.

"I hear you!" Frederick crept around the block, bending under a support girder.

"Hear this!" Blaine hissed, swinging the rock up.

Frederick doubled over as the rock and Blaine's balled fist connected with his midsection. An angry cloud of glowing, swirling metal exploded from his belly. Blaine stared wide-eyed as bits of it landed on her nearly transparent arm. The glowing green bits looked like hundreds of tiny lightning bugs with the same faint phosphorescent glow.

Frederick recovered quickly. He looked up with an angry scowl. "You shouldn't have done that, Stoker girl."

Blaine believed him. She scrambled out of her crouch and sprinted for the field surrounding the stands, dodging concrete blocks and metal support arms as she ran.

"Carlos!" Frederick shouted and followed, hot on her heels.

Blaine juked around a final iron bar, clearing the bleachers, looking back to track Frederick. She ran straight into Carlos who was lurking in the grass just outside. He grasped her roughly but she wiggled away. Blaine lost her balance and fell to the ground. She looked up at Carlos as Frederick joined him.

"The chase is over," Carlos growled. "Get up and come with us quietly... *now*."

Blaine gripped her eyelids together hard. *I have to get away, I have to get away,* she repeated to herself, concentrating with all her might to complete her change.

"Frederick, get her before she disappears."

Blaine opened her eyes and saw her hands and arms melting away but Frederick was on top of her as she prepared to bolt. As he stepped forward and gripped Blaine's shoulder, a giggling couple emerged from around the back of the bleachers and swayed right up to where Blaine and the two Grimm boys were having their confrontation. Frederick and Carlos glared at the kids, a girl and a boy.

"Oh, sorry," The boy said, hugging the girl next to him. He smiled. "We were just looking for some... ahem... private seats." The girl buried her face in his shoulder and sniggered loudly.

Blaine recognized the voice and laughed. It was Drake Harker and her sister, Vickie.

Ooo... Blaine thought. *Vickie was going to be so busted with Mom, wandering off with a boy at a football game!*

Frederick's grip tightened, re-focusing Blaine on her plight. Carlos stepped forward to distract Drake.

"There are no seats here," Carlos replied, leaning into Drake. "Go back to the Stadium, Romeo."

Carlos's voice was clear. He wanted them to leave. Vickie's embarrassed giggling ceased as she looked at the two Grimm students each staring at them icily. Drake stood unmoving, his easy smile transforming into a steely expression.

"Drake, let's just go back with the gang," she suggested, starting to pull him back toward the stands.

"What are you two doing back here?" Drake asked, not moving nor taking his eyes off Carlos. He let go of Vickie's hand.

"None of your business," Carlos growled.

Stepping shoulder to shoulder with the Grimm boy, Drake stared straight in his eyes, his disarming smile returning. "Maybe you two should leave," he retorted.

Carlos looked at Drake with a frigid expression, staring at the other's bright blue eyes. His face softened. He took a step back and looked at Drake in confusion. Carlos shook his head and looked from Drake to Frederick and back.

"Yes," Carlos murmured sleepily. "Yes, we will."

"Carlos!" Frederick hissed. Carlos turned and looked at his friend. His hard-etched face was slack and confused.

Frederick released his grip on Blaine and stepped forward toward Drake.

Blaine started to creep away into the grass, trying to stay quiet. She kept a close eye on Vickie, ready to swoop in and run away with her if things got out of hand. She didn't want her sister to find out about her invisibility but she was not leaving her here with these two psychopaths.

"What have you done to Carlos?" Frederick demanded. Drake stared at the other with the same cold blue eyes but easy smile. Frederick's aggressive expression relaxed and he also stepped away with the same muddled expression.

"Nothing," Drake answered coolly, "just like what you found back here, nothing." Frederick and Carlos nodded sluggishly.

"Now run along, before your friends wonder where you are," Drake commanded, nodding toward the stadium.

The two Brothers Grimm lingered for a moment and then shuffled toward the stands.

"That was weird," Vickie said, coming up to stand next to Drake. "Who were they?"

"I don't know," Drake said, watching the two Grimm boys round the nearby corner into the crowds. He turned to Vickie and smiled. "Why don't we get back to your friends, Vick…. probably better with so many weirdos around."

"Ok…Drake," Vickie replied, a little confused and disappointed.

Drake looked at a dark patch of ground where Blaine was crouched, invisible.

"I don't think it's a good idea for anyone to stay here for long," he said, putting his arm around Vickie and walking away. "No telling when those two will come back to their senses." He walked off with Vickie toward the lights and the crowds.

Blaine let the tension ease from her body. She looked down at her hands which were now completely invisible, the flickering and ghostly outline gone.

"That was weird," she whispered to herself.

Blaine had a sneaking suspicion there was more to Drake Harker than met the eye.

*****

Blaine waited for Vickie and Drake to clear out and crept around the far corner to the track and field beyond. The crowd was cheering as the Autumn's Hallow team returned the second half kick-off. The pep band blared horns and drums from the stands overhead and people were teeming everywhere. In the distance, several police officers were converged around the spot where Igor had confronted Blaine, questioning onlookers. There was no sign of the strange bent man anywhere. On the far end of the track, rounding a bend from the visitor's side, Blaine saw Carlos and Frederick. They were returning with several other Grimm students who looked suspiciously alike.

Not good... Blaine thought. She waited for a gap in the crowd and made her way to the snack stand, walking behind the back of the stands to avoid people. She had no idea what would happen if she accidently bumped into someone and turned their bag of popcorn or, worse yet, their rear end, invisible. She wasn't keen to find out.

The far end of the stadium roared and Autumn's Hallow groaned as Grimm Academy made a big defensive play, intercepting the ball and running it back for a touchdown. The Grimm cheer squad set off a small fireworks display and loosed their giant black bird mascot into the sky as their headmaster looked on approvingly. It circled overhead like a huge bird of prey, its wing span enormous.

Blaine stared out from behind the concessions area, eyeing the stadium exit. It looked clear. She tensed ready to make her move.

"They'll be waiting for you that way," a voice said casually from behind a giant jar of ketchup.

Blaine peered around the condiments tray and saw Drake putting mustard on a hotdog.

"Their mascot, that big black bird, can see you. Like many of the students at Grimm, it's not what it appears," he said, taking a bite. "Hi, by the way," he smiled.

Blaine stared at this strange boy, shocked. "Wait, you mean, you can see me?" she managed.

"Yup," he replied, taking another large bite and wiping a dab of mustard from the side of his mouth.

"And did you know this was happening to me all week?" Blaine asked. "The cafeteria, art class?

"Blaine, I'm here to keep an eye on you and your friends," Drake replied. "You're each very important."

"What do you mean important? How can you see me? What's happening to me?"

Drake put his sausage down and took a step away from the concessions stand. He saw a group of Grimm boys in the distance. Four broke off and headed for the stadium entrance while the remaining two headed their way.

"I promise I'll answer all of your questions once we get out of here. For now, though, we need to focus on getting you to safety. That bird can see you, which means von Frankenstein knows who you are. His lackey Igor is waiting outside the entrance to nab you."

Drake looked toward the stadium gate. "And with Tweedle Dee and Tweedle Dum coming back, that means they've probably figured out who I am as well."

"What are you talking about?" Blaine asked, standing up and looking toward the approaching Brothers Grimm. "And who are you? I mean really?"

"I'm who I said I am, Drake Harker," he said, taking her hand. His hand shimmered momentarily but remained normal.

"How can you see me? Why don't I affect you?"

Drake smiled. "Oh, you affect me," he answered, walking her toward the entrance. "But I have a couple tricks I can use. I'm like you, an heir."

"What is that? That creep Igor said that and so did those two Grimm morons," Blaine whispered, walking beside him.

"Heirs are the ancestors of a group of scientists who were given some incredible powers," Drake explained, continuing to walk. He scanned the crowd as he talked, watching for trouble.

"Scientists? Powers?"

"Yeah, I know it seems pretty hard to believe, but it's true. Where I'm taking you, we can explain more but first your friends are in trouble. We need to get you out of here and find them."

He paused as a group of Grimm students rounded the curve in the track. He turned to Blaine and blocked her from view, leaning his head down. The Grimm students walked by. They were dressed nicely but were otherwise normal.

"Are all the Grimm kids super-powered freakonauts?" Blaine asked, as Drake looked up.

"No, but their headmaster, von Frankenstein, can turn any of them into some really nasty suckers fast," Drake said, picking up the pace. "You've seen the glowing bugs?"

Blaine remembered the bits of glowing green metal that had exploded off Carlos.

She nodded.

"Those are von Frankenstein's. They're called nanobots. They can turn anyone into a monster. Trust me, I've had a lot of first-hand experience with them."

"Whoa," Blaine forced herself to stop. "Who is this von Frankenstein? And are you telling me that old guy from Grimm Academy can turn his students into monsters with glowing, fairy dust?

"Blaine, I'll explain later but for now, yes, von Frankenstein is the real name of Van Guiles, the Headmaster at Grimm. He is someone my mother and I have been tracking for a long time. He fell off the radar until a few years ago but has since been a major problem," Drake scanned the crowd warily. "He and his minions are not people you should take lightly."

"Your mother?"

"Yes, she can help. Her name is Mina, Mina Harker," Drake ducked down, acting like he was tying his shoe as four of the Grimm students who had been following Carlos and Frederick passed by toward the front gate.

He got back up and looked back to the concessions area. Carlos, Frederick, and a group of their lookalike lackeys were scouring the lines. They didn't have much time.

"Now, we have to get going," Drake said, staring directly at Blaine with his deep blue eyes. "No more questions and do whatever I tell you. Clear?"

Blaine nodded.

"Good, let's get going." As he turned, he bumped into Vickie.

"Hey, you! I have been looking all over for you!" she gushed.

"Vickie!" Drake replied, holding his hand back to stop Blaine.

"Who were you talking to?" Vickie asked, peering behind him.

"Just talking on my phone. My mom called, asking for me to get home. We've got family plans early tomorrow," Drake lied.

"Oh," Vickie said, disappointed. She looked down. "I could walk you home?"

Vickie! Blaine thought. *Stop being so desperate!*

"That is nice of you, but I'd hate to take you away from your friends…" Drake started.

He looked up in alarm as he saw Carlos and Frederick breaking through the crowd toward them. Just as they were on top of them, Drake grabbed Vickie, kissing her and holding her tight. Vickie gasped in surprise but melted into Drake's arms. He turned her around to point his face away from the Grimm Brothers who passed by, looking over the smooching couple for familiar faces in the crowd.

Drake released Vickie, who was blushing furiously. "Wow, Drake…" she breathed dreamily. "I didn't quite picture that as my first kiss but… wow!"

"*OMG!*" Blaine mouthed. *I just saw my sister have her first kiss with some teen superspy while two mutant cyborgs looked on*, she thought. *And, most importantly, I can hold it over her… forever!*

Drake tracked Carlos and Frederick as they headed toward the entrance.

"That was close," he muttered.

"I'll say," Vickie giggled.

"We have to get out of here. Come on." He grabbed Blaine by the wrist and tugged her forward.

"Drake, I'm right here!" Vickie said, following.

"We should go to my house."

Vickie hesitated.

"Well, that seems kind of fast…" Vickie said, catching up. "I like you… I mean, I really like you. But we should take it slow. Teen Cosmo says…"

Drake held up his hand.

Vickie stopped, startled. "That was a little rude," she muttered.

Drake surveyed the front entrance. Carlos, Frederick, and eight of their compatriots were lurking, eyeing everyone who went in and out. Overhead, the dark shadow of their mascot, the Grimm Reaper, cawed loudly as it circled overhead.

"We need a plan," Drake said, looking from Vickie to her invisible sister.

"Blaine, you take your sister's hand. I'll handle Carlos, Frederick, and friends."

"Blaine?" Vickie replied, confused. "My sister isn't here. And we really need to talk about your strange behavior. If we are going to be girlfriend and boyfriend…"

"Blaine, take her hand and I'll take things from there. Once you clear the gates, make a beeline for the woods to the left. I'll find you there."

"Hey!" Vickie said annoyed, pointing a finger at Drake's face. "I was talking to you... hold on, what's happening?!"

Blaine grabbed her sister's hand and instantly a silver wave washed over her fingers, arm, and body.

Vickie started to scream as she looked at her disappearing arm. Blaine put her hand quickly over her mouth, muffling her startled sister's outburst.

"Vickie," Blaine whispered. "It's okay, it's me."

"Blaine?" Vickie said in shock, her voice muffled thru Blaine's cupped hand.

"It's alright," Blaine said, taking her hand away from Vickie's mouth. "Just don't let go of my hand. It's very important."

Vickie nodded silently.

"We're ready," Blaine whispered to Drake.

"Stay here and wait for the fireworks to start," Drake said, looking at each, Blaine determined, Vickie frightened. "Once I have their attention, make a dash thru the gate and for the woods. I'll be following."

He took a step forward and cracked his fingers.

"It's show time."

Chapter 16: Drake

Drake strode through the crowd, directly to Carlos who was bossing around three of his lackeys. He tapped the other boy on the shoulder. Carlos turned with a sneer, which transitioned from recognition to shock as Drake drew back his fist and punched him in the nose. Immediately, the eight Grimm students around the gate exploded into action, grappling for him.

Drake ducked the first and knocked over a second. He made a dash for the open practice fields outside the stadium. Two Grimms dived after him from either side and one caught his shoulder, spinning him. A third pair came up and pinned him to the chain-link fence by the gate. Drake struggled to free himself but the two Grimm cyborgs held him fast, their eyes glinting an evil shade of green.

Carlos strode up to him sniffing his nose, which had a trickle of glowing emerald goo falling from one nostril. Frederick followed along with three others, shielding them from gawkers. "So... Drake Harker," Carlos spat on the ground. It sparkled with flakes of metallic lime. He punched Drake in the gut, doubling him over.

"Not so tough now, huh?" Carlos smiled. "My Master said to be wary of you, but you don't seem too hard to catch."

Drake looked up. His normally immaculate hair was a mess and he looked winded, but he smiled. His eyes glowed a bright blue. He glanced at each of the Grimms pinning him. "Who says you've caught me," he whispered.

The Grimm boys holding him let go, faces blank, drew back, and each hit Carlos squarely on the jaw. He reeled back, knocking Frederick and his gang off-balance.

Drake rolled on the fence toward open ground. He dodged one Grimm and came face-to-face with three steely faced boys approaching him. He stared down two. They blinked, shook their heads, and began to grapple with the third, clearing a path for him.

"Come on, Blaine, make your move."

He ran up to the gate. Two police officers were jogging up, muttering in walkie-talkies, responding to the scrum of students fighting near the entryway. Drake looked at them and said, "Those Grimm students, officers, they're fighting! Stop them, please!"

Without question, the policemen nodded and waded into the Grimms who were wrestling each other. Carlos and Frederick were underneath a dogpile with four of their compatriots.

Drake stood by the gate, prepared to cover Blaine and Vickie's tracks. True to his plan, he saw the two invisible figures ducking thru the gates and around onlookers, Blaine leading her bewildered sister by the hand. They were halfway to the woods when the dark shadow of the Grimm Reaper swooped down and screeched, its piercing caw cutting thru the noise of the crowd.

Blaine ducked and stumbled, the bird's talons missing her head by inches. She let go of her sister who tumbled onto her hands and knees, winking back into view onto the grass beyond.

Vickie got up shakily and looked at her now visible hands and body, relief flooding her face.

Blaine called out, "Vickie, run!"

From out of the woods, Igor emerged along with two Grimm cyborgs and an enraged Heinz. The bent, bedraggled man pointed to Vickie and the Grimms sprinted over to apprehend her. Before Blaine could react, he withdrew from his overcoat a small object and threw it toward them.

"Blaine! Dive for cover!" Drake shouted, as he sprinted toward her.

Igor's grenade spun thru the air and exploded on contact with the ground, emanating a thick purple fog that spread rapidly. The cloud reached Blaine, whose outline started to form in the mist.

"Get the other one!" Igor barked to Heinz, as he marched forward. "I will take care of the Harker boy."

Drake raced out of the entrance as the gate attendants stood transfixed between the fighting Grimms and policemen wrestling them apart inside the stadium and the purple cloud and light show outside. He grabbed Blaine's hand and raced with her to the woods. Blaine's outline still shown a faint purple from the receding grenade cloud.

"My sister!" she shouted.

"No time!" Drake yelled. "I'll circle back and get her once you're out of trouble!"

Heinz leapt after them, jumping ten feet in the air, covering a superhuman distance. He missed grasping Blaine and landed in a cat-like crouch, snarling.

Drake let go of Blaine and shouted, "Run!" He turned to face Heinz and Igor, who were trailing him, grasping a thin metal cylinder. The Grimm Reaper circled in low and landed on Igor's outstretched, gloved hand. The huge bird of prey twisted its head and eyed Drake with its inky black eyes, then cawed loudly.

Heinz immediately dived after Drake, throwing a flurry of punches. Drake moved with practiced ease, dodging an uppercut, left hook, and haymaker. He bent at the waist, leaned in, and flipped over the Grimm as he overreached, landing him on the ground hard behind him. Heinz let out a loud grunt as he bounced on the grass.

The Grimms, grasping a frightened Vickie, looked at their fallen leader with alarm. Drake stared at them with his eyes glowing a bright blue. They let go of her and stalked toward Igor who stood with the Grimm Reaper nearby. Igor let the bird fly with a flurry of feathers and talons and turned toward the two boys. He pointed the metal cylinder at the first. Drake heard a high-pitched whine and winced.

The targeted Grimm stared at his companion with alarm clouding his hard face. His companion hesitated as the first Grimm doubled over in pain and exploded in a swarming cloud of glowing green. The second Grimm stepped back in horror, covered in phosphorescent metallic bits. Igor pointed his wand at the second and he too exploded in a haze of swirling metal.

"Enough with your head games, Harker," Igor growled, turning to face Drake. He pointed his weapon at Drake and fired.

Drake doubled over in pain as he heard a high-pitched noise. Swirling black smoke emerged from his midsection where the invisible beam from Igor's wand impacted. As Igor concentrated the beam, the protective smoke evaporated quickly, exposing him to attack.

Igor clicked off his weapon and approached Drake, who had fallen to his knees, grasping his stomach in pain. Behind him, Heinz had risen and stood leering at his enemy with a twisted smile.

"This is an ultrasonic wand... a little toy of the Doctor's. It's a focused beam of sound that can mash your internal organs from the inside out," Igor sneered. "Not even your mother's gifts can protect you from it, whelp." He pointed the weapon at Drake who looked at his opponent in despair.

"The Doctor said to bring you in," Igor growled, preparing to push the trigger. "He never said anything about you needing to be alive." As Igor depressed the button, a faint purple glow swirled thru the air. Blaine had snuck up on the evil custodian and swung a tree branch like a cudgel at his head. It made contact with a satisfying crunch.

Igor crumpled. The beam missed Drake and hit a shocked Heinz who screamed in alarm as the lower half of his chest exploded in buzzing emerald metal, knocking him off his feet and into the underbrush of the woods beyond.

Blaine dropped her tree branch and ran to Drake.

"Are you OK?" she asked, bending down.

Drake looked up, pain streaking his handsome face. He got up with a grunt, taking Blaine's offered hand. "I've been better," he grimaced. He looked back toward the stadium gates where the Grimms were peeling off from the fight and heading their way. "We need to get out of here," he said.

A scream from above jerked Drake's attention to the sky. The Grimm Reaper was descending fast, its razor sharp talons extended.

WHACK!

The bird whirled away in pain as something hit it from the side. It floundered in the sky toward the nearby woods, cawing weakly.

Vickie stood with Blaine's tree branch grasped in both hands over her shoulder like she had hit the winning point at a Grand Slam event. "Five years of tennis lessons, you overgrown feather duster!" she called triumphantly. Blaine and Drake smiled.

"Come on," Drake said, jogging toward the parking lots. He was grasping his side and limping in pain. He looked back. "We won't get away from them on foot."

Blaine and Vickie followed. "How are we going to get out of here?" Blaine asked, offering him a shoulder.

"We take a car," Drake replied, grimly accepting her aid.

"A car! Are we going to call our parents?" Vickie said, catching up.

"Nope, I'll drive," he replied with a smile, wincing as he picked up the pace. "As I recall, Principle Marlowe has a nice ride."

*****

As the three friends passed quickly thru the dark field, two young boys wearing Grimm Academy sweatshirts walked in the opposite direction toward the stadium.

The first swatted at the back of his neck. "Ow!" he yelled.

"Emmit, what's wrong?" his friend asked.

"Something stung me!" the boy complained. Emmit looked at his palm and saw the remains of a large ugly bug and a splotch of glowing green ooze surrounding it.

180

"Disgusting," his buddy, Brent, commented.

"Yeah, hey there's more of them," Emmit said, rubbing his neck. They looked around as multiple green lights dotted the grassy area around them.

"Fireflies?" Brent asked.

"They don't sting and don't live this far West," Emmit replied, waving away a few of the strange phosphorescent bugs.

Brent slapped his forearm. "Ow... they're aggressive," he said, looking at an ugly red welt forming on his arm, "Let's get back to the game."

"Yeah...," Emmit's eyes widened as more and more of the glowing emerald dots winked to life. "Brent I think we might be in trouble."

A huge swarm suddenly lit up around Emmit. The boy tried to scream but his cry was cut off by the mass of glowing bugs swarming his skin, eyes, ears, and mouth. The bugs congealed and formed a churning cocoon around him. Brent backed away in shock as his friend was consumed, falling to the ground in a swarming mass. A lonely, glowing green bug landed on his neck and stung him.

Brent screamed, tearing away toward the parking lot in fear. Running in a panic, he tripped and fell. Brent turned and saw a figure emerge from the writhing mound on the ground lit eerily from the far off stadium lights. His friend Emmit had been transformed. Before there had been a diminutive brown-haired boy wearing a grey sweatshirt, now there stood a tall and athletic Nordic teen wearing a checkered shirt and spotless corduroys.

His former friend regarded Brent coldly, with steely blue eyes that glinted in the darkness. Emmit pointed at him and the swarm glowed menacingly, sizzling to life in an angry cloud that buzzed toward Brent.

"Emmit, no!" Brent screamed, before the mechanical cloud consumed him.

Emmit regarded the swarming mass as it did its work, transforming Brent into a cyborg like him. The mechanical bugs glowed and buzzed, rewiring Brent's DNA, adding circuitry and wiring to his nerves to make his senses acute, installing tiny motors and servos to his muscles to give him inhuman strength, and implanting probes and radios in his brain to put him under the Master's control.

Emmit turned toward the stadium and spoke aloud. "Doctor, the Harker boy and his two accomplices are escaping into the parking lot," he said, watching the three open a parked car door. Moments later, its brake lights glowed as the car revved to life.

"Follow them. We will join you soon," von Frankenstein replied.

"Yes, Master."

"Be wary of the Creature, he protects my heir. Use Carlos and Frederick's motor bikes to follow but do not engage until I arrive. It is time I took matters into my own hands."

"Yes, Master."

The sports car tore out of the parking lot and onto the main road. Emmit looked to the swarming mass of glowing green mechanical bugs. Brent emerged reformed, a near replica of himself. The boy flexed his arms and stretched his neck with a sharp crack.

"Come brother," Emmit said. "Now, we hunt."

The other's face broke into an evil leer. He walked from the swirling emerald mass of nanobots and joined his former friend as they jogged toward the parking lot to follow the fleeing Drake, Blaine, and Vickie.

*****

"OK, Obi-Wan Kenobi, time for some answers," Blaine announced from the passenger seat, as Drake fish-tailed the black vintage Mustang onto the highway and accelerated. "First up, what's up with the Jedi mind tricks?"

Drake flashed her a quick, dazzling smile.

"And where did you learn to hot wire a car and drive like Vin Diesel?" Vickie added, wedged uncomfortably in the backseat. "We're only in eighth grade!"

"I'm a bit older than I look," he had one hand on the wheel, the other arm waving lazily out the driver side window. "Man, I remember the year this car came out..."

"What do you mean you remember the year this car came out?" Vickie scoffed. "This car is ancient... like something from the 80s!"

Drake took a sharp turn onto a side road. "The 60's actually... a 1967 Mustang Spyder. Principal Marlowe has good taste in cars."

Vickie was about to object but Blaine cut her off.

"Quit changing the subject, Drake!" She pointed an accusing finger at him. "How did you do that to those Grimm boys and why are they, that creepy janitor, and that black condor stalking us?"

"It's a raven actually, like from the poem by Edgar Allen Poe." Drake took a turn at high speed spitting gravel into a nearby pasture. An idling cow mooed in protest.

"Start talking," Blaine growled.

"OK," Drake said, holding up his hands in mock surrender. The car approached a fence at high speed on the opposite side of an intersection.

"Grab the wheel!" Vickie shrieked.

Drake put his hands back on the steering wheel and expertly navigated the turn. He applied the handbrake and did a 180° swerve into a patch of gravel, surrounded by berry bushes, stopping the car and killing the low growl of the Mustang's engine.

"I think we have a few minutes, so here goes. Blaine, you're what von Frankenstein calls an heir. Your great grandfather, Edgewick Stoker, was a scientist who, along with three of his colleagues, made one of the most fantastic scientific discoveries in history. It not only changed our view of the universe, it also changed him and his friends forever... and you."

"What kind of discovery are you talking about? What could possibly have happened decades ago that causes me to disappear?"

"Yeah, how in the heck did Blaine make us invisible?" Vickie echoed.

"These scientists made first contact with an alien civilization, at least we thought it was the first contact. They found a craft and a strange pilot. The technology was beyond our understanding and in many ways still is. Their experience with the ship and its occupant changed them, giving them amazing powers and as it turns out, their descendants."

"How?" Blaine and Vickie said simultaneously.

"Those glowing green bugs you saw on the Grimm goons whenever they got hit, they're called nanobots. They are tiny machines that can manipulate anything

184

they touch, down to the molecular level. The technology is based on something light-years more advanced, which your great grandfather and friends discovered in the 1930's. It changed their DNA and it has changed yours."

Blaine took a calming breath. "Why does it make me invisible?"

"I don't know. The alien technology reacts differently to each person it touches. We all have unique DNA, the fabric that our cells are built from. It's that DNA blueprint which determines what the alien technology does to you and others it has affected."

"Why doesn't it affect me? I'm Blaine's sister."

"Her adopted sister," Drake clarified. "The changes are passed genetically. Blaine is the last survivor in the Stoker line."

"How do you know that?" Blaine said eagerly. She had always been curious about her past but never could find out more about her biological parents.

"Blaine, like I said," Drake explained, looking her in the eyes, "You and your friends are special. My mother, father, and I have made it our mission to protect and hide you."

"Are you with the government?" Blaine asked.

"When it's convenient," Drake replied.

"What do you mean when it's convenient?" Vickie said.

"My mother was one of the original four affected by the alien technology. She had awful things happen to her and the others. It's a long story and I was too young to remember but she and my father vowed to protect the heirs even if it meant hiding them from the government. We've been doing it for a long time now."

"What do you mean you were too young to remember?" Vickie said. "You're only 13, you barely remember a time before iPhones!"

Drake looked at Vickie seriously. "I'm over 70 years old, Vickie. I was born during World War Two."

"Whatever!"

"I'm serious. My mother, Mina Harker, is ageless. She looks the same now as when she was first in contact with the alien technology. I'm her son. It affects me differently since I am only half her and half my dad, who is a normal man... well, mostly normal. I might look like a teenager but I only age at about a fifth the rate that you and Blaine do."

"Seriously?" Vickie asked, dumbfounded.

"Seriously."

"*Ewwww.....*"

"What's wrong?" Blaine asked Vickie.

"I kissed a *grandpa*!" Vickie screeched.

"I might be over 70 years old, but physically I am just like you and Blaine," Drake replied, trying to hold back a smile.

"Whatever! I might as well have made out with the mall Santa Claus!" she hissed between her hands.

Drake sighed. "Give me a break. It's not like it's easy having puberty last for thirty years."

"Why are all these changes only starting to affect me now?" Blaine asked, ignoring her sister's tirade, something that came easy to her after years of practice. "All of a sudden, this week, everything started to happen."

"It's because of the Monster," Drake explained.

"Monster?" Vickie asked, incredulously.

"A robot that von Frankenstein stole from the US Government. I think Shelley has seen it. Those news reports about a bear in her neighborhood? That wasn't a bear."

"I know," Blaine murmured. "Shelley and Dash ran into it the other day."

"The Monster carries the alien nanotech. It is programmed to find and protect the heirs. Once von Frankenstein released it, it sought you and your friends out. It can sense you, even at incredible distances. By finding you, it brought you into contact with the alien technology and kindled your powers."

Blaine took a deep breath, thinking. "You mentioned others being affected and you thought my great-grandfather had been the first to come in contact with these aliens but you weren't so sure now. What did you mean?"

"Like I said, the alien technology works in strange ways and impacts everyone it touches differently," Drake answered. "Your grandfather and his friends weren't the first to come in contact with these aliens. There have been others throughout history."

"Like who?" Vickie asked.

"Pick a ghost story or monster legend and we think there is a good chance they were based on fact. Not all of them, but enough to make you a believer."

"Have you met one?" Blaine said.

Drake sighed. "Do you know that pop star from Canada, the one who all the blogs write about and is always getting into trouble?"

"Dorian Grey!" Vickie cooed. "He is adorable! I love his new song, 'Too Cool For Juvee!'"

"He's over 150 years old."

Vickie stared blankly, then buried her face into her hands again.

"I have his poster in my room!"

Blaine rolled her eyes.

"Why did the alien technology only affect the original four researchers? Why didn't it affect others as well? And where is it now?"

"I don't know. It bound itself to your ancestors' DNA when they first came into contact with it. Only they, or people with similar DNA, can get it to respond. No one else. It's like your DNA is some kind of key to a lock. That is partially what makes you crucial to von Frankenstein. You are a part of the puzzle to controlling whatever your great-grandfather and my mother found."

"How did von Frankenstein find out about this technology anyway?"

"He was one of the original four," Drake stated grimly.

"He has superpowers too?" Vickie said, sniffling.

"No, he found the craft's occupant, the robot. It's extremely powerful, advanced and dangerous. It's bound to him and only he and his kin can command it."

"His kin? Who is that?" Blaine interrupted.

"Your friend, Shelley. She is von Frankenstein's great-grandniece. Her great-grandmother was one of the chief researchers on the project after the war, Tempest van Helsing, von Frankenstein's niece. Van Helsing is Frankenstein's real name."

"Why do you call him von Frankenstein?" Vickie asked, poking her head forward.

"That was the code name the Nazis gave him in World War II," Drake said darkly. "Ian van Helsing, Shelley's great-uncle, is one of the most notorious traitors in history. He betrayed his country and his friends, including my mother."

Blaine sighed loudly, staring blankly forward. "This is too much to take in... monsters, aliens, secret agents, world wars, I'm freaking out over here!" Vickie nodded vigorously in agreement.

"Listen, we have to get moving," Drake turned the keys in the ignition and revved the engine. "Von Frankenstein and his lackeys are not going to give up looking for us and we need to find your friends."

He turned to Blaine. "Do you have your cell phone?"

"Yes," Blaine said, fishing it out of her back pocket.

"Call Shelley. Hopefully she and Dash are together. We'll go pick them up and head to my Mom and Dad's."

Blaine hit her speed dial and waited. "The call won't go through. I have four bars but all I get is a busy signal."

Drake took his phone out as well. "What's your number?"

Blaine told him and he dialed. No ring, just a busy signal.

"Von Frankenstein is probably jamming the cell towers. We'll need to find them the old-fashioned way."

"He can do that?" Vickie asked.

"That and a lot more, he has access to incredible resources." Drake pulled out of their parking spot and headed down the deserted road.

"I don't understand. Why didn't von Frankenstein round us all up before tonight or tear the town apart looking for us?" Blaine enquired, staring out the side window.

"The same reason we keep a low profile. He needs to act quietly and avoid getting the government involved.

The Feds are desperate to find him and he is desperate to get you out of the country before they zero in on him. The US Government has a lot of heavy hardware that would be difficult for even von Frankenstein to handle."

"Why us?" Blaine asked.

"Like I said, you and your DNA are the key. If von Frankenstein has you, Dash, Shelley, or me for that matter, he can do some terrible things. With all four us? Potentially really scary stuff."

"Like what?"

"Replicate your DNA, perfect his nanotech, and quite possibly access and activate the original alien objects your ancestors found," Drake said driving down the road, "and maybe much, much worse."

"I still don't understand," said Blaine.

"Listen, Blaine," Drake said, scanning the dark countryside, "I promise I will get you more answers, including what I can about your family. For now, we need to focus on finding your friends. Can you guys help me look for them? They were on foot and must be close by. We need to get to them before von Frankenstein does."

Blaine and Vickie nodded.

"Good, let's get to it," Drake gunned the deep, throaty engine of the Mustang and sped down the empty country lane.

*****

Dash, Kevin, Shelley, and the iron Monster emerged from the woods in a field near a road that crisscrossed thru farmland. It felt like they had been walking for hours, but it had been no more than thirty minutes.

Overhead, the sky had darkened with clouds obscuring the moon and stars.

Dash looked the worse for wear but was walking on his own now. He paused to rest as they reached the gravelly lane, leaning on a post. Kevin walked up the berm and looked up and down the road as Shelley waited with the large metal creature.

"It looks deserted."

Kevin slumped to the ground. It had been a long night for all of them.

"What now?" Dash asked.

"We could try my house," Shelley suggested, "with this thing following us, my Dad would have to believe us!" She pointed at the silent metal robot which stood motionless in the field, an oversized tin man straight out of Oz.

"I suppose. I wish he came with seats, though."

"Shelley, is your phone still on the fritz?" Kevin asked.

"Yeah, weird…" Shelley replied, staring at her screen. "Full signal, but I can't connect or even text."

"Me too," said Kevin, pocketing his phone.

In the distance, a crow cawed and landed in a lonely, skeletal tree in the middle of the field.

"I hate those birds," Dash muttered. "They are black and ugly and would steal candy from a baby if you let them."

"It's just a dumb bird, Dash," Kevin replied with a smile. He got up and did his best monster impression.

"Heck, if you don't like it why don't you jump fifty feet in the air and growl at it?"

Dash winced. "I wish I knew what was happening to me. Whenever the moon comes out, I lose it and when it goes behind a cloud, I feel drained."

"It'll be alright, Dash," Shelley said, patting him on the shoulder, "we'll find out what's happening." Dash smiled weakly in appreciation.

A second raven joined the first on a high branch and the two cawed at each other loudly.

"I still hate those birds," Dash grumbled.

"Hey, do you see that?" Kevin said, perking up. A light was rounding a far bend in the road and they could hear the low hum of an automobile coming down the lane.

"It's a car!" Dash said.

"What do you think we should do?" Shelley asked. "Hide?"

"Yeah, behind the metal dude and hope they don't notice," Kevin said doubtfully. "I say we flag them down and ask for help. Worst case, Optimus Prime over there covers our rears."

"Let's do it," Dash agreed. Shelley nodded her consent.

Kevin walked up to the side of the road and waved his arms. The car's headlights brightened, lighting Kevin on the side of the road. The throaty growl of its engines downshifted as it slowed. A classic black sports car pulled up next to him and the passenger side window rolled down.

"Need a lift?"

"Oh my gosh, Blaine!" Kevin exclaimed, an ear-to-ear grin creasing his face. "Hey, guys, it's Blaine!" Dash and Shelley walked up the steep berm, with Shelley helping to support Dash.

"Geeze, you look like you've been thru a war!" Blaine exclaimed. Each of their clothes was dirty and ripped from the woods. Dash in particular looked a mess.

"You don't know the half of it!" Dash sighed.

"Blaine, how did you get out here and who is with you?" Shelley asked smiling, happy to see her best friend. She gave her a hug thru the window.

"Hi!" Vickie waved from the back seat.

Drake flicked on the interior light. "Hey guys, it looks like you had a run-in with those psychos from Grimm Academy."

"And then some!" Kevin exclaimed. "Those guys are monsters! I mean literally, monsters!"

"I know."

"Wait, you know?" Shelley did a double-take.

Drake turned off the engine and got out of the driver's side door. He looked at Kevin, Dash, and Shelley.

"This is going to be a long story..."

Blaine got out of the passenger's side and cut him off.

"So we'll keep it short. Dash, Shelley, Drake, and I are all something called 'heirs'. The headmaster from Grimm Academy is a mad scientist with a mutant army and he wants to capture us. And, oh, by the way we each have superpowers. Oh yeah, and we stole Mr. Marlowe's car."

The three friends stared at her blankly. "You stole the Principal's car?" Kevin said dumbly.

Drake walked around the Mustang and looked into the dark field. He whistled.

"Well, it looks like you found Frankenstein's Monster," he said, staring at the giant iron golem standing silently in the field. "That's some serious hardware."

"I knew it!" Kevin hooted. "I know I said robot, Shelley, but the whole time I was hoping for Frankenstein's Monster! This is awesome!"

Dash looked at his friend and shook his head.

"Really, Kevin? *Awesome*? We were almost ripped apart by psychotic tween cyborgs, I'm some kind of werewolf from that stupid video game we play, Blaine randomly disappears, Shelley owns a pet monster, and a mad scientist is trying to kidnap us… and you think that is awesome?"

"It's *kinda* awesome," Kevin replied, sheepishly kicking a pebble off the road.

"Does it really obey you?" Drake asked Shelley, still marveling at the automaton.

"Yeah, so far anyway."

"It's amazing, I've never seen it in person before. It's been locked up all this time. My Mom has only told me about it."

"Locked up? Where?"

"A place called Area 51. It, along with the craft it landed in, were stored there for research."

"Hold on, what craft? Area 51?" Dash gaped. "You mean this thing is an alien?"

"Yes," Drake nodded.

"Oh my god! This is like the most amazing comic book ever! Small town kids. Amazing powers. A Frankenstein robot from a secret government installation…"

"Kevin!" the three friends shouted simultaneously.

Kevin stopped mid-sentence and shoved his hands in his pockets, looking down.

"Like I said, it's a long story," Drake stated. "For now we need to get you all someplace safe. Von Frankenstein isn't going to stop until he has you in his clutches so we need to get you and your families out of harm's way."

"Von Frankenstein?" Shelley asked.

"It's another long story, Shell," Blaine said, putting her arm around her friend. "I'll explain on the way."

"Come in, there's plenty of room in the back!" Vickie said, her knees pressed up by her cheeks in the crowded rear seat.

Drake scowled. "It's going to be a tough fit, but my Dad's place is close-by." In the distance a chorus of crows cawed.

Dash looked back at the tree in the middle of the field. "Say, wasn't there only two crows a minute ago?"

A murder of ravens had assembled on the branches of the lonely dead tree. They cawed loudly and their eyes glinted red in the night. They peered straight at the road as more and more of the inky black creatures joined their ranks.

"This is not good," Drake murmured.

"What's wrong Drake?" Blaine asked, cautiously.

"Those aren't crows," he answered, holding open the passenger door. "They're reapers."

"Reapers?" Kevin asked, crowding into the back seat next to Vickie.

"Grimm Reapers. Vickie, you're going to have sit on Dash and Kevin's lap. There's no room."

Vickie sighed and Kevin smiled stupidly as the attractive teen girl nestled atop his lap in the back seat.

The reapers began to caw louder, several took flight, circling the field and closing in on the car high overhead. The rest of the kids jammed themselves into the small sports car. Drake went to the other side, getting into the driver's seat.

"What about the robot?" Shelley asked. She was crammed uncomfortably next to Blaine in the front passenger seat.

"He'll either need to follow or we'll find him later," Drake said, turning on the ignition and revving the car to life. "He's programmed to find you guys, so should be easy to track down."

Overhead the few stars in the cloudy sky were blotted out as the crows crowded the night air. Their jeering caws overwhelmed even the loud rumble of the Mustang's engine.

Drake put the car into first and jammed the accelerator.

THUMP!

The car lurched in place as a giant metal hand grasped the rear bumper and lifted the wheels just off the ground. The Frankenstein's Monster had emerged from the field and was preventing the kids from escaping. The back tires churned helplessly, unable to gain purchase with the road.

Drake frantically twisted the steering wheel and revved the engine but the Metal Man held the car fast. Overhead the ravens cleared as a light flooded the sky and a low *WUMP-WUMP* sound drowned out the birds and muscle car engine. A sleek black helicopter landed on the road blocking them, lit up by the Mustang's headlights. Igor sat in the pilot's seat, a bandage covering half of his face. Dr. Victor von Frankenstein sat next to him, emerging from the vehicle as its rotors whipped the tall grass surrounding the country road.

"Get out. Now!" Drake commanded, cutting the engine.

He opened the driver's side door and jumped out in a crouch, shielding his eyes from the dirt and gravel churning from the helicopter and glare of its forward search lamps. Behind him, Blaine, Dash, Vickie, Shelley, and Kevin spilled out unceremoniously from the tilted vehicle still being held in place by the metal giant.

Von Frankenstein approached, wearing a black leather trench coat and trademark dark sunglasses. He looked every bit the evil madman. He nodded at the creature. The monster grasped the idled sports car with both massive steel hands and lifted it over its head. The robot turned with a crunch of gravel underfoot and threw the car tumbling in the air at the skeletal tree hundreds of feet away. It landed with a crash, knocking the tree over and scattering the remaining crows in protest of squawks.

"Wow, Principal Marlowe is going to be really ticked," Kevin muttered.

Drake looked behind him, searching for avenues of escape. Out of the darkness emerged two sleek gun-metal grey motorbikes with two look-alike Grimm cyborgs at the wheel, Emmit and Brent. They revved their engines wickedly. Down the road, in the inky darkness, Drake could see other headlamps approaching and heard the distant whirring of motorcycle engines. Reinforcements.

They were in it. Deep.

"It's no use!" von Frankenstein called. "You're surrounded."

Drake growled in frustration, looking side-to-side for options. Blaine and the others bunched nearby, looking fearfully from the helicopter to von Frankenstein, to the motorbikes, to the ravens overhead, to the gleaming steel monster behind.

"Help us!" Shelley called up at the iron giant.

It stood stone still, its green eyes passive, staring dead ahead.

"It's no use. Help will not come from the robot," von Frankenstein yelled over the whirring of the helicopter's blades. He approached the group of frightened friends with a wicked leer.

"The creature may listen to you but he obeys only his master... me."

"What do you want, Frankenstein?" Drake yelled defiantly, stepping in front of the other kids trying to shield them.

"The Harker boy... at long last. When was the last time we saw you? Milan? You and your mother were a few minutes too late, weren't you?" Drake made a move toward the Doctor but the other revealed a metallic wand, the same Igor had used on him earlier. Von Frankenstein shook his head.

"I wouldn't make any sudden moves, Mr. Harker. Nor you, Mr. Gaunt." Dash had started to creep forward, but froze.

"Now, two of my new boys, Emmit and Brent, are going to give you a few bracelets to wear... to temper your rude behavior," Frankenstein continued. "Each of you put on your manacles and come quietly and no one need get hurt."

Emmit and Brent dismounted from their bikes and moved toward the group. Each carried handcuffs with thin wires connecting them.

"Those are specially made to accommodate each of you and your unique abilities. If you make any sudden moves or try to activate your powers, you will get a taste of what one thousand volts of electricity feels like. I assure you it is most unpleasant." Von Frankenstein paused in front of them, covering them with his ultrasonic weapon.

"Once you are properly equipped you can join me for a little trip in my helicopter. We do like our students to wear the right uniforms at Grimm Academy."

The Doctor smiled at them while Emmit and Brent put handcuffs on Kevin and Vickie. Kevin tried to struggle but his captor lifted him up by the collar and threw him gruffly to the ground toward the chopper.

"Your turn, Mr. Harker," von Frankenstein offered, pointing the weapon at him.

Above, von Frankenstein's mutant ravens began to caw frantically as they circled in a frenzy. The Doctor turned his attention skyward, wondering what was amiss, aiming his wand into the air. Emmit and Brent paused, peering defensively into the darkness on all sides.

The darting reapers began to explode in puffs of metallic green, like cheap fireworks lighting the Fourth of July. They dived this way and that but it made no difference. Crow after crow disintegrated in sparkling emerald flame.

"Igor! Get the chopper going! We need to get out of here!" He turned to the two Grimm cyborgs. "Get them bound and to the helicopter immediately!"

Around them, a wall of black swirling smoke appeared and whirled around the helicopter like an inky cyclone. Von Frankenstein sneered and fired his weapon into the whirling vapor but even his high-tech toy seemed to have no effect.

Frankenstein's Monster shifted and peered back and forth, its eyes narrowing as the vapor solidified into a wall of roiling, oily black smoke. Emmit and Brent dropped their handcuffs and crouched in a battle position, preparing for an attack.

Brent looked at Emmit as a thick finger of vapor reached out from the dark cloud surrounding them. It wrapped itself around Emmit's face and snatched him into the darkness, giving him barely enough time to scream.

The chopper's blades began to squeal as it rotated faster and von Frankenstein backed toward it. He grabbed the bound Vickie and jerked Brent toward him, grasping a struggling Kevin.

"*Mina Harker...*" von Frankenstein growled as he retreated to the black airship.

The wall of darkness evaporated congealing into a single dense cloud between the children and von Frankenstein. From it emerged a beautiful, young woman with raven black hair, a golden nose ring, and piercing blue eyes.

"Ms. Poe?" Blaine said, in awe.

Drake smiled. "That's my mom, Mina Harker."

"Ian, give me the children!" Mina commanded from in front of them.

"Come and get them!" von Frankenstein jeered, pushing Kevin and Vickie into the rear of the chopper.

"Creature!" he roared over the swirling blades. "Get Harker!"

Frankenstein's Monster's eyes blazed into evil green slits and sprang into action as the mad scientist shut the helicopter door and Igor lifted the chopper into the sky.

Blaine, Dash, Shelley, and Drake dived for each side of the road as the creature stomped past. It creaked menacingly, taking a giant metal-fisted swipe at Mina.

Mina reacted with cat-like reflexes, turning into a cloud of vapor with scary shapes swirling in its midst like thousands of roiling magical bats. The creature's fist passed thru her. It stomped forward with surprising speed, trying to obliterate the inky blackness. Mina's cloud rose into the sky and swarmed over the creature's head, blinding it. The fog surrounding the monster's face pulsed and disintegrated as its eyes blazed a dazzling green. Mina tumbled to the ground, her body smoking.

Down the road, the whine of motorbikes approached, speeding down the country lane. The headlamps careened wildly off the road flipping over fences and spilling out onto the sides.

The helicopter lit the scene on the ground briefly as it turned and flew away. Mina got up just in time to avoid a giant foot landing with a thud where she had been laying. She backed away from the kids, keeping them safe from the iron golem's attacks.

Headlamps rounded the corner and an old pickup truck emerged, skidding to a stop in front of the kids. An old man in a red trucker's cap leaned out the driver's side window and yelled, "Get in!"

"Old Man Murphy?" Dash marveled at the old-timer with his slobbering dog next to him.

"Yeah. That's my Dad, a real character!"

Dash, Shelley, Blaine, and Drake scrambled into the back of the truck as Mina battled Frankenstein's Monster on the road ahead. The creature swatted viciously but Mina either dodged or used her vapor ability to counter the robot's brute force.

"Grab onto something! Those goons of von Frankenstein's will recover quickly!" Peter Murphy yelled back to the kids. "I managed to knock them off the road but they are tough sons of guns!"

He gunned the engine of his old Ford. "Now, let's help out the Missus!" he yelled with a wheezy laugh. The pickup truck leapt forward and rammed into the iron golem just as it was throwing a wild punch at Mina. The truck knocked the monster off-balance and sent it flailing into the ditch by the side of the road.

"Get in!" Murphy yelled.

Mina picked herself up from the ground and climbed into the rear of the truck, hunkering down next to the kids. Peter peeled out as the Monster rose from the ditch and the headlamps of motorbikes approached. He headed at breakneck speed into the night.

Mina looked at each of the kids. Blaine, Dash, and Shelley stared at her with alarm. Drake just grinned broadly.

"Hello, children, I hope each of you finished your homework because I think this is going to be a busy weekend."

Chapter 17: Peter

Fifteen months after the incident at Roswell…

Peter sighed as he rested his hands on the desk of the small quarters he shared with his wife. On it set a picture of them smiling on a beach boardwalk. Mina's head poked thru a cut-out of a mermaid trapped in a net while Peter gaped at her thru a cartoon fisherman. He smiled and saw a scarf she had been wearing draped over some papers. He picked it up and breathed in deeply the scent of Mina's favorite perfume.

A pen rolled off the desk onto the floor. He bent down to retrieve it and opened the desk drawer to put it away. In it was some loose change, pencils, stationary, and a well-worn leather-bound book, Mina's journal. Peter had seen her writing in it often. He flipped through the pages. A tear formed in the corner of his eye as he got to the spread with a paper menu folded in between. It had been from the Italian restaurant he had asked Mina to marry him in. The restaurant had specially printed the daily specials page with his proposal. Peter remembered Mina's coy smile as she had asked the waiter if they had any calamari instead.

She was a heckuva gal, Peter thought.

He opened the book and read:

*March 27*th

> *Peter asked me to marry him! I did what any proper girl would do, I waited for the big goof to get on his knee and ask properly but, of course, I said yes! We decided to set the*

big day this summer in his hometown in Oregon, assuming we get permission to leave our new home. Lots to do to prepare! The last year and a half with him have been the happiest of my life, albeit one of the strangest.

The move to Grooms Lake has gone well but you can tell there is a tension among all of us. We still don't understand why the changes Lonn, Edge, and I have experienced are happening or how to stop them. Every day some new wrinkle happens. Ian is researching furiously but seems increasingly withdrawn. Our Army hosts are nice enough, but distant. While we're told we are part of a team sometimes it seems like we are more inmates than researchers.

Peter frowned and flipped a few pages forward:

April 19th

After several arguments with the Major, we finally have permission from the Colonel to leave the base for a few weeks to get married. Of course, we won't be allowed to leave alone. We will have an escort wherever we go to assure knowledge of my new abilities stays secret. While the facilities and staff at Grooms Lake are amazing, the attitude of the Army is maddening. They see us as lab rats, testing our powers day after day and trying to reactivate the alien spaceship we recovered at Roswell.

Nothing we do seems to be able to turn the ship back on. It was heavily damaged on re-entry and its last act seems to have been to probe us before shutting down permanently. We suspect somehow the beam transformed us but we don't know how. Ian says he has a theory he is working on but won't say more. Ever since Peter and I announced our engagement, he refuses to talk to me, though his niece, Tempest, is a delight who is starting to come into her own as part of the research team.

Peter skipped forward in the journal, several entries focused on their wedding and brief honeymoon.

June 9th

Peter and I have returned from a wonderful wedding! His family is amazing as is the charming home town he comes from. When all of this madness with powers and aliens passes we have promised to return there and start a family together. I couldn't think of a nicer place to settle down.

We have been away for a month and much has changed at the base we now call home. The Army has doubled security and increased the staff. There are rumors that Germany and their dictator, Adolph Hitler, is preparing for war in Europe. While the US government said we will stay neutral, you couldn't tell by how the staff at Grooms Lake are acting. The Colonel and his team are desperate to learn what has happened to us, how we can activate the alien craft, and how we can use the technology as part of our military program.

Ian has had a breakthrough. He claims the ship and its robot pilot are made of billions and billions of tiny machines he calls nanobots. He thinks these artificial creatures are the key to re-activating the ship and figuring out how Lonn, Edge and I have been transformed. We've offered to help him with his research but he refuses our offers. He won't even talk with most of us now, including his niece. Whenever we have a chance for free time, he disappears.

Peter frowned... the nanobots. Ian claimed they were the key to this whole thing and ordered a lot of expensive equipment be flown in from Chicago to investigate them. Colonel Dickinson obliged but everyone had been growing worried about the scientist's state of mind. He had grown hostile and combative and whenever there was a weekend pass, Ian always seemed to mysteriously disappear.

Peter read ahead:

July 7th

Ian had a meltdown today. He is obsessed with his theory on the nanobots. He flew into a rage when Colonel Dickinson would not allow him to undertake human testing with his new equipment. He wants to replicate what the aliens did to us with others on the base! He believes he can create a superhuman, harnessing these tiny mechanisms and possibly replicate more of them.

Colonel Dickinson tried to calm him down, as did Peter, but he told them they lacked vision, whatever that means, and they could not see this was the next stage in human evolution. I explained the dangers to the subjects were too high but Ian shouted me down. He claims the rewards justify the risks.

Our powers seem to grow daily. Edge can render himself invisible and for the first time an object he touched! Lonn's strength grows, as does his speed and agility. He seems to have some connection to the cycles of the moon. The closer we come to a full moon, the stronger and more uncontrollable he becomes.

My powers are manifesting and it troubles me. I seem to be able to turn myself into some form of vapor which makes me impervious to heat, cold, or ballistic damage. It is frightening. When I change, I feel invincible and free. I worry that if I change too much, will I ever want to come back to my true form. And what about having children? What would they be like? And could they even survive what is happening to me? I want to talk to Peter about this but I am afraid. He is so kind, but these changes are so overwhelming...

"Oh, Mina," Peter sighed, "of course you could have talked with me."

He moved on to the next entry:

August 4th

Ian has been arrested and sent to the brig for insubordination and putting at risk Area 51 staff. He took a bird, a crow, he found outside the base and subjected it to an experiment. Somehow, using the nuclear equipment from Chicago and the robot, he was able to produce some form of reaction. The crow reacted badly, growing, mutating, breaking out of its cage and injuring a researcher before dying.

Ian tried to escape the base with his research papers using the robot to clear a path for him. It was only with Tempest's help, who the creature also seems to listen to, that we were able to subdue him.

I tried to talk with him but he would not speak to me. He kept accusing us all of not understanding and needing a place that appreciated his vision. I'm concerned about him. I think the stresses of the project have proven too much.

The world seems destined for war. Hitler's armies are eying Poland and he's in league with the Reds from Russia. I worry if war

starts what will become of our program. It is
clear the Army has designs similar to Ian's.
They may not tolerate the same approach but
they want to turn us all into weapons. This is
not about science any longer, it is about war.

Most important, Diary, I think I am
pregnant. I should be happy! I've wanted this
with Peter for so long, but if I feel like a
guinea pig, what will that make my unborn
child? What will my powers do to my baby?
And how do I tell Peter? He doesn't know...

Peter set the journal down in shock. Mina was pregnant!
But how?

On second thought, Peter knew how. But why hadn't
she told him! It made the news of the past day all the
worse. *A child!*

Peter put his head in his hands and felt tears flowing
freely. It was all he could do to keep the pain away and
maintain control.

"Why Mina?" he sobbed. "*Why?*"

He gripped the desk, anger for his loss overtaking his
sadness, his knuckles were white with the effort.

He picked the journal back up and read the final entry.
It was from three days ago, written just before Mina and
the team had boarded that fateful plane.

September 2ⁿᵈ

The world is at war. Hitler and the Soviets
have invaded Poland. Britain and France
have declared war on Germany. I have not
solved my dilemma of how to tell Peter about

my condition and the changes that have been affecting us for the last year continue to roil our lives, but a glimmer of hope seems to have emerged.

We received news of another alien craft sighting, this one in South America, at the southern tip of Argentina. The land is barren there but a local geographic expedition reports finding something in a remote mountain glacier. The team is being sent to investigate! Ian, who has been acting more like his old self these past few weeks, has been asked to join us. The Colonel believes we will need his expertise and the assistance of the robot in the expedition.

I can't wait to leave Grooms Lake and Area 51. Peter is to stay behind, but it will be good for me to get some distance and to think about the problems we face from a new perspective. Hopefully, what we find in South America will give us answers and maybe a cure for the strange changes that are overwhelming us.

Peter set the journal down in the drawer and closed it. He walked away and stared into a mirror by the coat rack near their apartment door. His eyes were bloodshot from loss of sleep, worry, and tears. The expedition had been sent three days ago and had not been heard from for over 24 hours since their plane entered Argentine airspace. The team at Area 51 feared the worst.

A knock at the door interrupted Peter. He turned and opened it. It was Tempest van Helsing. "Tempest," Peter said, clearing his throat. "Sorry, I look a wreck… come in." Tempest walked in and gave Peter a quick hug.

"Has there been any word on the team?"

"No, no word since they left Buenos Aires. The locals haven't been able to find them. The land in Tiera Del Fuego is remote and the air currents unpredictable, particularly in the winter."

"I'm sorry, Peter," Tempest said, a tear welling up in her eye.

"Thanks," Peter sighed. He motioned her into the apartment. "Can I get you some tea or coffee?"

Tempest entered and shook her head. "No, thanks." She hesitated. "Peter, I have something I want to show you and it's urgent. It's about my uncle and I didn't know who else to turn to." Tempest handed him a folder she removed from the inside of her coat.

"I found this in Ian's quarters. I went there after I heard the team may have been lost. I don't know why, I just wanted to be near things that reminded me of him."

"I understand," Peter replied, taking the thin manila folder.

"His room was a mess, like he hadn't been taking care of it or himself for a while," Tempest continued. "I found this. It was under his couch. It looks like it had fallen under it by accident. The contents are… *troubling*."

Peter opened the folder. A single sheet of paper lay inside. The paper had a series of numbers and letters in an odd pattern. Below it was scrawled Ian's handwriting.

"It looks like a code?" Peter said. "The words are German. Can you read it?"

Tempest took the paper. "Our family is second generation Austrian. Ian was born in the fatherland as a young boy. Let me translate."

"Operation Werewolf is a go. Stop. You are to bring the creature. An opportunity will present itself soon. Stop. The three must survive. Consider all others expendable. Stop. By order of the Fuhrer. Stop."

"Oh my god," Peter exhaled, his face turning pale.

"I know."

"This means…"

"I know."

There was a knock at the door, which startled them both.

"Lt. Murphy," Major Belcher said, "we have news of the team." Peter opened the door to let the Major in.

"What? What have you found?" he asked urgently.

"It's not good…" the Major said bleakly. "A wreckage has been found in the mountains. Bodies badly burned."

Peter stared at the Major with eyes of steel.

"No survivors," the Major continued.

"The Monster was not in the wreckage, but the crash site is extensive. It could be anywhere in a several mile radius."

"You won't find it," Peter answered, grabbing his hat and coat. "And we need to act quickly, Major. The team isn't dead."

Major Belcher paused and gripped Peter by the shoulder. "Listen, Pete, I know this is hard, but you have to accept the facts. We all do."

"Tempest, give the Major the document from your Uncle's quarters," Peter replied icily. "Major, I think you'll want a linguistic expert to read this carefully."

"What do you mean? What document?" Belcher sputtered.

"Ian van Helsing is a traitor. The whole South America expedition was a set up. And if we want our people back, we need to act fast."

Peter walked out of his apartment and strode down the hall toward the Area 51 command center. Tempest and Belcher stared at his back as he left.

Peter had one thing on his mind, to get his wife and unborn child back safely.

Chapter 18: Mina

"Ian betrayed us that day," Mina said, finishing her story as the truck pulled up to the tool shed in Murphy's Scrap Yard. "The South American expedition was a trap. German agents intercepted and kidnapped us and Ian revealed himself as a traitor, jealous of his friends who had been given strange new abilities, and frustrated by the rules placed on him by the Army."

"We tried to fight back, but with the Monster and the Nazis we were overwhelmed. Peter looked frantically for us to mount a rescue, but that was not to come for some time. Lonn, Edge, and I spent the War in the hands of the Nazis and Ian, who was referred to by his code name, von Frankenstein. That was a terrible time. The Nazis were cruel and Ian was relentless."

The kids stared at her for a moment, huddled in the bed of the truck. Crickets chirped in the grass surrounding the scrap yard as Peter cut off the truck's engine.

Peter's dog, Chuckles, ran up eagerly to the back of the truck, leapt in, and gave a big slobbery kiss to his mistress.

"How are you holding up, Peter?" Mina asked, ruffling Chuckles' floppy ears.

"Pretty good for pushing the century mark!" Peter exclaimed, hobbling to the back. He grabbed Mina's hand and helped her down from the truck.

"Hold on..." Shelley asked. "You two are married?"

The three kids stared at the spindly old man in the dirty coveralls and trucker's hat standing next to the beautiful woman with the skin-tight black outfit.

"I grant you I am the envy of all the old-timers down at the Kiwanis Club. Being married to a vampire has its benefits," Peter added with a proud sigh. "But I think the secret to my youthful good looks is in the genes... and a high fiber diet, amazing what a little tender-loving colon care can do for a man!"

"Vampire?" Shelley said, blankly.

"Colon care?" Dash and Blaine mouthed.

Peter laughed, a dry old man cackle. "Well, what else would you call her? She flies like a cloud of bats, walks around in a mysterious black vapor, shies away from bright light, and can melt a man's willpower with a single glance. Sounds as close to the bride of Dracula as I can figure."

"So, you, my great-grandfather, Dash's great-grandpa, Shelley's great-grand uncle who is this Frankenstein dude, were all members of an alien hunting club called the Monster Squad?" Blaine asked.

"That's right," Mina nodded.

"And each of you had amazing powers like out of the Gothic game Kevin and I play?" Dash asked.

"Now you're tracking, son!"

"And my ancestor, Ian van Helsing now called Frankenstein, turned on you? And now he's after us?" Shelley finished.

"That about sums it up," Drake said, hopping down from the truck, standing next to his parents.

"So do you drink blood?" Dash asked. Blaine shoved him, shaking her head.

"Do you eat doggie biscuits?" Mina shot back.

"No..."

"Don't believe everything Hollywood tells you then." Blaine grinned.

Shelley was concerned. "How do we get Vickie and Kevin back?" she asked.

"Good question," Mina replied. "Peter, are you sure we lost Frankenstein's crew?"

Peter nodded. "I'm pretty sure. Those scooter jockeys of his don't worry me. We doubled back enough to keep those chuckle-heads guessing and you made sure most of those robot chickens ended up extra crispy. The Monster's another matter. He's like a tick on a bloodhound."

"Then we'll need to act quickly," Mina said.

She turned to the kids. "Come inside. We need to make sure you're uninjured and think about how to get your friends back."

Dash, Blaine, and Shelley followed Peter, Mina, and Drake into the back door of the two-story house. Mina tried the lights. They wouldn't turn on. She picked up a phone near the door. It was dead.

"Ian's cut the power and the phones, probably in the whole region. He wants us isolated. Drake, help your father get the generator going."

"Sure, Mom," he said, walking out with the crotchety old man.

"Let me take a look at each of you." She lined up the three by the kitchen table and inspected them in the faint moonlight of the night sky.

"How can you see anything?" Blaine asked as Mina looked her over.

"Well, I'm not a vampire dear. That's just Peter's little joke, but I seem to have many of the same abilities you might associate with one." Mina checked Blaine's right arm and wrist. "It's not a big stretch to assume that I can see in the dark."

"How?" Shelley asked, leaning in.

"Infrared vision," Mina turned to Dash. "The nanotech allows me to see a light spectrum invisible to most human eyes. You have a number of bad scrapes and bruises, Dash. We'll need to get you cleaned up and apply some bandages. Like your grandfather you will heal up quickly, but we need to keep those cuts clean."

Dash winced as Mina felt a sensitive spot on his lower chest.

"Cracked ribs…"

"So, you knew our great-grandparents?" he asked, thru gritted teeth.

"Yes, and your grandparents and parents as well," Mina said. Outside they could hear Peter cursing as he and Drake worked on the nearby generator.

"I wish he would stop saying words like that around Drake but then again, he is nearly seventy-five… I suppose Drake was born before that last one was even invented," Mina shook her head.

"You know our parents?" Blaine said interested.

"Yes, some of them," Mina replied, finishing her inspection of Dash and walking to a nearby cupboard. She took out a first aid kit and retrieved a fresh towel and soap from the sink. She turned to Blaine and her eyes shined a bright blue.

"It was you," Blaine whispered. "I should have known from your eyes, you were the woman at the orphanage."

"Yes, dear," Mina paused. "Your parents were close friends of mine. They helped in our work." She turned to Dash and handed him the towel and soap.

"Dash, please go in the bathroom and clean up. The lights will be on in a minute."

On cue, the generator roared to life and the lights of the kitchen flickered on.

"Yes, ma'am."

"When you're done, wrap this bandage around your ribs. Make sure it's tight," Mina instructed. Dash took the first aid kit and retreated to the bathroom.

"How did you know them?" Blaine asked, taking a seat on a stool by the worn, laminate kitchen counter.

Shelley joined her on an adjoining stool. "Yeah, how did you and Mr. Murphy become involved in all of this?"

"It's no accident that each of you and your families are here in Autumn's Hallow, particularly after we learned von Frankenstein had returned," Mina said. "The war was hard on each of us. The Nazis turned us into lab rats, and in many ways made what happened to us worse, accelerating the changes. Ian was their lead researcher. He was bent on replicating the alien technology and unlocking its secrets, no matter the cost."

Dash rejoined them and sat at the table opposite Mina.

"Feeling better?"

He nodded.

"After the war, we thought von Frankenstein had been lost and his experiments with him. The Russians captured him in a terrible battle and we assumed the worst. Peter was able to rescue me and retrieve the Monster ahead of the Red Army but Edge and Lonn, they didn't make it."

She paused sadly. "They were good friends."

Peter walked inside and stood behind Mina as she told the story. Drake followed and leaned on the counter next to the girls.

"We returned after the war and vowed to make sure nothing like that would happen to our families or friends. We hid Lonn and Edge's families and helped them assume new identities. Shelley, your great-grandmother, Tempest van Helsing, she didn't need assistance. She was the lead researcher at our old facility, Area 51, and stayed there a long time, which left Peter, Drake, and me to lead a quiet, ordinary life, or as quiet and ordinary as people like us can lead."

She smiled and patted Peter's hand. "But things began to change. The Cold War, the Space Race, the Red Menace. The government was desperate to gain any advantage it could. I was forced out of retirement and we moved away from our home here in Autumn's Hallow. It was time to move anyway, there were only so many nephews visiting from out of town who I could pass off as Drake... who because of his powers was a toddler for the balance of the 1950s."

"I helped the US government. Peter worked with me and together we raised Drake. For a time, we lost track of the decedents of the original four. But that all changed when we learned von Frankenstein had returned."

Mina stood and offered her chair to Peter. He sat down resting his old legs. She leaned on the chair behind him.

"At first, it was just rumors. Someone was trying to steal objects with mysterious origins. Whispers about strange purchases on the black market. Urban myths about horrible creatures that stalked dark corners. A dangerous old man with crazy ideas and a blank checkbook."

"But the rumors started to get more concrete. Specific names were mentioned - Gaunt, Stoker, van Helsing,

Harker. The objects that were being stolen weren't just random, they were connected with rumors of alien landings and other-worldly origins. And the black market purchases pointed to technology that only one person knew how to put together, Ian van Helsing, von Frankenstein returned. Not only had the Russians not killed him at the end of the war but wherever they had captured him it was clear he had escaped and was now more dangerous than ever."

"Frankenstein was trying to put back together Project Werewolf," Peter added.

"Project Werewolf?" Dash asked.

"The name of the secret project he led for the Nazis during the war. It was a super-soldier initiative, the centerpiece of the Nazi's human testing program. They would raise an army of supermen and make the Fuhrer live forever."

Mina nodded gravely. She looked at Blaine and picked up her story.

"And then he went after you, Blaine. Your parents were living in Italy at the time. They were scholars, just like your great-grandfather. Your father was able to save you and your mother using powers he found incredible and scary, long-rumored in his family but not seen since his grandfather before the war. He escaped with you and sought Peter and me out. He and your mother were brave, wonderful people and loving parents, dear. Together we worked to trap von Frankenstein before he learned the identities of the other heirs."

"Frankenstein separated us and was able to get to your parents before I could save them. It was all I could do to get to you before he closed in."

Blaine paused, staring at Mina. Her eyes were bright and wet.

"Von Frankenstein killed my parents?" she whispered softly.

"Yes," Mina said quietly. "From that day forward, Peter and I resolved we needed to guard the remaining heirs closely. We worked hard to get you and your families all together here. Peter could watch over you while Drake and I worked to find and stop von Frankenstein."

"But now he's found us," Dash murmured.

"And he's got our friends," Shelley added.

"Several weeks ago he reclaimed his Monster, the robot," Mina nodded. "He raided a very secure and secret installation, proving the depth of his resources. Whomever or whatever is backing him has power and considerable resources. We tried to stop him but the iron creature is formidable. Once Ian had his pet, it was only a matter of time until it found all of you. We knew it was headed here. Since it was on foot, we had a few weeks but we needed to act."

"So you assumed the identity of a new teacher and Drake a student?" Shelley said.

"Yes, that was easy. Drake and I can be convincing when we want to be."

"So I noticed," Blaine said quietly. Drake put a hand on her shoulder in comfort. She smiled weakly.

"We needed to keep an eye on each of you," Drake said. "Assuming identities at school helped us be close in case you needed us."

"We could also monitor how much Ian knew," Mina added. "The Monster directed him to this town but not to each of you. That gave us some time to understand his

221

plans and his local resources. It also forced him to be careful. He knows Drake and I can be challenging to deal with and we were likely close by."

"We had to avoid his lackey, Igor, at school," Drake said. "That was fairly easy, as he was focused on finding you three."

"Plus, Frankenstein isn't overly fond of getting the government involved," Peter grumbled. "He might have a whole bunch of fancy pants technology but he's on the run. He needed to keep a low profile until he was sure who each of you were."

"Yes, it's just a matter of time before Uncle Sam closes in," Mina continued. "The speed at which he moved is alarming but, unfortunately, not surprising."

"So what's our next move?" Dash asked. His stomach growled. "By the way, err... can I have a sandwich?"

Shelley smiled and Blaine shook her head.

"Of course, Daschle," Mina replied, turning to the fridge and removing ingredients.

"Vickie must be freaking out," Blaine fretted.

"Yeah," Dash added. "I think Kevin's learning the hard way, real life doesn't play out like a videogame."

"We'll get your friends back," Peter assured them. He retrieved a root beer from the refrigerator. "Von Frankenstein's tough, but we've been on this merry-go-round before."

"We need a game plan," Drake confirmed, taking his father's chair.

Mina placed a plate of sandwiches on the table. Each of the kids took one. Dash greedily stuffing one in his mouth, blobs of mayo and mustard coating the corners of his lips. Blaine and Shelley looked on in amazement at a thirteen year old boy's appetite. It was like watching the sandwich version of the Cookie Monster on a snicker-doodle fueled bender.

"Shelley, von Frankenstein gave you a device this morning at school," Mina said, wiping off her hands on a towel. "Do you still have it?"

Shelley nodded and removed the leather satchel around her shoulders and placed it on the table. She fished out the rolled up iScroll that Frankenstein had given her in the Principal's office. The B-shaped logo on its top was pulsing a faint electric blue. She tapped the logo and the device unrolled automatically, stiffening into a tablet. An email program automatically opened.

"There's a message," Shelley said as the others crowded around the device. "It's from Frankenstein!"

Mina

I have your two students.

If you value their lives, you and the heirs will give yourselves up by 9 A.M. sharp tomorrow at the gates of Grimm Academy. Come or they will die. We will be watching. Test me and I will annihilate this whole town, molecule by molecule, starting with the Stoker girls' family.

Do not try my patience, Ian

"What do we do?" Dash asked.

"I have to call my Mom!" Blaine fretted.

Mina paused and considered the message. "We give Ian what he wants. But we make sure he can't keep it." She huddled them together.

"We have much to discuss," Mina said, her tone serious and business-like. "Once we understand our plan and each of you is ready to do your part, we are going to have to make sure that each of your families is safe. Are you all ready?"

She looked each of them in the eye. They nodded back grimly.

"Okay, here's what we'll do…"

*****

The next morning Mina, Drake, Dash, Blaine, and Shelley approached the gates of Grimm Academy. The plan was simple and they worked hard all night to prepare with Mina, Drake, and Peter instructing the kids in the use of their new powers.

Peter dropped them off a quarter mile down the road near the edge of the forest neighboring the Grimm Academy grounds. He remained close by on a rise overlooking the school, monitoring them via a shortwave radio transmitter in Mina's ear. As Mina and the kids approached, the two-way radio broke into static.

"So much for Plan A," Mina murmured, discarding the earpiece. "Let's keep moving."

Fancy black iron gates opened before them as they turned onto the school entrance lane. The grounds were a lush green with trees gently swaying in the ocean breeze. In the distance, the small football stadium was starting to buzz with activity with the coming Middle School football game. The two teams were already on the field warming up for kick off an hour later with a few students and staff milling around.

Dash sighed heavily as he saw the teams prepping. Today was opening day and he was starting halfback. He would not have a chance to play and didn't even get a chance to tell his coach. Despite the danger to himself and his friends, letting down his team gnawed at him.

Grimm Academy looked the perfect seaside prep school. If it weren't for the ugly grey manor house dominating the background and the bent and gnarled figure of Igor standing by the gate, the scene would be like one from a painting. Adding to the discord, two of the Brothers Grimm, Carlos and Frederick, along with another Grimm cyborg, Brent, flanked Igor, their expressions snide.

"Search them," Igor barked, arms crossed. Brent, Frederick, and Carlos walked forward and frisked the kids and Mina, whisking flat metal detectors over them.

"Where are the children?" Mina asked, ignoring the Grimms.

"Where's my sister?" Blaine urged.

"They are safe for now. Don't get cute and you'll see them soon."

"Where's your leader, that cozy guy, Heinz?" Drake said, daring Carlos as the cyborg searched him. "Still in the shop or did Humpty-Dumpty not have enough pieces left to put him back together?"

Carlos pushed Drake with his shoulder but didn't look him in the eye.

Drake smiled.

"Hey, Drake," Dash piled on eyeing Brent as he patted him down. "Looks like Frankenstein cooked himself up a new goon."

He sniffed as Drake grinned. "He still has that new thug smell."

Brent turned violently and tried to grab Dash by the t-shirt. Dash pulled away from the Grimm, growling.

"Bring it on!" Dash snarled.

"Dash," Shelley cautioned.

"Enough," Igor said, brandishing a silver wand, the same he used the night prior. "You will come quietly or your friends will suffer. Put these on to make sure you behave."

Dash backed down, as Igor threw several sets of silver handcuffs on the ground connected with thin wires. As a demonstration, Igor pushed a button on a small remote control and the cuffs hissed with an electric blue current coursing over them. He let go of the button and the high-tech shackles returned to normal, the smell of fresh ozone drifting from them.

"One wrong move and you'll know what it's like to be microwave popcorn."

The Grimms picked up the cuffs and attached them to each of the kids, ending with Mina who they approached cautiously.

"They are ready," Frederick announced, lining their prisoners up in a row.

"Good... then let me be the first to welcome you," Igor announced, gesturing grandly, "to Grimm Academy... The Doctor and your friends await."

Chapter 19: Shelley

Von Frankenstein's lab was located in a long, gleaming white building ending in a brilliant circular glass dome on a pier over the ocean with large pylons that protected it from the pounding surf. Next to it was a tall crane anchored to the ocean floor, with Frankenstein's black helicopter positioned on a floating dock. On the beach were several tools and large boxes covered in tarps. Judging from its appearance, the building was in the final stages of construction.

As the kids approached the complex they saw a shiny bronze plaque at its entrance which read *Grimm Science Annex* with another that listed several donors. Topping the list was Black Labs. A large red ribbon was tied around each double glass door with a sign that read *OPENING SOON* in block letters.

The shiny new complex stood below the main Manor House, connected by a glass elevator shaft that went up the cliffside. Hugging the shaft was a twisting set of metal stairs that descended over several stories of rock to the gravelly beach below. The modern structure stood out from the drab granite and greying wood of more traditional buildings overhead. Sunlight shone off it brightly. Underneath, the cold waters of the northern Pacific frothed.

The kids walked inside, guarded by Igor and the Grimm Brothers. No one stirred. Inside were rows of never before used classrooms and labs, gleaming in the morning light, connected by a long hallway in fancy enameled wood. A few tools and painting ladders dotted the recently completed hallway. At the far end of the corridor was a pair of thick, metal double doors that led into a large, private lab. The main room of the complex dominated the far end of the pier, opening into a large, glass circular room.

Igor marched the kids and Mina, handcuffed, single file into the imposing globe. The outer walls of the lab were made of glass and raised three stories high, arching to a dome. Thick silvery metal connected the windows and came to an apex in an observatory four stories up that could be accessed only by an elegant spiral staircase that raised from the center of the room. On its top was a large telescope suspended in the air on a rotatable platform big enough for a clutch of people.

Surrounding the staircase in a semi-circle were five ugly machines wrapped in wire and metal. Each had a thick black metal base. Rising from the base was a clear tube big enough for an adult to stand in. Blaine shivered, she thought they looked like plastic coffins. Connected to each tube was a set of blinking lights, digital read-outs, and a series of smaller tubes and wires that spider-webbed together. They led to a master console and set of large white tanks on the other edge of the room. Each tank had a set of warning markers punctuated by electric bolts and skull and cross bones. The tanks steamed menacingly while the facility hummed with electricity.

Dash gulped. This place was a curious toddler's worst nightmare. If the sparking wires didn't get junior, the smoking tubes and mysterious smoke were sure to do the job.

Von Frankenstein stood in a lab coat, spindly and hunched, waiting expectantly near a bay of computer terminals. His characteristic sunglasses dominated his craggy face. Standing watch near him was his Monster, silver and gleaming in the morning sun, its green eyes narrow and unexpressive.

To his side, were three large tables. On one lay the third Brother Grimm, Heinz. His eyes were open, unblinking, his perfect hair disheveled, as a set of robot arms whirred over him picking at a large dark hole in his chest. Next to him, on two operating tables, were a writhing mass of Frankenstein's green mechanical nano-bugs. They buzzed wickedly, moving like two giant alien Jell-O molds well past their expiration dates.

Igor pushed his captors forward.

Von Frankenstein approached them, his grim face mimicking a smile.

"Welcome! Do you like my new lab? It has all my latest toys." He walked over to Mina and eyed her closely. He stroked her chin with one gloved hand and she jerked back, eyeing the Doctor in warning. He removed his hand and smiled back, stepping to a safe distance.

"My dear. It has been too long since we have seen each other. You've changed your hair, no?"

"Where are Kevin and Vickie?" Mina asked, ignoring his question.

"Oh, your two friends," von Frankenstein pressed a control pad and the mounds of nanobots parted revealing the faces of Vickie and Kevin unconscious underneath.

"Vickie!" Blaine gasped.

"Kevin!" Dash yelled and struggled with his manacles. Frederick sought to restrain him but Dash pushed the other away, making a move toward his friend.

Frankenstein glanced at him and pressed another button. Dash's handcuffs flashed a brilliant electric blue as it sent a shock coursing through his system. The boy gritted his teeth as he dropped to the floor in pain.

"Ian!" Mina warned.

Frankenstein depressed the button. "That will be enough, Mr. Gaunt."

Dash dropped his head, breathing heavily. Shelley knelt to check on him.

The mad doctor pressed another button and the green bugs sickeningly congealed over Vickie and Kevin's passive faces.

"As for your friends," Frankenstein continued. "They are quite safe, and will continue to be, so long as each of you cooperates."

"You said you would let them go!" Shelley accused, looking up at Frankenstein as she hovered over Dash.

"Oh, but I shall... Shelley, isn't it?" Frankenstein approached. He leered at her with a malevolent expression, leaning in close, eyeing her up and down.

"You look so much like my dear Tempest, Ms. Merry. Do you know that?"

"I never met my great-grandmother," Shelley said uncomfortably, wincing every time Frankenstein moved to peer at her from a new angle.

"Don't fear me," Frankenstein whispered. Shelley could see her frightened expression mirrored in his dark sunglasses.

"Why should I fear you?" Shelley asked quietly.

"You shouldn't. Not you, I have plans for you, dear. You are my flesh and blood, my last link. For a man that works in genetics, twisting the fabric of nature, purity is so rare."

"Leave her alone!" Drake said. He stood shackled next to Shelley.

Von Frankenstein looked up and sneered at Drake. He stared at him long and hard.

"Murphy's son," Frankenstein growled. "It has been decades since I last saw you. You were just a baby and now you are little more than a boy."

Drake stared back at von Frankenstein, unblinking and without fear.

"Are you surprised I can stare into those blue eyes of yours without falling under your trance?"

Frankenstein removed his wide sunglasses and Drake's expression changed, his eyes widening. Von Frankenstein turned and faced the others. Where his eyes should have been were two gaping black holes with thick scabs etched over the sides of his temples. Over each ear were two small metal plates.

Von Frankenstein smiled and put his sunglasses back on. The ends clicked into the metal connectors.

"A present from the Russians. I had to design these glasses to see again," he said.

He turned to Mina. "You didn't know the tortures they subjected me to," he added, tilting his head to her at a crazy angle. His voice started to come unhinged.

"You and Peter conveniently forgot about me, left me for dead, thinking the Russians would finish your dirty work at the end of the war." He walked toward his bank of computers. "Well, you did worse than that. The Russians captured me, broken and cornered. They tortured me, subjected me to the cruelest punishments, wanting me to talk, but wouldn't let me die."

He clicked a few buttons and the tubes on each of the machines surrounding the stairwell raised in a sickening hiss as gears on the base units crunched.

"The Russians didn't know who I was or what we were doing at Castle Dracul. They just thought I was some Nazi stooge. I spent seventy years rotting in Siberia, eyes gouged out, barely surviving in darkness, lucky if they even remembered to feed me."

Mina whispered, "What you did to us, Ian, to your friends… it was unforgiveable. You deserved whatever you got after the war."

"Ian… you are the only person who calls me that anymore…" Frankenstein replied in a menacing whisper.

He took a deep breath to control himself but failed. His face twisted into a fury.

"I DESERVED A MEDAL!" Frankenstein screamed. "I deserved *RESPECT!*"

He strode forward and eyed all of them with a desperate, made expression. "I was on the verge of unlocking the secret of life itself!" He paused and breathed heavily, the veins in his neck bulging. "The Nazis were just a means to an end… just like each of you…"

He paused slicking back his thin white hair over his skeletal head and continued in more measured tones. "What we can do with these powers, with this technology, is beyond the pale of man. We can be God. We have the potential to all be gods."

He stared at Mina. "If in the process of becoming gods we need to sacrifice a few for the benefit of the many, then I'm prepared to make that trade."

He sighed heavily. "I regret you never understood this."

"You're a monster," Mina said, gritting her teeth.

"No, Mina," Frankenstein replied, pointing at her and the children. "You are wrong. I was never a monster. That was always *you* and your friends... and now your children's children."

He shook his head and smiled. "I was just a man. You are the monsters. You are the *freaks*, and now it is time my research begins anew."

"Let me show you my new lab," Frankenstein said, gesturing toward the nefarious looking tubes. "We've made advancements since our time with the Germans, no?"

"What do you want with us?" Drake asked.

"I want what makes you special, Mr. Harker. How about this? I offer you a trade, your powers in exchange for a normal life. Sounds like a fair deal, eh?"

"What are you talking about?" Blaine asked, baffled.

"You will each enter these tubes. My equipment will conduct some tests and, if successful, separate the nanos that have changed you and return your DNA to normal."

"And if not successful?" Mina asked.

"Well, sacrifices sometimes have to be made in the spirit of progress..."

"How do we know you'll free our friends?" Dash said, rising from the ground.

"Ms. Merry will vouch for your friends' safety. She will not be part of these tests. Once you have started the procedure, she and your friends will be free to go."

"I don't trust you," Drake growled.

"You don't have a choice."

"If you double cross us I will make sure you pay," Mina warned stepping forward.

Von Frankenstein stared at her with disdain.

"Igor, fetch the box."

"Yes, master," Igor muttered and shuffled to the rear of the room.

He and Carlos hauled a large metal chest forward, strapped together with thick chains and padlocks. They placed the container on the ground and unlocked it. Frankenstein opened the top of the chest with his boot.

The inside glowed and sparkled a rich yellow. Frankenstein lifted out a fist-sized rock. It looked like a large hunk of gold, except its structure was clear and it emitted a bright golden light. He placed it on the ground in front of the kids.

Everyone stared at it. Mina's already pale skin blanched. She began to sweat and doubled over in pain.

"What is that?" she uttered, holding her side.

Frankenstein paced behind the stone. "This is a curious artifact the Russians found around the beginning of World War I," he explained, smiling. "The stone is very beautiful. It's like a little piece of the sun, isn't it?"

Mina swooned. Blaine helped her remain standing.

"What is it doing to her?" she pleaded.

"Oh, this rock is special. It is from a region called Tunguska, a place very close to where I was imprisoned in Siberia. It, along with what the Russians thought at the time was a small comet, crashed to Earth over a century ago. I learned about it from the whispers of the prison guards."

He picked up the stone and held it out for them to see more closely. Mina moaned as it passed close to her. Frankenstein placed it back in its metal container but kept the lid open allowing its golden light to spill out.

"It is alien in origin, I believe from the same aliens who crash landed years ago in Roswell. It has many curious properties. For one, it helped me to recover from the ravages of my Russian prison, but it affects people differently. For some, it offers strength and healing." He looked at Mina without an ounce of pity registering on his face. "For others, it is like sunlight to a vampire…"

He turned to address Drake. "So, whelp, your only ace is gone. You will do as I say or I will destroy your mother while you stand and watch."

The mad scientist smiled triumphantly.

"Igor, Creature, escort our guests into the nano-chambers!"

"Yes, Master," Igor nodded. He and the Grimms pushed Dash, Drake, and Blaine into the large, clear tubes. The Monster's eyes lit up. He stomped forward, picked Mina up in his arms, and carried her to the nearest of Frankenstein's nasty-looking machines. He laid her gently inside.

"Watch it, buddy!" Blaine snapped, as Brent shoved her toward her tube.

"Move or your sister pays," Brent snarled.

Blaine shot a quick glance to the table holding Vickie and obeyed begrudgingly. She ducked her head under the thick, clear plastic and turned around as the door on the tube slithered shut, sealing with a hiss. The other tubes echoed her own as Mina and the boys entered theirs. Blaine pressed on the plastic barrier, her eyes widening. She shouted and started to pound on the clear walls, the sounds muted under the thick material.

The Creature turned and walked behind Shelley as Frankenstein pressed buttons at his master terminal. The Brothers Grimm and Igor fanned out on the sides of the lab, keeping watch.

"What are you going to do to them?" Shelley asked urgently, seeing her friends struggle in the tubes.

Frankenstein looked up from his control panel. Behind him, a large LCD showed bars rising and a countdown clock beginning. In the distance, the large white tanks steamed and began to vibrate loudly as tesla coils above snapped with tendrils of electricity.

He smiled. "I am going to break down their DNA, my dear, molecule by molecule, harvest it, clone it, and recombine it for my own purposes."

"Will it hurt them?" Shelley asked. She moved toward the machines but the Monster restrained her with two giant metal hands.

Frankenstein considered his reply. "At first… but they will die quickly."

He peered at Mina, unconscious in her tube. "A pity…"

Chapter 20: Shelley

"Die!?" Shelley shrieked. "You promised you weren't going to hurt them!"

"But I won't," Frankenstein replied, "the same technology that gave them their gifts will take it away. Unfortunately my nanos won't just stop with harvesting their powers. They are hungry. Once they feed, they cannot be satisfied. All of this equipment is merely to contain them and keep us safe." He pressed a button and a claxon blared as lights flared around each testing apparatus. "Here, watch."

The giant white tanks shuddered and the piping leading to the large storage tanks pulsed. Blaine, Dash, and Drake looked frantically around as each tank began to shake and spit with steam. Mina was still in a stupor slumped in her own. A purple gas began to flood each testing tube, punctuated by glowing green dots that buzzed rapidly inside, the nanos.

Shelley heard the pounding on each tube intensify. Dash's tube rocked as he smashed the sides using every ounce of nano-enhanced strength. The sturdy base of his machine held him fast but the clear plastic of his tube began to crack. He continued to pound but slowly the gas overwhelmed him, his strikes weakening.

Blaine shrieked as her face disappeared in a cloud of swirling purple gas and then was silent. Drake looked at his Mom in the next tube stoically.

Shelley looked at Frankenstein frantically who was absorbed in his monitors and then at the large creature who held her fast.

"You have to let me go!" she begged the giant steel robot.

The Monster regarded her silently, his grip unchanged.

"They are hurting my friends!" she sobbed. "You must listen to me!"

"The Creature only has one true master," Frankenstein chuckled. "You may be my heir, but I am still in control."

The purple gas in the tubes swirled faster and more green speckles of light joined the mix as the LCDs overhead showed each of their red status bars at full. The lights under each machine gleamed bright and steam rose from them as they rattled with the intensity of the hurricane of nanobots swarming inside.

"The process begins. I will harvest their powers and build my own perfect beings. The keys to immortality, life and ultimate power shall soon be *mine*!"

The three kids shouted in panic and pain, desperately clawing at their tubes. Even Mina stirred from her torpor, moaning as the nanos whirled around her, probing the cells of her body.

Shelley wrenched free of her jacket and backpack and tumbled away from the Robot whose eyes widened into circles. She raced for the nearest machine and grabbed a valve, twisting it rapidly. The base began to shake and white smoke rose from a console.

"Igor, stop her!" Frankenstein screeched.

Igor moved in, along with Brent. Each grabbed her gruffly and yanked her away. They hauled her toward their Master.

"I told you to obey," Frankenstein warned, leaning in close. "Don't force me to make you suffer like your friends."

"How's this for suffering!" Shelley kicked up with one knee and caught the leering Frankenstein squarely in the groin. He doubled over in agony. Igor watched in shock as Carlos and Frederick lurched back in sympathy pain. Frankenstein jerked his head up with a look of loathing. He pushed Shelley back, sending her reeling across the floor.

"Put her in a tube!" Frankenstein growled thru gritted teeth, still bent over, nursing a throbbing pain. "I should have known not to trust a half-breed like you! Your genes are no longer pure!"

Igor and Brent stalked toward Shelley who lay dazed on the floor. Behind her stood the iron creature who had silently taken in the scene. He still held Shelley's jacket and leather satchel in each giant hand. Shelley looked up at the robot with pleading in her eyes. "*Please...*" she pleaded.

Brent and Igor closed in, dragging Shelley away to the fifth test tube. On either side, the machines gleamed bright green as millions of nanos swirled around her screaming, struggling friends. Shelley bent her head, closed her eyes and gave up hope.

WHUMP! CRASH!

She looked up. Behind where Brent had been standing was a Brent-shaped hole in the glass leading to the sea beyond. Frankenstein's Monster bent down and handed Shelley her jacket and bag. He raised to his full height, his eyes narrowing into bright lime slits, eyeing Igor dangerously.

"Master…" Igor muttered nervously before the Creature grabbed him in one iron fist and flung him across the room into a web of tubes which broke apart in a fog of steam and smoke.

Carlos and Frederick flanked the creature on each side. Frankenstein straightened and stalked toward his pet robot. "*Enough!*" he howled. "Stand down this instant, I command you!"

The creature regarded his Master, its eyes rounding in submission and turned and looked at Shelley who was struggling to rise. Her hair was a mess and the side of her cheek had a big red welt where the demented scientist had struck her.

"You know what's right," she urged the robot, climbing unsteadily to her feet.

Frederick and Carlos closed in.

"Stand down, you piece of scrap!" Frankenstein growled, pointing a warning finger directly at the robot's face.

The creature looked at the Doctor, whose face was evil and crazed, and its eyes narrowed. Von Frankenstein flinched in alarm. The Monster punched sideways and sent Carlos careening into Dash's tube. Carlos hit the machine with a bone-crunching 'thud', evaporating in a swarm of swirling green as the tube spider-webbed. Bright purple gas hissed out, followed by thousands of phosphorescent specks as the nanos escaped their confinement.

Frederick leapt away in fright as the Monster eyed him. The creature turned to peer at Frankenstein who was backing away, his angry expression melting to fear.

"You must obey me!" Frankenstein sputtered. "You have *always* obeyed me!"

The Monster stepped forward and stood between Frankenstein and Shelley.

"Not anymore, Dr. von Freak," Shelley announced. She looked up to the creature.

"Can you help me free my friends?" The robot nodded in reply.

"No!" Frankenstein shouted. He backed away as the creature eyed him in warning.

"If you release the nanos there will be no controlling them!" Frankenstein pleaded. "They'll destroy everything once out of their tubes. We'll all be finished!"

"Do it," Shelley urged.

The robot shoved Frankenstein away, sending him flying into a bank of terminals near a stunned Igor, and with one hand grasped the cracked casing of Dash's tube and crunched it to pieces. Immediately, a claxon started to blare throughout the complex and a calm female computer voice announced *"Containment breach. Emergency protocols activated."* Red security lights began to flash over every window and door.

Shelley moved to help Dash who slumped over the thick plastic-like tubing. The purple gas and glowing green nanos swirled overhead as emergency fans suspended above turned on automatically and fire valves started to douse the lab equipment in coats of water.

The once sparkling state-of-the-art lab descended into chaos. The creature moved from tube to tube, ripping off the doors and placing the kids on the ground a few feet away. Shelley tended to them, making sure each was still alive and breathing.

Frankenstein wasted no time as he saw his pet robot turn on him and his lab transformed into a wet, smoking ruin. "Igor, retrieve the box! Frederick, help me with the Harker woman!"

As the creature rounded the spiral staircase to the final testing apparatus, Frederick and von Frankenstein released the outer door and removed the unconscious figure of Mina from her plastic tomb. Igor joined them, carrying the metal box with the strange glowing golden rock. They retreated to the rear entrance of the lab leading to the dock and helicopter pad outside. The robot stalked forward, attempting to block their escape.

Von Frankenstein hesitated a moment, timing his next move just right. He pressed a button on a small panel on his belt and above them a huge explosion wracked the ceiling. The telescope, suspended overhead, fell and smashed down onto the Monster. The combined weight of the large telescope, the steel girders, and the robot was too much for the floor to bear. The creature fell into the churning sea below as the concrete and wood beneath gave way in a massive *CRACK!*

The power immediately gave out in the lab, and the remaining piping and tubes creaked and vibrated ominously. Von Frankenstein retrieved a small silver tube near the giant white tanks as Igor and Frederick hurried toward the awaiting helicopter, Mina in tow.

Shelley looked up from across the way, separated from von Frankenstein by the giant crack in the floor. The creature was nowhere to be seen lost in the dark grey ocean below. Dash, Drake, and Blaine were just starting to stir, shaking their heads and moaning softly.

"Congratulations!" von Frankenstein yelled over the whirring of chopper blades. "You have won, but I think you will find your victory short-lived. In seconds, this entire facility will explode in a violent cloud of uncontrollable nanos. These aren't like the others you have encountered. They are designed only to break down, to destroy. They will consume you, this campus, and this whole town."

"Run, if you like," he said leaving. "But it will do no good."

"Auf wiedersehen!" he shouted, and ducked thru the door to the helicopter beyond.

The large white tanks rumbled and gushed out huge plumes of bright purple gas, their surface dimpling with pressure. The floor buckled as one side of the dock which was supporting the building gave way, teetering ominously downward.

"Jerk," Shelley grumbled. Dash, Blaine, and Drake slowly began to rise. "Come on guys," she urged. "We've got to get out of here."

"What happened?" Drake asked.

"No time for explanations!" Shelley urged. "This whole place is going to blow. Not only that, if we don't find some way to stop these nanobots from escaping, the whole town is in danger."

"So, no pressure then," Blaine muttered, standing up and shaking the cobwebs from her head.

"First, we have to get Kevin and Vickie," Dash said, running to the tables where their two friends lay.

"How do we free them?" he asked, urgently.

"Let me try," Drake said. He placed one hand in each swirling mass of green. Grey smoke started to swirl around his arms and expand over the writhing mass of nanobugs. Drake's face twisted in concentration as sweat began to bead on his forehead. Slowly, the nanos receded as the smoke expanded, revealing their friends underneath.

"Get them," Drake grunted.

Blaine and Shelley grabbed Vickie, removing her from the swirling pile of bugs, while Dash put Kevin's arm over his shoulder. Once they were safely away, Drake snatched back his hands from each pile. He breathed heavily.

"I'm not as strong as my mother," he said, "but sometimes I can make do in a pinch."

Shelley smiled at him as Dash and Blaine hovered over their friends. Kevin and Vickie began to stir. "Wha? What happened?" Kevin slurred.

"No Channing, I shouldn't. OK, just this once..." Vickie murmured, making a sleepy kissy-face.

"What's that about?" Dash wondered.

"She talks in her sleep," Blaine sighed, "and she has a huge crush on that guy from 21 Jump Street." Blaine bent over her sister and clapped her hands beside her ear.

"Time to wake up Princess!"

Vickie's eyes opened wide. She had a worried look on her face. "What did I say?"

"It was the Magic Mike dream again," Blaine grinned, despite herself.

Vickie rolled on her side and tried to get up. She winced. "Ooo... what happened to me?"

"You were the creamy center of a glowing spacebug-flavored Twinkie," Blaine explained, pointing to the dying piles of nanobots on the nearby tables.

"Oh, my gawd! Those things were in my hair?"

"She's fine," Blaine announced.

"Dash, is that you?" Kevin asked, rising to his elbows, squinting. "Man, I had the weirdest dream. You were Teen Wolf minus the 80s head band, and Blaine was the

Invisible Girl. There was this giant robot, a mad scientist and a preppy kid driving an awesome car..."

Kevin looked around at the ruined lab. Clouds of nanos and purple gas were filling the ceiling. Drake stood nearby flashing a brilliant smile, his eyes glowing bright blue. Blaine wave at him shyly, her hand invisible from the wrist upwards and there was a monster-sized hole in the floor several feet away.

His skin drained of color. "I wasn't just playing too much Gothic, was I?"

Dash smiled and helped up his friend. "No, buddy. You weren't."

"*Two minutes to total containment breach.*" A calm female voice announced from overhead. The emergency lights began to flash a deep red, mixing with the morning daylight from outside. The tanks in the far corner shook loudly while the purple gas and tiny glowing lights from the ruined test chambers gushed unabated. Overhead, the lights started to converge on the steel rafters and wooden ceiling. The whole building began to creak ominously as bits of daylight began to poke thru from tiny holes above.

"The nanos are escaping," Drake said grimly, "and they're eating thru the building. We need to get out of here now because when those tanks blow, we are going to be in some deep *doo-doo*!"

Except he didn't say doo-doo...

Chapter 21: Mina

U Boat 679, the Atlantic

Mina awoke groggily. Her eyelids were thick and sleepy, her thoughts soupy. She moaned softly as she shifted, her arms and body felt unnaturally slow.

Breathe, she thought, *breathe.*

She struggled to open her eyes but a thick film coated everything, making the shapes surrounding her dull and blurry.

Concentrate.

She blinked hard, gritted her teeth and opened her eyes again. The haze lifted. Surrounding her were thick grey bars. She tried to rise but felt a weight around her ankles and wrists. She looked down. Shiny manacles bound her arms and legs, rattling against the bars. She shifted, seeking slack in her bindings, but found little.

Where am I?

She looked around, trying to keep her focus. It was difficult at first but as she concentrated it became easier to make heads and tails of her surroundings. She breathed in deeply. Bad idea. The smell was horrible. Her gag reflexes kicked in, causing her to wretch. She made a sour face, trying to hold her breath, inhaling only when necessary through her mouth. The only benefit to the acrid stench was it helped to pierce the strange veil clouding her senses.

She shifted. She was in a small cage, something built for an animal, lying on a dirty, smelly cot. The cage was low, giving her barely enough room to rise onto her elbows and look around. She raised and immediately felt woozy. She shut her eyes and counted to five trying to stop the spinning. She opened her eyes and exhaled slowly, careful not to breathe in deeply.

The long, narrow room she found herself in was poorly lit with a weak red light bulb at one end shining dimly over a slim portal with a thick metal door. The cell was tight with barely enough room for her cage and a narrow walkway to one side. Crisscrossing the ceiling of her tomb were pipes and gaskets from one end to the other. If she didn't know better, she would have thought she was caged in the belly of some mechanical beast, Jonah and the iron Whale.

Steel, pipes, humming... where am I? she thought, gripping her forehead and trying to burn thru the fog that constantly fought to cloud her mind. She looked down at her body and saw red puncture marks on each arm above where the shiny manacles chafed her wrists. She raised one arm, her chains scraping, and recoiled at the foul aroma emanating from her wounds.

"Medicine," she coughed, her nostrils burning. She lowered her arm heavily and sighed, her head hanging low.

"Good morning, lass..." a voice called softly from nearby.

Mina jerked up startled and hit the top of her head hard on a cast iron bar of her cage's roof. She collapsed back down onto her soiled cot, nursing her throbbing noggin.

"Sorry, I did that twice already today, meself."

Mina tried to focus. There was someone chained like Mina to the sides of another cage next to her. Mina could just make out a face... it was Lonn! Mina could also see the outline of a similar cage near the red light and portal.

"Edge?" she whispered. Her throat felt bone dry. Suddenly she was ravenously thirsty.

"Aye. Take your time. Get your bearings."

"I'm so thirsty," Mina whispered, "is there water?"

"It's the tranquilizers they dose us with," Edge answered, his voice was quiet and sad. "Truth be told, I'd suck the sweat out of a tinker's sock right now. But those rat Nazi gits are nowhere to be seen."

"Nazis?" Mina muttered.

"We're their guests. Been knocked out cold for I'd guess for days."

"Where are we?" Mina coughed.

"Either they found their own spaceship at Roswell or my guess is some kind of sea vessel. With our luck it's probably some kind of ruddy submarine, Jules Verne be damned."

"A submarine..." Mina whispered.

"50,000 leagues under the sea and me without my swim trunks," Edge quipped sullenly.

And then it all came back to her...

The trip to Argentina. The stop-over in Buenos Aires. A strange man with haunting black eyes, bone white skin. Who was he? Ian. The robot. What happened? Had the robot attacked them? Had Ian ordered it? Yes! And then... and then what?

Mina shook her head again, trying to clear her memory from the befuddling haze. Whatever the Nazis had injected in her was still affecting her thoughts. The room began to spin. She clenched her eyes shut and concentrated, and her hand gripped a nearby bar, her knuckles whitening. Slowly, the fog burned away. Mina opened her eyes and concentrated on her hand clutching the cage as an anchor. Thin tendrils of black smoke emerged from between her fingers as the strange powers she had been trying to control took on a mind of their own. The black smoke grew thicker. As her power grew, her mind cleared and the thick haze of the medicine parted. She released her grip and stared at the bar, breathing slowly. It glowed a bright red, hot to the touch. Slowly it cooled and a calm clarity settled over her mind.

"Ian betrayed us," she said simply, "he set his Monster and a group of Nazi goons against us, led by a strange man in a black suit."

"Herr Major, aye," Edge replied. Mina could hear the chains from his cage rattle as he shifted on his cot.

"Lonn tried to defend us but they came at us from all sides," Mina paused, staring at the cage separating them. "Is he alright?"

Lonn turned in his crate and let out a long snort, followed by another rather less pleasant snorting sound from another part of his body.

"Well, other than a touch of morning body ordor and a bad snoring problem," Edge sniffed distastefully, "I think the big man's no worse for wear. He's a brave lad, though, I'll grant you. Fought Ian and his goons to the end."

"Where are the Germans? Where's Ian?" Mina asked.

They both turned as the door at the far side of the room clunked loudly and squealed open. A bright light forced Edge and Mina to shield their eyes. Lonn stirred in surprise, rising from his slumber and bumped his head hard on his cell. He cursed loudly in German.

"Why Professor Cheney, you should watch your language, *mein freund*," a voice clucked from the open portal. A thin shadowy figure passed into the room.

"Ian…" Mina hissed.

"Good, you're awake Ms. Harker," Ian van Helsing replied. "I'm afraid you'll need to start calling me by my proper name now… Dr. Victor von Frankenstein."

He walked into the cell holding a handheld torch, surveying each of his former colleagues like prizes in a private collection. His expression was smug.

"I don't care what you want to be called, *Ian*. As far as I'm concerned you always have been and always will be a gammy dosser!" Edge thundered. "Now what have you done to me and our friends, you traitor!" He reached out with one arm to grasp Ian. In response, a bright light flared near Edge's cage and he howled in pain.

"Edge!" Lonn whispered hoarsely.

"That will be enough, Dr. Stoker," a second voice, haunting and distinctly German, said as a new shadow passed thru the bright doorway.

Following Ian was a pale man clad in a midnight black Nazi uniform. His hair was neat, combed and bone white. His skin was as pale as a ghost's. In one gloved hand, he held a long metal prod. He pressed a button and a bright blue tendril of electricity arched between two evil-looking prongs. The light revealed his face more clearly. Mina shrank back in her cell. His eyes. They were like two shiny black holes edge-to-edge.

He released the button on his weapon with the faint wisps of a smile touching his pale face. The portal behind him closed. The cell returned to red-tinged darkness, the features of the strange German masked by the soft light of the chamber's lone bulb.

Edge moaned softly and the Nazi officer jammed his prod between the bars again, the blue light of his prod revealing a crazed look on the strange German's face. Their friend's shrieks echoed off the metal walls of the room.

"Stop, you're hurting him!" Mina called. Suddenly, her arms flared to life in billowing tendrils of black smoke. Ian shrank away from her cell, the smug expression melting into fear. Mina gripped her bars and the black smoke hungrily consumed her cage, melting the iron in searing heat. Mina looked down in surprise at the alien power she barely understood but continued to tear apart the bars of her cage. She was determined to win her freedom and save her friends.

"Herr Major…," Ian quaked.

The black-clad Nazi looked up from his torture of Edge and strode toward Mina, with Ian retreating behind him toward the door. He looked down as Mina tore thru another two bars, snapped the chains binding her wrists and struggled to wedge herself thru an opening in her cage.

"Fascinating…," the Major muttered as Mina reached toward him, her hand flaring with thick black smoke.

"Let's see how you like this, you goose-stepping slime ball!" she snarled.

Mina gripped the Major's leg and prepared to burn thru the terrible Nazi tormentor like the bars of her cage. The Major did nothing to stop her. He stood and watched as Ian quaked behind him in worry. Tendrils of smoke rose around the Major's black clad leg, wrapping around him as Mina concentrated with all her might to incinerate him.

The smoke thickened and an eerie green glow emanated from the Major's leg. The Major looked at her with his empty black eyes and all hope seemed to drain out of her. The smoke surrounding his leg and Mina's arm began to weaken and dissipate until it evaporated in a few weak puffs. Mina felt weak and drained. Where she gripped the Major her hand was pale and draining of heat and color. She released his leg and recoiled into her cage.

The Major looked down and tutted. "As you will soon learn, you are not the only one with power, my dear Ms. Harker. Do not make me use my toys on you. The Fuhrer would prefer you and your friends arrive in Germany alive, but he did not *insist*." The Major pointed to the pipes and gaskets above them crisscrossing the room.

"As you have no doubt surmised, you are in the belly of a German U-Boat. If you or your friends try to escape again or do any harm to Herr Frankenstein or my men, we will flood this compartment with ten thousand gallons of icy cold sea water."

The Major paused, smiling as he tapped his electric prod in one hand.

"It will be an experiment. You're familiar with those. Did the aliens grant you the power to breathe underwater or not? Herr Frankenstein believes they didn't... But tempt me and I will take the opportunity to see if they did."

"Who are you?" Mina whispered, still nursing her ice-cold arm.

"I am your new warden," the Major said, squatting down to look her face-to-face, making sure she could see clearly the cold, depthless black of his eyes. "Cooperate and you and your friends will live. Resist... well... resistance is futile."

"Where are you taking us?" Lonn said hoarsely.

The Major stared at him and rose, a cold smile etched on his face, wrinkling his solid black eyes.

"I think you'll like it. It's quiet, secure, remote. Protected from any prying eyes or attempts at rescue... or escape. Dr. von Frankenstein, tell our guests where their new home will be."

Ian joined the Major, smiling evilly, his confidence renewed. "In Transylvania," he cooed. "The ancestral home of Vlad the Impaler, Castle Dracul."

"What are you going to do with us?" Mina muttered.

"You will be prize subjects in a vast research program personally sponsored by the Fuhrer," the Major replied. "You should be honored. Our work is central to the goals of the Wehrmacht."

"And what if we don't want to be your lab rats?" Lonn growled.

"Ask a lab rat how much say he has in the matter, Professor Cheney. As I said, resistance is futile."

The Major rapped on the thick iron portal leading out of their cell. It opened and the bright light from without streamed in, blinding Mina and her friends.

"I would suggest that each of you rest and enjoy the remainder of our journey. Once we arrive in the Fatherland, you will be quite busy. Herr Doctor, after you?" Von Frankenstein left the lab with a chuckle, the Major following. The portal shut with a resounding *CLUNK!*

Lonn growled while Edge moaned in his cell. Mina's anger grew to a hot boil.

"*Ian!*" she shouted. Her voice echoed helplessly against the walls of their steel tomb.

Resistance was futile.

Chapter 22: Dash

"We have to get out of here!" Shelley said, looking around ideas. "Vickie, Kevin, are you okay to walk?"

"I think so," they answered in unison as Blaine and Dash helped them to their feet.

"Then let's go. If the elevator is offline, we can take the stairs."

Dash looked at the hole in the floor. "What about the big guy?" he asked.

"We'll have to catch up with him later," Drake replied. "He's programmed to find us. I don't think a bath is going to stop him and if what Frankenstein said is true, we have bigger fish to fry."

"Yeah, there are still a bunch of kids in this school," Shelley fretted.

"And the entire football team," Dash whispered, "and our family and friends here to watch the game. Kick-off is any minute now!"

"Hey, guys," Blaine said, raising her voice. They all turned.

"What happened to the third Brother Grimm?" she asked, pointing to the operating table. It was empty.

"He was there a minute ago," Dash muttered.

A desk flew thru the air and slammed into Dash who was flung across the room and crushed against a support beam for the spiral staircase.

"Dash!" Blaine yelled.

"Fetch, dog!" a voice mocked from the shadows.

Bright yellow eyes emerged from a darkened corner revealing Heinz in a ripped shirt and pants, limping into view. The center of his chest glowed like a dazzling emerald as thousands of nanos buzzed inside a gaping hole in his torso. A bright green beating heart thumped behind a slowly congealing phosphorescent ribcage as the nanos did their work, knitting the cyborg-boy back together.

"Everyone, behind me," Drake ordered. He turned to face Heinz.

"Heinz, we've got no beef with you. Let us by and you can do whatever floats your boat, steal candy from toddlers, torture ants with magnifying glasses, buy groceries with loose pennies…"

"Shut up!" Heinz snarled. "This *IS* personal. My chest is blasted open. You have destroyed my brothers. My Master has abandoned me. I and every other servant of Frankenstein remaining at this school will see you all destroyed."

"It doesn't have to be that way," Drake cautioned, "this whole lab is about to blow and you with it. Let's work together to save everyone."

Heinz laughed. Green nanos swarmed out of his chest as he wheezed. "I'm already dead. Come and get me, Daywalker. And if you get past me, I have already alerted my comrades. They will destroy you if the Master's nanos don't."

Heinz leapt thru the air with a crazed look contorting his boyish face. He slammed into Drake sending him sprawling to the floor. He hunched over, hacking loudly. Phosphorescent nanos streamed from his mouth in sickly clouds with each cough. Blaine, Vickie, Shelley, and Kevin backed away as he leered with a crazed smile. Heinz grabbed a table and with superhuman strength, tore away a metal leg. He held it over his head, ready to strike, smiling like a madman, bugs trickling from his mouth and the gaping hole in his chest.

"Who's next?" he growled.

"You!" Dash roared from across the room as the desk he was pinned behind came hurtling across the room, smashing into Heinz's upper body.

The force of the blow tore the cyborg in half sending Heinz's upper body sailing across the room with the desk while his lower half remained planted in place. Green light and streams of brightly glowing nanos fountained above his lower body, searching for the rest of Heinz. The light quickly faded and the nanos fell to the ground, turning to dusty ash. Heinz's legs fell over lifeless. Across the lab, the lights surrounding his top half winked out as Heinz disintegrated into dust.

"And stay down, punk," Dash said, limping forward. He offered Drake a hand who gratefully accepted.

"He called you a Daywalker because you are that woman's son from last night, aren't you?" Kevin asked enthusiastically as the two joined them. "You're half-vampire!"

"We can talk about my family history later Kevin," Drake said. "We've got to get out of here."

To underline the point, the calm computer voice announced, "*One minute to total containment breach. Emergency back-up systems failed.*"

"Come on," Shelley yelled, urging them toward the exit to the main hallway. "We can take the elevator back up to the main campus." The others followed her and raced down the hallway of the Grimm Science complex. They dashed out of the main entry to the walkway and glass elevator that hugged the cliff.

"Uh oh," Blaine muttered as they reached the elevator console, jamming the 'up' button.

"What?" Dash asked.

"Two things. First, power is off. The elevator buttons don't work. Second, look up."

Dash and the others peered skyward and saw more than two dozen identically-dressed, blonde-haired, blue-eyed boys descending the stairs, jumping from ledge to ledge with superhuman grace. The last of the Grimm cyborgs, the ones Heinz had summoned, were converging on them.

"Not good," Kevin whispered.

WHUMP!

Behind them, a huge geyser of purple gas, polka-dotted with glowing green, exploded from the roof of the giant glass globe at the opposite end of the science complex. The sides of the main lab exploded in a shower of broken glass that sparkled in the morning sun. The entire end of the building began to sink into the ocean. The glowing green nanos radiated out from the lab, covering the far end of the building. As they did, everything they touched disintegrated into ash.

A seagull made the mistake of being too slow. At the first explosion, it took flight from the nearby pier. A tendril of the purple gas coiled out and engulfed the bird. In an instant it was consumed, eaten up molecule-by-molecule by a million hungry nanos.

"*Really* not good," Kevin gulped.

"We've got to get off this beach and to that school," said Drake, searching up and down the coastline for options. Cliffs rose up for miles in each direction. The only path out was right in front of them, covered with quickly converging cyborgs.

"Holy moly!" Shelley said. "Those bugs are chewing up the whole pier, the entire building and the ocean itself."

"We've got to fight our way up," Dash said. "It's the only option."

"How about that crane?" Blaine suggested.

"It's too far away," Drake shook his head. "It won't reach."

The first of the Grimms dropped down to the beach. Blaine grabbed Vickie and immediately activated her invisibility powers, pushing her sister out of the way to safety. She grabbed a shovel from a nearby pile of tools and slammed it into a Grimm's head, sending him flying. Dash confronted the next two, sending one hurtling down the beach and another wind-milling toward the science complex. A plume of green nanos caught the cyborg who evaporated in a cloud of ash.

For every one the kids dispatched, two more cyborgs were at the ready. The Grimms pushed the kids away from the elevator toward the Science Complex. Several yards separated them as the Grimms made room for more of their comrades to join them to finish the kids.

Dash looked up in despair as a swarm of Grimms were climbing down the catwalks, preparing to attack. Behind them, the cloud of deadly green nanos rapidly approached.

CRASH!

Behind them the crane smashed into the sea as a swarm of nanos began to chew apart the helicopter pad. The kids turned their attention to the cyborgs who were now grouping into formation for their final assault.

"Prepare to die," the lead Grimm snarled as he signaled for his brethren to charge.

Dash, Drake, Blaine, Shelley, Vickie, and Kevin crouched, preparing to take them on.

From out of the water a giant lance of metal crashed into the oncoming Grimms like a freight train.

"It's the Monster!" Shelley shouted.

The giant iron robot grasped the four-story crane in both hands, wielding it like a massive club, emerging from the frothy waves. The Grimms descending the stairs slowed and began to scurry for the safety of the main school complex.

The robot swung the crane and demolished the rickety stairwell, sending the Grimms flying. Unfortunately, he also smashed the elevator and any chance of escape for the kids.

"Great, saved by the Monster but killed by the bugs," Kevin moaned.

"No, look!" Vickie shouted.

The robot twisted the crane back down and slowly rested it on the pier near the six friends. The robot's eyes widened as it brought the crane's tip to a stop in front of them.

"What's he doing?" Dash asked.

"He wants us to grab on!" Shelley shouted. "He'll be our elevator."

The Monster nodded.

Behind them, another explosion shook the pier as the middle of the science complex crumpled. Inside, the new science center lay in ruins as purple smoke and billowing clouds of nanos licked just feet away from them, devouring everything in their path.

"Beam me up, Scotty!" Blaine grabbed onto one of the crane's metal girders. The others followed as the pier rocked from another explosion and groaned ominously, listing.

"Hold on tight!" Shelley warned.

She turned to the Monster. "OK! That's everyone. Get us to the top!"

The robot's eyes creased as it gripped the base of the crane, tilting Shelley and her friends upward. The Science Complex exploded, sending shards of glass and glowing green bugs everywhere, narrowly missing the kids. Tendrils of green nanos attached themselves in patches to the lower regions of the iron crane. The hungry machines began to chew thru the metal, creating puffs of grey residue that spider-webbed across the struts.

"He'd better hurry!" Kevin yelled, lifting his sneakers from a nearby smudge of nanos who were rapidly expanding.

The crane creaked, weakening. Below Vickie, a large girder groaned and broke away in a puff of dust. A tendril of green bugs chewed their way across, closing in on her left hand as she struggled to hang on. She screamed.

"Vickie!" Blaine yelled, trying to navigate closer to her sister, monkey bar-style.

Vickie shrieked and let go with one hand as the green bugs ate away the bar she was holding. She hung precariously as the robot raised the tip toward the cliff, her grip slipping. Drake got to her just in time. He snatched her dangling free hand and swung her to him, embracing her tightly. His other hand billowed black smoke which clung to his section of crane, keeping the hungry nanos at bay.

CREAK...

The top quarter of the crane came to rest on solid rock and the kids scrambled off. The top half of the crane teetered and went crashing to the rocks below. A few nanos were left in the yard, covering the rear section of the huge Grimm Manor house and nearby dorms. The machines began to chew up sections of the grass, turning the healthy plant life dry and yellow as they sought out more food for their insatiable appetites.

Below them the pier sank into the boiling ocean. The remnants of the elevator shaft and rickety staircase were covered in green as the nanos swarmed up the cliff side. The robot threw the bottom third of the crane into the sea and looked at the kids, its arms extended. A cloud of nanos blanketed the robot and soon it was lost in a fog of glowing green and purple gas.

"No!" Shelley shouted. "He saved us! We have to help him."

"Shelley!" Dash yelled, snatching her from the cliff's edge as a section cleaved away. "He's gone."

Outside Grimm Manor, students in pajamas and weekend wear were beginning to emerge from the buildings, flanking the cliff. Inside, fire alarms blared and teachers and staff were milling around trying to bring order to the situation. A couple students in bathrobes peered over the side of the cliff as the new Science Complex sank into the ocean, emitting one final large explosion in protest.

"Was that a robot?" one wide-eyed young boy asked.

The yard they stood on rumbled and Blaine and Vickie grabbed the boys and moved them away from the cliff's edge as more sections of rock tumbled over the edge. The nanos continued their ascent.

"We've got to get these kids and their teachers out of here!" Blaine shouted.

In the distance, cheers and sounds of a marching band rose over the tumult below.

"The football game," Dash breathed. He checked his watch. "It's kick off time!"

"Drake!"

The kids looked up as they heard Drake's name hollered from across the yard. Emerging from a dorm hobbled Peter Murphy, followed by a group of Grimm staff.

Peter came up and gave his son a gruff hug before looking down the cliff side. He whistled loudly, titling his trucker's hat back. The whole Grimm Academy grounds shook precariously.

"After the radio failed, I managed to keep an eye on you kids from down the coast," Peter said. "When the helicopter took off and the smoke started to rise, I figured there was trouble, hustled down here in the truck and threw a couple fire alarms on the way in to make sure the locals started to clear out."

He paused. "Where's your mother?"

The kids looked down sadly. "They took her, Mr. Murphy," Shelley explained.

Peter looked over the ocean and again at the purple gas cloud sparkling with green flecks. It was rising and nearly at the lip of the cliff. Rocks and dirt tumbled below as tendrils licked upward. "It's not the first time," he grumbled. He looked at the kids, eyeing each one to make sure they were alright.

"The important thing is you're each safe." He turned and indicated the few adults who had followed him out of the building. "These are the residential advisors for

Grimm Academy. They watch the students on the weekends. Not surprisingly, several went home due to Labor Day but we still have kids many hanging around. We need to move them to safety."

One of the R.A.s looked over the cliff to the Science Complex below.

"It was that Guiles creep, wasn't it?" he asked.

The kids nodded.

"He was bad from the word 'go'. No one could figure out how he became Headmaster other than bringing in a truck full of money from those shady characters at Black Labs."

"Now it looks like everything he built is ruined," said another. "What is that smoke?"

"Drake, help me out here," Peter asked.

"Sure, Dad," he turned to the counselors, his eyes shining bright. "That smoke is dangerous. We must get the children and staff as far away from it as possible. You must follow my father's every direction."

"Who is your father?" a counselor asked dreamily as Drake weaved his hypnotic spell.

"That man right there," Drake said, pointing to Peter.

"But he is so old and grumpy?" the counselors asked in a sleepy chorus.

Vickie and Blaine turned to each other and blushed.

Drake smiled. "Listen to everything he says and get the kids and staff to safety."

"We will listen to everything the old, grumpy man says and get the kids and staff to safety," they repeated robotically.

The cliff rumbled again and this time a huge chunk broke away, taking the remains of the elevator station with it. Purple gas began to bubble over the lip and spread across the grass, instantly turning the green lawn into a shriveled wasteland.

"Alright, enough," Peter barked. "Let's get these kids out of here. Shelley, Vickie, Blaine, I could use your help with herding these cats." The three girls nodded.

"Drake, there's a bunch of folks in that football stadium. I need you to figure out how to get them out of there."

"Will do, Dad."

"We'll meet in the parking lot outside the stadium, near the big scoreboard and television screen," Peter finished. He nodded and walked toward the milling students, barking orders.

"Sign?" Kevin asked.

"Yeah, they have a great stadium for such a small school. They even have one of those big Jumbotron scoreboards," Dash answered, as the three boys started to jog toward the football field. "Too bad it's about to become nano-chow."

"And how did you do that to those adults, Drake?" Kevin asked.

"If I can see people, I can influence them. Tell them what to do, what to remember."

"Yeah, you're the Daywalker, part-vampire, part-human," Kevin mused. "Say… that gives me an idea… Come on!"

As the three ran, he explained his plan to Dash and Drake.

Chapter 23: Drake

TWEET!

The referee blew his whistle to signal kick-off for the opening middle school game between the Yowling Sasquatch of Autumn's Hallow and the Grimm Academy Ravens. The Ravens were kicking off and their kicker was making the final preparations at the 35-yard line. His teammates were getting into position to sprint down the field in chase, while the Autumn's Hallow squad looked on, preparing to return the ball.

Dotting the stands were friends and family out to cheer on their friends. While there were nowhere near the numbers as the high school game the night before, there was still a couple hundred people inside the small stadium. On the far end, the LCD Jumbotron looming over the bleachers zoomed in on the kicker as the Grimm Academy A.V. club manned the cameras and announced the game.

THUMP!

The kicker raced forward and socked the ball solidly, sending it spinning thru the air in a high arc. Near the 10 yard-line, the Sasquatch runner watched the ball, readying for his return as the Ravens ran down the line, preparing to stop the visiting team deep in their own territory.

As the ball was about to land in his arms, the Autumn's Hallow player was pushed gruffly out of the way and another boy caught the ball in a dead sprint, running as fast as a cheetah.

"Sorry, Brian!" Dash yelled as he whizzed by, using every ounce of his nano-activated speed to propel him forward.

Brian got up from the ground confused. He whispered *"Dash?"* as he watched his teammate running down the field, juking players at an impossible speed, wearing his street clothes. Around him, the Autumn's Hallow players slowed down, wondering what had happened while the Ravens tried haplessly to catch him.

Dash twisted around a Raven defender and hurdled over two others who made a crazy dive trying to tackle him. The others slowed down as they realized he wasn't a member of either team. Dash screeched to a halt by the visitor's sideline in a spray of Astroturf. His teammates stared at him dumbfounded. The coach, a big burly ex-football player, was chewing a wad of gum and looked at Dash stupidly. His eyes widened as he recognized the boy standing in front of him and his mouth fell open, his gum falling out.

"Gaunt?" he asked, thunder stuck.

"Hi Coach!" Dash said, huffing and puffing. Two Grimm players attempted to tackle him but he ducked out of their way sending them flying into the water cooler on the sidelines.

"What are you doing?" Dash's coach demanded. "Why aren't you suited up?"

"No time to explain. We've got to get everyone out of here. This whole place is about to fall into the ocean!" The referee came running up the line, trilling his whistle repeatedly.

"What's going on here, coach?" he said, red in the face from blowing the whistle. The other boys from both sides jogged in to see what was going on.

Dash's coach ignored the ref. "What do you mean fall into the ocean?"

Before Dash could respond, the whole stadium shook violently. At the far end, an empty section of bleachers buckled, crashing to the ground. Several people began to run for the exits.

"This whole place is in trouble!" Dash yelled. "We have to get everyone out of here, now!"

The Ravens' coach jogged over from his sideline, followed by his team.

"Ref, Coach. What's happening? Who is this kid?"

Dash's coach looked up at the Ravens' coach and the referee. The stadium rumbled again and in the far end a few puffs of purple smoke started to lick thru the gates leading toward the Grimm Manor house and nearby dorms.

"We've got to get the kids out of here, Frank. It looks like there's some kind of earthquake going on."

Peeking above the back wall of the stadium, a four-story Victorian-style tower in one wing of the Grimm Manor crumpled in a great cloud of dust. Next to it, the roof of a dorm building began to evaporate, blowing away on the ocean wind in dusty grey dimpled with flecks of glowing green.

"What the..." The Ravens' coach said, backing away.

"Listen, we have to go... NOW!" Dash urged.

Around them, kids and parents screamed as the purple smoke expanded and the wall of the far end of the stadium collapsed. Swarms of glowing green bugs zoomed from out of an expanding purple cloud, consuming everything in its path. The crowd could nervously make out the vague outlines of the Grimm dorm building and the main Manor House. Each silhouette was dissolving before their eyes, falling away as the nanos consumed them.

"Oh man…," Dash whispered. "Run!"

The coaches, referee, and players didn't need more convincing. They started to run in a dead sprint toward the entryway underneath the giant scoreboard leading to the parking lot. The crowd of onlookers followed.

Dash looked back to make sure all the people were clear. He heard another grinding sound of metal twisting as the hungry smoke moved forward, chewing apart the bleachers, followed by a woman's scream.

A lone mother was struggling to remove her baby from a carriage wedged into a lower section of bleacher crumpled inward, trapping the carriage between two metal benches. She clawed at the baby seat trying to get her trapped infant to safety. The metal bars of the benches were slowly inching together, crushing the plastic carriage.

Dash felt his muscles tighten and endorphins fire as his hair stood on end. He poured on the speed and raced to the mother and her stranded child. He jumped the fence separating the field and the bleachers with superhuman grace and landed next to the woman clawing for her child's life. He gripped the bleacher and ripped at the benches trapping the car seat, freeing the crying infant.

The mother grabbed her baby and ran down the benches as the purple smoke and speckled green nano bugs rapidly chewed thru sections. She nearly lost her balance, but Dash gripped her wrist and steadied her, helping her to the track circling the field below.

"Thank you!" the woman cried as they reached steady ground.

"You're welcome," Dash gulped. He looked back as the bleachers crashed down. The fence surrounding them glowed a bright green as the nanos chewed thru them, leaving ash in their wake.

"We need to get out of here! Come on." They raced down the track outdistancing the hungry bugs and joined the scrum of football players and their families trying to crowd thru the narrow exits. The cloud of nanos enveloped the opposite side of the stadium chewing thru the fields, walls, and bleachers. It moved in a churning mass with green flashes of lightning flaring inside its interior.

"We're too late," Dash murmured. There's no way they would make it out in time with so many people scrambling for safety. Above them, the jumbo LCD screen winked on and a giant bright blue field filled the screen. The camera zoomed out, revealing Drake Harker's blurry face.

"Man, this camera is different from my Dad's," someone muttered over the PA. It was Kevin. Finally, the scene on the screen came into focus, settling on a close-up of Drake's eyes.

"Okay, Drake," Kevin said into the mic. "Showtime!"

"Everyone!" Drake commanded, his voice booming over the stadium speakers. "Look up into the screen!" At first people only looked in ones and twos as they swarmed desperately to escape. But soon everyone was staring at the giant scoreboard screen, dumbfounded. Drake's mesmerizing bright blue eyes stared back.

"You will obey me," Drake boomed. "If you are outside the stadium, you will walk calmly up the parking lot. If you are inside, you will walk out of the exit single file in an orderly fashion, helping others if they need it."

The people stopped fighting each other and lined up. People began to stream out into the parking lot as chaos turned to order.

The cloud of nanos continued to stream forward, passing the 50 yard line. Another minute and it would consume the entire stadium.

"Okay, Kevin, now what?" Drake asked, his voice muffled as he turned away from the mic.

"I don't know," Kevin replied. "Hey, wait, what's *that*?"

Emerging from the menacing haze of purple, grey and green, a bright blue light shone in its center. It was small at first but began to grow in size and intensity. The nano cloud began to buckle violently. The hungry fog's tendrils stopped at the 30 yard line and convulsed and shriveled. The blue energy grew brighter and the nano cloud swirled inward, the green lights of the bugs turning sickly, winking out.

Dash covered his eyes as he watched. Dust and dirt whirled, kicked up by the retreating swirl of dying nanos. From the parking lot, the cliffs, the oceans below, and the building to either side, the haze of purple and the phosphorescent micro-machines floating inside, retreated and died. In its wake, the chewed-up remains of the stadium and Grimm Academy was in ruins. Thick grey dust was everywhere.

The blue light flared and the last of the cloud died, retreating into the center of its sapphire corona. Dash looked on as the Monster stood up. Its silver chest panel was open revealing a bright blue slash of light flashing brilliantly where its heart should have been. The panel sealed and the Monster stood tall in the midst of the destruction Frankenstein's nanos had wrought.

The crowd turned and looked at the Monster. People stood in awe of the huge, shining metal robot standing in a field of swirling grey ruin.

"Is that from Japan?" an adult asked near Dash.

Drake returned to the microphone, his voice booming. "OK people. Everyone look up at the scoreboard again. We've got some explaining to do."

Chapter 24: Dash

"I think I took care of everyone's memories," Drake said, meeting up with his friends and father. Kevin followed.

"As far as everyone knows it was an earthquake and a fire that did all of this. The Grimm staff were the heroes."

"Kevin, that was a really good idea!" Shelley said, smiling, showing off her silvery braces.

"Yeah, Poindexter," Old Man Murphy confirmed. "That was fast thinking, saved a lot of lives."

Kevin looked down bashfully as Dash clapped him on the back. "Thanks," he said grinning.

"The police and fire department are on their way and should be here any minute," Blaine added. "Mr. Murphy called them once we gave the Monster instructions."

"He'll meet us back at your house, Drake," Shelley continued. "But now we need to figure out what to do next."

"What's the plan, Dad?" Drake asked.

"With your mom gone, I think it's time for reinforcements," Peter replied, pulling out an old cell phone. It was big and ancient, like an old-fashioned walkie-talkie.

"What's that?" Vickie asked.

"It's a phone, Debbie Debutante," Peter quipped. "Had it since Apple went public."

"It looks more like a microwave oven," she said dubiously.

Peter ignored her and dialed.

"Who are you calling?" Dash asked.

"Agent Crane. We're going to need some help and he's as reliable as they come."

"Who does he work for?" Blaine asked.

"The US government," Peter grunted.

"Which part?" Shelley asked.

"Every part."

The phone picked up. "Ichabod," Peter said into the microphone. "It's Murphy. I need a favor... I need a plane. What do you mean turn around?"

They turned and saw a tall, slender man emerging from a dark sedan that had just pulled up behind them. He was dressed in a form-fitting black suit and white shirt. His hair was dark brown and his face was thin with a hawk-like nose. He removed his sunglasses and walked up to shake Peter's hand with his large gawky hands.

"Agent Ichabod Crane," Peter said loudly.

"Peter Murphy," Ichabod said, a grin creasing his narrow face. "And these are?"

"I think you know," Peter replied coyly.

"Ah," Agent Crane murmured, "your new Monster Squad."

Peter nodded.

"So where is the robot and Frankenstein?" Crane asked, surveying the scene. Police cars and ambulances were turning into the parking lot and two more black sedans followed closely with similarly-dressed agents joining the police and fire department crews. People were milling about confused and frightened.

"The robot's safe, but Frankenstein is gone. He has Mina... How did you know we were here?"

Ichabod smiled. "You, Mina, and Drake each qualify for your very own personal satellite surveillance, my friend," Agent Crane replied, putting his sunglasses back on. The morning sun shone brightly thru the grey dusty haze left over after the nano's wrath.

"After last night's hijinks, we were bound to investigate. I take it things didn't work out the way you wanted."

"No," Peter answered. "Frankenstein is on the run and I need help to track him down. I suspect he's mixed up with those shady characters at Black Labs."

"Peter. I can let you go and maybe even help out with transport, but I can't help you outright. I'll be in trouble as it is."

"I know," Peter said nodding. "I was thinking Jekyll."

Crane grunted. "You know he's not to be trusted."

"I know, but if we are dealing with Black Labs we need equally shady characters to find out where they are holing up."

"I can get a jet for you inside of an hour, but I'm going to need the Monster back."

"After we find Mina, he's all yours."

Ichabod pausing looking each of the kids and Peter up and down.

"Fair enough," He finally nodded. "I'll mop up here. I assume your boy took care of everyone's memories?" Peter nodded, patting Drake on the back.

"Good. See you in an hour and make sure you deal with these kids' parents before you take them out of the country. Use that son of yours to create plausible cover stories and make sure this whole adventure stays quiet."

"Thanks, Ichabod. I owe you."

"Add it to the list. Just make sure you handle von Frankenstein." He turned and walked away, barking instructions to his agents gathering at the scene.

"What now?" Dash said. The other kids looked at Peter expectantly.

"We go to find an old colleague of mine, two actually," Murphy answered, "in London."

"We need to have Drake pay a visit to each of your parents. You're each coming, aren't you?" The kids nodded.

Kevin and Vickie stepped forward. "We're coming too!" he announced. Vickie stood next to him, her face set.

Peter smiled. "Wouldn't dream of the trip without you," he grumbled.

"Who are we going to see, anyway?" Blaine asked.

"Two old war buddies," Peter replied, his voice gravelly. "Dr. Jekyll and Mr. Hyde."

*****

Dash closed the door to his small home with a glum look. His gran was still in bed and looking worse than ever. Drake talked with her using his vampire mojo. While unwell, she was happy her grandson had been selected for a special exchange program in Europe. As far as she knew, Dash was leaving for an all-expenses paid trip to England for a Young Olympian program. He could be gone a few days or a few weeks. Dash promised to keep in touch every day, but he felt horrible leaving her when she was unwell, even if it was for her safety.

"Are you okay?" Blaine asked as he put a duffel bag into the back of Old Man Murphy's truck and took a seat on the rusty rear bumper.

"I'm really worried about Gran. Ever since Mom left her health has been going downhill. Now I'm leaving her too, and who knows when we'll be back."

"Dash, my dad agreed to check in on her every day," Shelley said.

"My parents too!" Kevin added.

"Thanks guys," Dash said. He tried to perk up but it was difficult. He appreciated what his friends and their families were doing for his Gran but he still felt troubled.

"My mom comes here all the time for her real estate stuff," Blaine added. "She'll make sure she's taken care of. Heck, she is over the moon her two daughters were accepted into the Imperial Clown School or whatever Drake made up."

Vickie scowled. She was not a fan of the Davis girls' cover story.

Drake raised his hands defensively. "Hey, I didn't exactly have a lot of time to think up a brilliant alibi."

"But, clown school? Really?" Vickie scoffed. "Drake, I know you are like 99 and a half and clowns were pretty cool back when Lincoln was emperor or whenever you were born, but honestly. How about the Parisian Academy of Modelling? Or the French Fashion Institute Young Designer's award? Or a junior internship at Elle?"

"Yeah, Drake you are so heartlessly lame," Kevin teased, laughing.

Drake mock scowled at his smaller friend and smiled. "Vickie, I promise the next time I hypnotize your parents before you go off and save the world from an evil madman, I'll consult with you beforehand about your cover."

"Whatever," she huffed and turned away.

"I love my cover story," Kevin announced. "An internship at the Royal Games Academy! I plan to code Gothic 2 and make millions, retiring to my private island lair with a likeness of me carved into the local volcano... all before the age of 13."

"Right," Dash laughed, shaking his head. You could always count on Kevin to get his mind off his problems.

"What? Do you think the volcano is a little overdone? How about a man-made archipelago that reads *KEVIN IS AWESOME* from space..."

They all laughed.

"So what now?" Blaine asked.

"We head to the airport," Shelley said. "Mr. Crane has secured a private plane."

"London," Dash added. "Man, I haven't even been to Seattle, let alone England."

"I know, it is exciting!" Vickie gushed. "I hope von Frankenstein took your Mom to Paris, Drake!" She punched at the air, making a tough girl face. "We could fight him on the Eiffel Tower and then celebrate with crepes and new Louboutin shoes!"

"Right," Blaine muttered.

"How are you holding up, Drake?" Dash asked. "This has to be hard on you and your dad."

"My mom's been in a lot of tough scrapes," Drake replied, looking serious but confident. "We'll get her back." He looked at each of them and smiled. "Besides, with the *Monster Squad*, how could we fail?" They all chuckled.

"So who are these Jekyll and Hyde dudes we're trying to find?" Kevin asked.

"I don't know," Drake admitted. "My Dad's never mentioned them."

"Strange, two guys from a war fought over sixty years ago," Shelley mused.

"Something tells me these are more than a couple of my Dad's horseshoe-throwing buddies down at the Kiwanis Club."

"Well, I hope these old timers pack some serious heat," Dash said. "We're going to need it if we're playing von Frankenstein on his home turf."

"You whippersnappers ready to go?" Peter asked, as he hobbled into view. He had been inside talking with Dash's Granny.

They all nodded.

Murphy walked over to Dash and clapped him on the back. "Your Gran is a fine woman, Dash. She's got iron in her bones, all of your kin does. She'll be alright. And she'll understand... she knows you're special."

"Thanks, Mr. Murphy," Dash replied.

"Ok, let's load up," Murphy announced. "Wallis, you sure your folks can handle Chuckles while we're gone?"

"Yes sir," Kevin replied, referring to Mr. Murphy's giant slobbery dog staying at his place while they were away.

"I just hope they don't feed him any dairy," Murphy chuckled, "that's like loading him with a live mortar round."

"I'll make sure to call before we leave..." Kevin said uncertainly.

"Alright, Monster Squad," Peter announced, "next stop London and Dr. Henry Jekyll and Mr. Edward Hyde!"

Epilogue

The small private jet bucked as it flew thru a rough patch of turbulence. Outside, the night was clear with stars winking brightly in the sky. Mina slouched in her seat, her arms wrapped tightly in reinforced steel cuffs. Beside her a lock box lay open with the bright golden glow of the Tunguska Stone irradiating her, stripping her of her powers like sunlight paralyzing a vampire. She could barely move with the strange fragment nearby.

Across from her von Frankenstein sat, eyeing her closely. "So we find ourselves in a small room crossing the Atlantic again," he chuckled. "After all these years."

"You make me sick," Mina muttered, her voice weak. Even talking was an effort that made her dizzy.

"Oh, my dear, it's the nanos in your blood that make you sick," von Frankenstein leaned forward, the light from the stone shining on his face, reflecting off his dark glasses. He breathed in deeply. "That stone helped to heal me after all those years with the Russians, repair what damage it could, keep me younger than my years. Curious, the same aliens who make you invincible with one gift, take it all away with another."

"Where are you taking me?" Mina asked.

"I wouldn't want to ruin the surprise," he said darkly.

"What do you want with those children? Haven't you ruined enough lives?"

Von Frankenstein leaned back and sighed. "You never understood. Progress requires pain, sacrifice, loss. What we did together in the war, that was amazing."

"It was monstrous!" Mina spat.

"No, my dear, you are monstrous. I'm a visionary, and what I have planned will change this world forever."

"You're insane…"

Von Frankenstein smiled. "It doesn't really matter what you think. All that matters is the heirs."

"Peter won't let you get near them. He'll stop you. He has friends who can stop you."

"I am well aware of his friends," von Frankenstein muttered, his voice ominous. "I have friends too, you know."

"Peter will save me."

"We shall see."

"You will fail," Mina coughed.

Von Frankenstein rose and walked to a trolley at the edge of the small cabin. He poured a drink and stared out the window as he drained its contents. He set the glass back down listening to the ice in the glass jingle. He looked back at Mina who coughed helplessly barely able to stir in her chair.

"I don't think so, not this time, my dear."

He resumed his watch of the night sky and smiled as a shooting star dashed across the distant horizon.

"Come if you will, Peter. Our game has just begun."

End of Book 1 of **Monster Squad: The Iron Golem**.

More exciting adventures can be found in Book 2 of **Monster Squad: Jekyll & Hyde**

Coming soon!

PREVIEW: Book 2

Extract from the next exciting book in the series

Monster Squad: Jekyll & Hyde

The double doors to the Spa's sumptuous head office opened and a sharply-dressed, middle-aged man entered, wearing a white lab coat. He had slicked back hair, a thin athletic frame and a haughty air about him.

"Peter!" the man exclaimed. "My god, man, it's been a long time! Smashing to see you!"

"Henry," Murphy replied, "long time indeed."

"And who are these friends of yours?" the man asked, moving forward to greet Dash and Blaine. "Allow me to introduce myself. I'm Dr. Henry Jekyll, proprietor of this establishment."

"Hi," Blaine and Dash both mumbled.

"Can I interest any of you in a cucumber-infused mineral water?" Jekyll asked, approaching his desk.

"No, Jekyll," Peter replied. "We're here on business and in a bit of a hurry."

"Always so straightforward, Peter, that is what I adore about you," Jekyll replied, pouring himself a glass. "Before we get to the dirty details, where is that fetching wife of yours? She always does such a good job of softening your rough edges."

"That's why we're here," Murphy coughed.

"Oh," Jekyll replied, setting down his glass, "I see. Always getting into a spot of trouble, aren't you?" Jekyll leaned back on his desk.

"What can the good doctor help you with?"

"Frankenstein is back. We need to find him."

Jekyll grew serious and eyed Peter studiously. "And why would you think I would know the whereabouts of this Frankenstein chap?"

"Come on, Henry," Peter leaned forward on his cane, "you always have your fingers in the game."

Jekyll paused. "And where is Mina?" He picked up a set of relaxation balls from his desk, each black and white, and shifted them in one hand.

"Frankenstein has her. We need to get her back and were hoping you could help."

Blaine sneezed and excused herself. Jekyll looked up at her and Dash, considering them critically, his eyes narrowing.

"Ah, our two young friends. I almost forgot you." Jekyll sighed, smiling slyly. He approached Dash and Blaine. "My, my, Peter, they do so remind me of some people we once knew."

The kids looked at one another. Dr. Jekyll walked around them as Peter watched. He continued to move the relaxation balls in his hands as he paced around them. He returned to his desk and set the balls back down, the black sides up.

"So, you found the heirs. I'd be surprised if you haven't been hiding them all this time. Frankenstein resurfaced, came after them, and things didn't go as planned." He regarded Peter. "Am I right?"

"You've got the general drift," replied Peter.

"Getting the old band back to together then, eh? That is the American expression, isn't it?" Jekyll said. Peter simply nodded.

"What did you call them before?" Jekyll tapped his chin. "Ah, yes, the Monster Squad."

"I don't understand," Blaine said, confused. "Mr. Murphy, I thought you said you knew Dr. Jekyll and Mr. Hyde from World War II. Dr. Jekyll seems younger than my Dad."

Jekyll grinned. "My dear, my partner, Edward Hyde, and I have special abilities as well. Peter may look a bit shabby now but I assure you we worked closely together during the War, and for some time after."

He stepped closer to Blaine. "By the color of your hair and your deep chocolate eyes, I would say you're related to Edgewick Stoker, a pre-eminent scientist and, what you Americans would call, the Invisible Man."

He looked at Dash. "And you, a strapping young lad with thick, sandy hair, and big shoulders. I would guess you are the great-great grandson of Lonn Cheney, another famous scientist, and the Wolf Man, if I do recall his popularized name."

He walked away. Dash and Blaine shifted uncomfortably.

"Right on all counts," Peter said.

"And they possess their ancestors' powers?"

"Blaine…" Peter indicated.

Blaine held up her hand. Jekyll and Peter watched as a silver light washed over it, rendering her fingers and palm invisible. She approached Jekyll and picked up one of his relaxation balls. It winked out of existence. She placed it down, white side up, next to its mate and the silvery light washed away. Her hand returned to normal.

"Quite impressive, young lady," Jekyll said, nodding.

"Thanks," Blaine muttered, returning to stand next to Dash.

Jekyll watched Peter for a moment, thinking. "Well, Peter," he said, picking up a piece of paper and writing something. "You must understand I am a legitimate businessman now. But I would like to be of some small service. Perhaps I could point you to a contact who may be helpful."

A knock at the door interrupted him. Dr. Jekyll's assistant poked her head through.

"Excuse me, Doctor," she said politely, "but Mr. Hyde's two o'clock appointment is here for him." She closed the door and entered the room.

Jekyll stopped writing and the color drained from his face. "Oh dear…"

Jekyll gripped the sides of his desk and bent down in pain. The veins on his neck tightened as he gripped the thick glass tabletop. The muscles on his back and arms began to convulse as he grunted and cried out in pain.

"Doctor?" Blaine asked, approaching.

Peter walked over and grabbed her by the hand, moving her back to Dash.

"What's happening to him?" Dash asked.

"He looks like he's hurt!" Blaine said.

"Keep clear," Peter ordered, putting his cane in front of them.

The top of the glass desk spider-webbed as Jekyll's grip tightened like a vice, followed by a low gurgling growl. His hands grew large and hairy while his back, arms, and legs bulged unnaturally. Before their eyes Jekyll seemed to grow by four feet and three hundred pounds with muscle, hair, and bone sprouting everywhere. The doctor's clothes tightened, swelling outward, ripping his pant legs and sleeves.

"Holy shiitake mushrooms…" Dash breathed, watching the doctor transform.

A hulking beast of a man stood before them, bent over the ruined desk, back turned. His shoulders heaved up and down as the behemoth huffed and grunted.

"Dr. Jekyll?" Blaine asked, tentatively stepping closer.

The giant turned and regarded her with a single piercing blue eye, the other shut tight. Where Jekyll's face had been smooth, clean shaven, and sophisticated it was now knotty, furrowed, and studded with thick, bristly stubble. His hair was wild and his chest and body were huge. His arms were unnaturally long, like a gorilla's, hung at his sides, rippling with muscle and thick mats of hair. He stood up tall and towered over them. He grunted and pushed his hair back, flexing his muscles.

He took one massive hand and flipped the table over, sending it careening to the other end of the spartan office. He regarded Blaine, Peter, and Dash and sneered.

"The name's not Jekyll," the giant huffed in a thick booming voice laced with a heavy street accent.

"Hyde," Peter muttered.

"What?" Blaine asked, fearful of the big man.

"Hide!" Peter yelled.

"The name's Mr. Hyde!" the giant boomed.

Hyde leapt at Blaine who instantly coated herself in invisibility and dodged to one side. He hit the floor heavily, shaking the fancy pictures on the wall. He lifted his head and roared, sending spittle flying.

"Blaine!" Dash shouted, moving to intercept Mr. Hyde. The large misshapen man regarded him critically.

"Hello there, buttercup," the giant said, thickly. "Come to have a go, eh?"

"I don't want to hurt you," Dash said, feeling his endorphins racing and muscles tightening.

Hyde chuckled a deep phlegmy laugh. "And I don't think you will, lad."

Mr. Hyde moved with incredible speed. He snatched forward and grabbed Dash by the shirt before he could react, flinging him to one side. Dash landed like a rag doll, spilling over a couch into a collection of plastic ferns. Hyde stalked toward Peter, his feet pounding heavily on the wooden floor.

"Peter Murphy," he barked. "And what did you want with that two-faced Nancy-boy, Jekyll?"

Peter backed away. "We need help with Mina, Edward…"

"Hmm…" Hyde muttered, looking at Murphy closely. "You've gotten old, mate."

"Some of us age, Ed."

"Not my problem."

"Can I talk to Jekyll again?" Murphy asked.

Hyde's face screwed up and turned red. "Why would you want to talk to him?" He bellowed.

Blaine was standing behind Hyde and swung a floor lamp solidly at the big man's back, revealing herself as she did so. The lamp hit Hyde hard, yet he didn't flinch. Blaine's eyes widened as the giant turned around and stared at her, smirking.

"I don't like you, Peter. Never did." He looked at Blaine. "I think I'm going to take this one for a jaunt, she's got steel."

Blaine started to back away but Hyde reached out and grabbed her. She tried to struggle but the giant thug held her firm. He turned and jumped from where he was standing thru the front glass window, landing on the street below, sending people entering the spa scattering, including Monty who was lounging by his car.

Peter hobbled over and saw Hyde bounding away quickly down the block, Blaine screaming in his grasp. Dash struggled out of the ferns and got a glimpse of Hyde as he and Blaine rounded a corner.

"Get after her," Peter ordered. "Monty and I will follow. Keep in touch on that phone I gave you."

Dash nodded and with a running jump, flung himself thru the hole in the window, landing lightly on the street below. He sprinted down the block in pursuit.

Peter shouted down to Monty to get the car ready. The double doors opened and Jekyll's assistant came rushing in to stand beside him, staring out the window.

She had her hands on her hips and shook her head, an annoyed look spreading across her pretty features.

"Oh no," she sighed, "not again."

About The Author

Christian Page loves stories that combine fun, action and adventure. A father of two, he lives in the Pacific Northwest of the United States with his wife, son, daughter, overly plump cat and under-behaved dog.

You can visit the author to learn more about his stories and upcoming work at www.chrispage.com or follow him on Facebook (Chris Page) or Twitter (@cpagewriter).

For My Mom, Carole, who gave me a lifelong love of great stories and my kids, Mason & Emery, who inspired me to tell some

Acknowledgements

I'd like to thank several people in the creation of this book. Firstly, my wife, Maya, who gave me the support and allowed me the time to research and write it. Second, my kids, Emery and Mason, who were my chief critics and the first readers of the story. Next, my group of proofreaders who gave me early feedback, in particular Scott, Ethan, Nathaniel, Stephen and Neal. And my agent, Darin, and early editor, Kari, who helped guide a rough manuscript to a more finished product.

CPSIA information can be obtained at www.ICGtesting.com
Printed in the USA
LVOW08s1705080115

422026LV00009B/1085/P